Seeds of Death

Rubbie Jones

Published by Clink Street Publishing 2022

Copyright © 2022

First edition.

ISBN:
978-1-915229-78-6 - paperback
978-1-915229-79-3 - ebook

CHAPTER 1

It was close to midnight by the time Mia finished her rigorous, high intensity, hard body workout and was pleased with her bag work after a long day of business meetings.

She was alone in the gym privately owned by her mentor and sponsor Pietro Allard, who afforded her private use and set of keys due to the hectic and demanding schedules she partly imposed on herself.

As lead researcher for one of Allard's private skin care laboratories, 'Skintakt', she was on her monthly business update meeting visit to the Malaysian capital Kuala Lumpur (KL), an overnight stay, and had showered, slipped into a pair of skin-tight spandex leggings and trainers and was about to put on a T over her bra when she heard a noise coming from the emergency-lit, gym area she had recently vacated.

She stopped immediately and stood still in the changing room listening, when she thought she heard the turning of a lock at the main door. Then, checking, she realised to her horror, her mobile phone was left in the car outside and could not call for help.

Very 'Cat like' alert and taking a deep breath she entered the gym area, "Who's there?" she shouted, "the gym is closed, this is private property." Nothing. Again, "I know someone's here, show yourself."

Hearing a shuffle behind her from the shadows, she turned, but too late, she was pushed to the floor and standing over her, a male around 178cm tall, of stocky build, around 80kg and late twenties; wearing shorts, trainers and hoody.

"I've been watching you come here sometimes and always at night," he said, "and I like what I've seen, a girl like you would have no interest in a guy like me so, I'm thinking help myself."

He was right, Mia was a statuesque beauty of a young woman, 23 years old, half Japanese and half Italian. Around 173cm tall and 60kg with long, jet black hair, dark brown eyes to slowly drown in, with long slender, toned legs, a beautifully formed ass and shapely hips with firm rounded breasts, coupled with smouldering looks and flawless skin, she was a beauty.

Beauty or not, Mia was in danger and her survival instincts from seemingly tedious hours of mixed martial arts training cleared her head.

"Listen, nothing has happened so far, please think what you are doing and leave now," she suggested.

"Oh, I know what I'm doing," he replied, "quite a plan to get you here on your own and I'm not wasting it."

Mia, acrobatically, flipped to her feet in one movement, she realised he had managed to lock the door and decided the only way was to confront him.

She distanced herself from him in a fighting, sideways stance, hands raised, chin tucked in and elbows lowered as if about to begin the first round of an MMA cage fight against a formidable opponent.

He lunged forward, but she deftly sidestepped his advance and landed a punch behind his ear as he passed. The punch made good connection, but not enough to put him down and he reeled back up, angry like a man possessed.

"I love resistance," he chided, "and this fancy kung fu shit doesn't bother me; you'll have to kill me to stop me, because I will just keep coming."

He threw himself at her in a rugby style tackle catching her in the midriff and they both tumbled to the floor with him landing on top of her. Mia was vulnerable in this position. He was heavier than her, but she managed to catch him in the nose with a well-placed elbow strike, bloodying his nose, but it made him angrier. He got his hands to her throat squeezing her larynx, she responded with blows, but he was like a wild animal.

Her senses were departing, the grip on her throat was intense and she knew she was wearying. She pretended to fade and let go her grip on his hands at which point he released her, stood up and removed his shorts. He was sporting a huge erection and then, his mistake, as he leaned back down to try to remove her leggings. She arched her back throwing her hips upwards and wrapping her legs around his neck in a figure four triangle choke. He was taken by surprise, the choke was in, but he was still over her. Pulling down on the foot of her trailing leg with her hand and in one movement she flipped over to a dominant position seated on his throat, her slender muscled legs coiled tightly around his neck like an Anaconda squeezing its prey.

She adjusted herself on his throat moving her seated leg tighter into his side creating a more efficient choke hold.

She leaned forward to increase the effectiveness and squeezed every muscle in her thighs and calves. He knew he was in trouble as she looked down at his bloodied angry face, but he was very resilient and spat angrily, "I'm going to rape you when you're dead now, he spluttered."

Mia knew she had to end this, no compromise, no mistakes, he would keep on coming until he physically could not. She knew her choke was in tight and crushing both sides of his carotid arteries which no man could fight, but this wasn't a tournament fight, it could be life or death.

She was right, the choke began taking its toll on him and every relaxing inch he gave she took up, coiling her legs around his neck tightening her lethal grip.

His hands stopped fighting and instead went to her legs desperately trying to gain some release, but there was none. Mia closed her eyes and poured on every ounce of pressure she had feeling his hands now going to her hips desperately pushing in panic now, flapping, tapping her, but she ignored everything.

The tapping became lightly pushing, weak and failing, and his eyes began to roll into the top of his head. She continued her choke, her shiny leggings so deep and tight around the trapped neck between them.

His hands fell away limp, his lower body thrashing involuntarily, and at that exact moment she felt a warm splattering of liquid on her lower back.

In that moment she thought nothing of it as she unravelled her legs from around his neck and he lay completely still, obviously dead, eyes open, eyeballs in the top of his head and mouth open, totally choked to death. She reached to her lower back thinking somehow blood had splattered on to her, but as she smeared it with her fingers, she realised that it was sperm, the filthy scum had orgasmed and shot his seed at the exact moment he finally gave in to death.

She just sat and cried, grateful to be alive and safe, but distraught at what had just happened, something she had only ever read about or seen on the news.

Her mind drifted as to why she had taken up martial arts in the first place and how, this time, it had all been worth the long hours in the gym and had probably saved her life. Her thoughts wandered as to how she had gotten to this place, right now, at this time.

CHAPTER 2

Mia had never really known her birth parents, orphaned at three years old, she was born to an Italian father and Japanese mother in Singapore who were tragically killed in a boating accident off Kusu Island and void of any other relatives was sent to an orphanage. She inherited her mother's exotic oriental features, jet black hair, the deepest brown alluringly beautiful eyes, and her father's statuesque physique and olive skin.

She spent the next eight years of her life in the orphanage under a strict regime and attended school, becoming a very dedicated scholar with early interest in the human body and 'what made things work' in the form of sciences.

It was standard policy at the orphanage to find permanent foster parents but being three years old made it difficult. Couples looked for babies to take on as their own from birth, however, as she just turned 11, one day, the matron told her to make herself, more than usually, presentable. A family: husband, wife and their 15-year-old son would be coming to the orphanage later that day with a view to taking her into the family.

She had gotten used to the life she had, kept herself to herself and studied hard and was not happy about going to live with a family. However, the couple were quite wealthy and had decided to offer their status to someone in need and quite often Mia found herself 'wanting' financially.

The meeting was set in the Matron's office and Mia was a little nervous as she entered. The Matron was sat behind her antique desk, a donation made by the local council offices on refurbishment back in the eighties and in front of her on three matching antique oak chairs, the potential family.

Mia quickly recognised they were of European descent, later confirmed as Dutch. The husband, Marco, was medium build, blonde receding hair, in his late thirties and dressed smartly in a light blue casual suit, obviously a business type. The wife,

Lieke, was petite, attractive and wore a flower-patterned jump suit again in her late thirties. Then, the son Daan, Mia caught his stare and smug look and didn't like from that second as he looked her up and down. He was quite chubby, thick wavy hair, and from her school experiences, the capacity trademark of a bully.

Introductions were made as Mr and Mrs De Jong and the husband and wife were both very warm and receptive, complimenting her appearance and manners.

The couple explained that the husband had a very successful shipping business and had now reached the stage where the wife, company secretary, could back away and devote more time to the home and her hobbies. This left the space for an additional family member and she was looking for the daughter she could not have following a serious, bacterial, infection of her womb when she was younger leaving her unable to conceive.

For Mia it seemed that Marco was just placating his wife, trying to compensate for something and Daan was fearing giving up status as being 'the only child'.

They could offer Mia long term security, her own room, and afford to buy her the things she, mostly, only witnessed the other kids had at school like expensive mobile phones and designer clothes. She was by no means materialistic, but every girl her age felt the need to belong.

The meeting went well and despite Mia's initial reluctance, she could see benefits for her going forward, although, concerns regarding her potential 'step-brother' already plagued her mind.

The assembly ended with the Matron saying she would discuss with Mia and her thoughts, evaluate the whole initial gathering, and, if everything appeared positive for all, they would reconvene in one week.

Two weeks later, Mia was being shown around her new home and settling in with her meagre belongings.

Her new home was a delightful, single storey house located in a very serene and leafy suburb of the City. Although set up on one level, Mia's room was annexed, separated from the main building by a corridor, but beautifully appointed, everything she needed including privacy.

The second day Mia was taken shopping by Lieke who treated her to new trainers, jeans, tops and some dresses all chosen by herself; something she was not used to at all. Then some tech, a new phone with a package and an iPad.

For once she felt truly connected.

Mia fitted into the family life, eating meals together, attending school with a dedicated study of her chosen, science-related subjects.

Lieke spent time with her, they shared their interest in plants, biology, chemistry and, as it transpired, her own specialty and area of interest when she was younger.

Mia had suffered from mild eczema for a while on both her shins and Lieke, on examination of her ailment, introduced her to Aloe Vera and its magical properties. This natural, plant-based, phenomenon fascinated Mia as within two weeks, the eczema disappeared completely, and she marvelled at the potential healing ability of naturally occurring substances. It opened her eyes to the reality that not every cure or remedy was necessarily of man-made origin.

CHAPTER 3

As she turned 12, Mia took on human biology and chemistry as her main subjects and became an upstanding, naturally gifted academic, excelling in every area of her study. She was dedicated and from this early age, with Lieke's help, began making her own skin care potions using natural extracts, mainly Aloe Vera based.

Then Daan, he was now 16 years old, spotty complexion, and overweight with hormones driving a virility only thwarted by his unpopular position with girls from his school; he resented their rejection of him and his chauvinistic attitude.

He became irritable and was increasingly rude to Mia, made lewd comments and became disrespectful. Lieke had noticed this uncomfortably offensive trait and brought it to Marco's attention, but he brushed it aside, saying the boy was just growing into a man.

Mia often thought that Lieke had suffered a fair share of abuse from her husband and basically 'did as she was told' from her, also chauvinistic and bigoted, husband, she had formed quite a bond with her and was saddened by it.

Anyhow, this was their family history, nothing she could do could alter that and for Mia as long as 'the creepy' Daan stayed away from her that was ok but then, one night, when Lieke and Marco were staying out late on a retirement function, he had abhorrent plans of his own.

Time had reached close to midnight; Mia had been watching a Netflix film in bed and just turned off the bedside light when her door creaked open. Lit by the light from the corridor it was Daan standing in the doorway.

"What do you want?" Mia asked him.

"I want to come in," he said.

She never had cause to lock the door before but was beginning to wish she had and found herself trembling.

Before she could move Daan quickly climbed into her bed, she turned over, so she wasn't facing him, but he put his arm around her, he was strong, and she said, "Get out or I'll scream."

"No one will hear you," he said confidently in her ear. "I don't want to hurt you I just want to be close." Mia realised that he had been drinking, possibly whiskey with the stench on his breath.

Then, she felt something against her bare leg, something she was unfamiliar with, it was warm, hard and pulsating. "Get off me!" she cried.

"I just want to feel your skin on my penis," he said.

"Get off me I will tell Lieke," she warned him.

"If you breathe a word to her I will tell Dad and he will make sure she doesn't say anything, he always sticks up for me," he replied confidently.

Daan began working his erect penis against the back of her thigh, gripping her tightly so she could not move and at this point, although sickened and horrified, she decided not to resist.

He began to make noises reminding her of someone asleep in the middle of a nightmare, she thought, and a few seconds later felt his warm sperm, spew on to her leg as he groaned to a sordid climax. He released his hold on her then quickly got out of the bed.

"Not a word," he said, "or there will be trouble for everyone including you and especially your best friend Lieke," he added, smirking.

Mia rushed out of the bed and threw herself into the shower to wash his filth from her body. She was frightfully aware of what had just taken place but was relieved he had not tried to penetrate her in any way. With that, came the harsh realisation of how fragile and vulnerable she was to a creep such as Daan. She had never resorted to any kind of violence before, but, decided from that point, to ensure no one would take such advantage of her in that way ever again.

Lieke had noticed Mia was not herself when they returned as she went to her room to check on her.

She noticed she had changed her bed linen and asked if everything was ok.

"Everything is fine thank-you, I had an accident, you know, 'Ladies accident'," she tutted embarrassingly.

"Oh, that's ok, dear, happened to all of us," she replied. "I'll get them laundered for you tomorrow."

"Already in the washing machine, I didn't want things left lingering around," she replied.

"Sure, you are ok, dear?" Lieke repeated.

'Yes, I'm fine, I haven't seen much of you today and I've been meaning to ask, I have been considering taking up self-defence and wondered if you had any objection to me joining the local Dojo, you know, as a hobby?" Lieke was surprised and wondered at the timing, but thought it would be good for discipline, health and at the same time, learn to protect herself.

It was very rare that Mia was ever alone with Daan so, till now it had only been a one off, but she was adamant it would not happen again.

CHAPTER 4

For the next six months, Mia studied hard at school and trained extra hours in the Dojo gaining belts as she progressed. The martial art gave her confidence and promoted awareness of who was around her at any time.

Daan continued to be arrogant and rude, his girl skills lacking on every level and she was always weary of him.

Mia had a family 13th birthday and celebrated with a meal out at a favourite Asian restaurant. Daan had been told by his father he had to go and, as usual, was obnoxious throughout the meal even though he ate like a pig. He was still very insecure and although sexually 'straight', still did not seem to do well with the opposite sex and no girlfriend.

Mia was a little apprehensive as they reached home to hear that something urgent had occurred at Marco's offices, there had been some kind of break in, the Police had requested attendance by the two Directors so, Mia and Daan were to be dropped off back at home.

She decided not to stay in her room after changing into comfortable clothes of leggings and a T shirt and instead watched TV in the main lounge relieved to see Daan go straight to his room, but not for long.

Some minutes later he came back and sat opposite Mia on an armchair wearing only a dressing gown and just staring at her.

Mia continued to watch TV but kept a wary eye on him, she believed Marco and Lieke would not be too long and thought it best to stay in a larger open space with him around.

Her cautiousness was well founded as Daan, making out he was going to the kitchen, suddenly diverted his course and lunged at her as she sat, legs under her, at one end of the couch. He pulled her backwards onto the couch and she smelled alcohol, he had been drinking again. Daan was holding her in a bear hug, but this time, Mia was not going to give in to him no matter what the consequences.

Her coach had recently gone through some grappling, ground defensive work and with a twist of her hips they both ended up on the carpet. He was compromised because of his dressing gown, hardly the attire for any kind of ground fighting. Mia was first up on her knees and Daan was sat upright wondering how she had dared to fight him, but he had underestimated her.

Before he could recover, Mia was behind him and wrapped her slender arms around his neck in a perfectly executed rear naked choke. In the same movement she wrapped her legs tightly around his waist and pulled him back, so he was lying on top of her. She adjusted the choke, locking her arms, and squeezed.

The choke was perfect and deep, Daan's hands went to her arms to try to pry them apart and just before he could end the sentence "You crazy bi—" he convulsed and was asleep, literally snoring in Mia's arms, completely unconscious.

Mia released him and he flopped to the floor, amazed at how she had applied the sleeper hold taught by her coach in a real-life situation.

At that point she saw car headlights on the drive through the netted curtains and knew that Marco and Lieke were home, how would she explain this?

When they entered the room, Mia was over his prostate form, shaking him, "Are you ok, Daan?" she asked. "What is it, Daan, you just collapsed." He came around wondering what had just happened of course, very confused from being put to sleep he couldn't recall very much at that point.

Lieke rushed over, "What happened?" she said worryingly.

"I don't really know," Mia replied, "he came into here and basically passed out, but I can smell whiskey or something on his breath."

Marco took over and was angry and ashamed believing his son was totally drunk. "Lieke!" he barked. "Help me get him to bed so, he can sleep off his drinking."

Daan was shaken and confused, but otherwise ok and his parents helped him into bed.

Lieke came back and said to Mia, "That was strange I knew he sneaked the odd drink but didn't think he ever drank so much."

"I'm not sure," Mia said, "I'm going to bed, too much excitement for one night."

"Yes of course, I hope you enjoyed your birthday, dear, despite this," she said.

"Very much," Mia replied, smiling, "turned out better than I could ever have imagined."

"Good night Lieke."

Mia was buzzing and knew that was the last time he would ever try anything again, a typical Bully, give it back and it ends. Mia slept like a baby that night, but the evening's events made her more determined to train even harder on her martial arts.

Daan never bothered Mia again.

CHAPTER 5

The next few years literally flew by for Mia, she was turning into a confident, highly intelligent young woman with entrepreneurial tendencies.

She absolutely excelled scholastically and extraordinarily and at 18 years old achieved doctorate degrees in both Biomedical Science and Chemistry. Her martial arts hobby was just as successful, winning many amateur tournaments in Singapore, Japan and Malaysia. She became known as the 'Sleeptress' with many of her opponents finishing up snoring in her arms or between her powerful legs. Once the hold was on, they were 'going out' and she sadistically loved the moment an opponent gave in to her anaconda-like sleeper holds and lost consciousness. She had mastered the technique to such a degree that many of her opponents were asleep before they realised in time to tap out. Of course, everything was in a strictly controlled, professionally monitored environment and, aside from the odd opponent peeing themselves whilst going out, all recovered within minutes to fight another day.

Highly qualified academically, Mia had been working part time in a laboratory investigating new advances in skin care products, a passion she shared with her stepmother Lieke, whom, she still maintained contact with after the couple funded a single bed apartment for her.

She blossomed as a woman and leaned naturally towards men in her early sex life and there was never any shortage of would be suitors, Mia was a stunner. However, her looks attracted the shallow, gigolo types, some very ostentatious characters enjoying the fruits of their parents' labours.

She recalled one such example after being invited by a friend of friend who had complimentary tickets, to a 'singles' cocktail extravaganza held at one of the most expensive and elaborate venues in the city; it wasn't really her thing, but her friend had asked her to go as she was a little nervous and so agreed.

The three young Ladies laughed and giggled as they showed their VIP passes to the doormen and marvelled at the high-end cars being valet parked for their designer-dressed drivers, Ferraris, a McLaren and even a Bugatti. None of them had ever been to a venue like this before; it was as if the whole place was filled with beautiful people and the fixtures and fittings appeared solid gold and crystal everywhere, from tastefully modern chandeliers to the brilliantly illuminated cut glasses at the bar areas.

They were shown to their own booth and the VIP passes were inclusive of one complimentary bottle of Champagne so, they raised a glass to each other as her friend announced, "Cheers and here's to finding my rich Knight in Shining Armour."

Mia was totally unconvinced with that, but she played along as the trio chatted and giggled, seemingly only sipping their Champagne then, quickly realising the bottle was empty as she tipped the final drops into her friend's glass flute.

They looked at each other dejectedly and with a further bottle costing around $400 Sing wondered if their night was going to be a short one as far as the alcohol was concerned but then,

"Two more bottles over here please!" a voice piped up.

Three guys in their twenties had noticed the beautiful quarry, out of depth money wise, and the leader had spied the empty Champagne glasses and somewhat disappointed faces of the three friends.

"It's ok thank-you, we are fine," said Mia but her friend had other ideas.

"What she meant was, we are fine with that, why don't you join us?" she invited them, winking at one of the boys.

Seating was arranged Boy, Girl, Boy, Girl and, although not thrilled with the new arrangement, Mia went along.

The Champagne flowed and she had to admit that, initially, it was a civilised gathering. The guy next to her was polite and respectful but noticed that her friend seemed more under the influence of alcohol and she didn't like the guy plying her with it. He became more than friendly, his hand was under her short skirt, he was kissing her neck and she was unresponsive to his advances. The music was loud, and the intensity of the flashing lights had an almost hypnotic strobe type effect and it was obvious to Mia that her friend had been drugged with something. The guy all over her friend reminded her of Daan, a total creep having to resort to underhand moves to get what he wanted, and she was well out of it.

Mia could not sit and watch her friend literally being abused in front of her eyes.

She stood up and went over to the couple who were seated at the end of the group as the other two guys looked on. She grabbed the hand that was busy under the skirt of her friend and twisted his forearm in a Japanese Aikido style wrist lock.

"You, fucking crazy bitch; you're breaking my arm," he screamed in absolute agony.

"That's not all I will break if you don't get up and get away from us you cunt!" she replied calmly.

"And I'm sure the authorities and ultimately your parents will be interested to know what drug you have used on her."

He looked over to his friend as if for direction and he shook his head.

"Ok we are going, let me go," he said, grimacing in pain.

Mia was in fight mode, totally sober and fixed and they realised also that she wasn't to be messed with.

She released the hold and the three of them scurried away to find alternative, less resistant, victims, leaving the girls at their table.

Mia comforted her friend who hadn't comprehended what had just happened, but the other girl was very sympathetic and grateful Mia could look after herself and had noticed what was happening.

The evening was over, and they left, Mia making sure her friend got well hydrated and back to her apartment where, the drug began to wear off.

She didn't have time for things like this, flashy creeps believing they were God's gifts to women and, on the other side, needy guys searching for long term relationships.

She played the game to suit her own needs, sometimes finding uncomplicated relief with same sex adventures, either way she never got serious and chose her career goals over relationships.

CHAPTER 6

She began formulating her own skin care compounds and it was at a beauty exhibition where Mia was introduced to Pietro Allard, a 40-year-old French National, multi-millionaire philanthropist and multiple business owner in the health and beauty/lifestyle industry.

Allard was immediately taken by this young beautiful scientist whom he later discovered could also kick his ass if she wanted to and, following a few business and dinner meetings, offered her the chance to work in one of his R&D laboratories located on Tengah Island, part of an entity called 'Skintakt'. This Lab was used to develop new skincare products for the brand of the same name and supported the topical cream manufacturing facility in Singapore.

He discerned the future potential of this young biochemist straight away, a knack which had got him to where he was today, retaining a strong, dedicated and loyal workforce.

Mia threw herself at the opportunity, unattached and absolutely passionate about her work, she relocated to the Island where she was given beautiful living quarters. On site, a fully equipped gym, and of course a state-of-the-art laboratory which was staffed by six who also lived on the Island. Together with, support staff and two security guards, in total, 18 people ran the facility.

The laboratory, situated on the private island Tengah, used to be a tourist attraction until, following the global pandemic of Covid 19 in 2021, Pietro purchased it and turned it into one of his research facilities. Completely self-contained, barring the weekly supply ship docking at its own, purpose built, jetty and a small airstrip for his private Lear Jet, it was the perfect haven for uninterrupted and dedicated research. The incumbent Hotel type facilities had been converted into staff living quarters and the main Lab complex built in what used to be the main banqueting hall. The existent kitchen/restaurants had been renewed for use as café and canteen facilities and retained an Italian style outlet for those wishing to indulge a little and enjoy themselves between their shifts on the Island.

Mia had always worked with Aloe Vera compounds and the Lab had its own acreage of the plant managed by two resident agricultural hands and used exclusively for the research she was conducting.

This was a dream position for Mia, and she threw herself into her work. Pietro visited occasionally, but did not interfere, he had taken her under his wing, treated her like a daughter and knew she was working hard, developing innovative, future products for his business.

Following an ordinary hard day's work in the Lab and an even more gruelling session in the gym, almost destroying the kick bag, Mia had showered and was looking at her naked body in the full-length mirror.

She was a perfectionist and beautiful, but despite this, the single 'flaw' which really bothered her was a faded burn mark just over 2cm in diameter, to the left of her lower back just above her 'bum cheek' as she referred to it. She had gotten experimental with her hair a few years ago whilst home alone. She had borrowed Lieke's hair straighteners, misplaced them carelessly on the bed and inadvertently rolled over onto them, singing her skin painfully. Despite the first aid of Aloe Vera, the burn had scarred and to her was a blot on an otherwise beautiful landscape.

Barring surgery she had always hoped for some magical cream that would remove it naturally and had tried many of her experimental compounds and mixtures, but as expected, to little or no effect.

CHAPTER 7

Mia blinked her eyes as if waking from a dream and snapped out of her reminiscing, finally gathering herself with a stark realisation of where she was and what had just taken place. The first call she made was to the man she considered her father and guardian, Pietro, and the second to the authorities. She was desperate for a shower to wash away the filth of her attacker, but also wanted to help with any forensic protocols at the scene.

She needed psychological assurance, personal attention, and was grateful when Pietro arrived at the same time as the Police.

He was horrified at what he found and his gym security guard who had been paid to leave early that night would not be returning; that was a certainty.

His main concern was Mia and she flung her arms around him sobbing and distraught.

"Thank god," Pietro sighed, "thank god," he repeated.

It was late into the early hours of morning by the time the Police had secured the gym, they interviewed Mia at the scene and later at the Police station. Satisfied they didn't need her anymore at this time and, of course being with the influential and upstanding Pietro Allard, they allowed her to return to her Hotel.

He escorted Mia to her room and stayed while she spent at least an hour under the shower trying to wash away the male degenerate who had assaulted her.

She alighted from the shower and was absolutely, physically and mentally drained and not that aware, but she happened to glance backwards into the mirror.

Was this her mind paying tricks? Her exhaustion, tiredness, fatigue? Where was her burn scar?

She put it down to sheer exhaustion, slept the whole day and when she finally awoke in the late afternoon, Pietro was sitting in a chair by her bed fast asleep, he had stayed watching over her.

She rubbed her eyes wondering if it had all been a dream, but then the reality came back, and she realised it had all been true and horrifically real.

Pietro awoke and was happy to see her fit and well.

"I can't believe what happened to me," she said, "it all happened so fast and I, I killed someone," she stammered tearfully.

"Don't concern yourself with that right now," he told her. "You were the victim, you need rest, I have arranged with the investigating official that I will get you back to Tengah and if they need you again, they will contact me, right now they are satisfied you acted in self- defence."

The assailant had been identified by the Police as being known to them and was listed on a sex offenders register, another case of dangerous, known, violent scum being allowed to mix with law abiding and gentle folk, a story the world over propagated by 'do-gooders'. For average citizens the world was now one depraved pervert less to fear for the safety of their children and womenfolk.

Pietro flew Mia back to Tengah with a security guard just to give her more reassurance that she was safe now. He had a million and one things to do in the capital before flying on to Jakarta for more business meetings, but was certain Mia was ok.

CHAPTER 8

Mia felt comfortable in familiar surroundings, there was a bond between the whole team on Tengah and colleagues offered their support to anything she might need, but all she desired was sleep, so, she went to her rooms and did just that, only materialising the following day.

As she awoke and adjusted to her now safe and familiar surroundings, she recalled what she thought must have been a dream experienced during her long sleep, but was it a dream?

Mia threw off the covers and literally, flew out of bed and into the bathroom where she turned herself to gaze at her rear, lower torso in the mirror.

"No!" she cried. "It, it just can't be." But it was. The scar Mia had carried since her teens was completely gone, vanished without a trace, just as if it had never existed. This was impossible, it didn't make any sense. How? Why? When? Who? What? All the expected open- ended questions requiring answers for a professional, scientific researcher's mind and brain to ignite and plunge headlong into overdrive appeared.

"Too much!" she thought and backslid to the trusted mindset gained from her scientific, martial arts training and meditation techniques. She accepted that there would be a tangible, logical explanation, but dealing with this phenomenon at this time was too much on top of everything else. She put it to the back of her mind, calmed herself, showered, dressed, not for the Lab today, and then ate some breakfast of salmon, poached eggs and avocado with her favourite Columbian blend coffee.

She took the time to catch up on some social stuff. Pietro called reassuring her everything was ok with the authorities and she should take as much recuperation time as she needed. Mia had never once ruminated Marco as a father figure, but she had a mother/daughter type bond and relationship with Lieke, and it had been a while since they last spoke.

Lieke was happy to hear her voice but was very distraught as Mia explained what had happened over the past two days. Mia assured her she was fine, and they began to talk about what was happening back in Singapore.

She could tell Lieke was troubled as she began talking about how Daan had become a bigger problem, dropping out of his expensive high-end education, over-eating, with no job and no intention of finding one.

She explained cleaning his room was a dreadful affair all he did was play video games, watch pornography, drink spirits and blamed the opposite sex for all his problems, saying 'those bitches' had caused his miserable and depressive state. Marco, although not happy with the situation, was over supportive in the circumstances and didn't really chastise him enough into doing anything about it. As a mother, she was worried about his mental stability and health wellbeing.

Mia was sorry for Lieke. She imagined how hard it must have been for her, but, she said, she spent a lot of time with her hobbies and asked if Mia had discovered a new skin cream cure for all ails, jokingly.

"Not yet," Mia laughed, "but you won't believe this." And she went on to tell Lieke about how her burn scar had miraculously vanished.

"That's impossible," Lieke said, "things like that are permanent unless removed surgically and that can often lead to complications; have you no idea what could have caused this to happen?"

"No," replied Mia, but she did. "Oh my God!" she stammered. "No, that's just not possible."

"What is, I mean isn't?" Lieke asked, confused.

Mia couldn't tell her what she was thinking right now, not at this time.

"Oh, nothing," she stuttered, "you know how I get carried away with my thoughts," she quipped, laughing.

"Always did and always will," teased Lieke.

They parted mutually happy they had chatted, but she needed to get back into the Lab.

CHAPTER 9

For the rest of the day Mia couldn't reconcile what she had suddenly contemplated, it made no sense; scientifically, biomedically, topically or anything else for that matter. However, one fact remained, the only unknown substance to have come into contact with her burn scar was, the sperm she had inadvertently spread on her lower back from the would-be rapist as she choked him to death between her legs.

She was first into the Lab the next day and didn't know where to start but had to see if she could find anything supporting her theory.

Of course, sperm was life and she had never really examined the male reproductive cell any further than her earlier basic studies in human biology. She knew it was quite complex, created by male procreative organs and made up mainly of water, plasma, mucus, a few calories and some commonly found nutrients. There was, however, no suggestion that it possessed properties other than the human reproduction of life. Frozen properly it had an almost indefinite life although 10 years was normally the maximum for fertility use. Outside the body, however, even in the right conditions it could only remain alive for 15–30 minutes. The word 'Reproduction' parked itself in her mind, could it be responsible for reproducing and regenerating damaged skin or cells, like her awful scar? This could be an absolutely earth-shattering development in skin care advancement, something she could not even begin to imagine the possibilities of. The only lead was this unknown substance she had experienced that had propagated more than just reproduction of life, but that wasn't much help to her at this stage.

Undeterred, she researched everything she could find about the male sperm and arranged for some Lab samples for testing, easily obtained via Pietro's premier infertility clinic based in Zurich. The only disadvantage, it would be frozen, but it was somewhere to start.

CHAPTER 10

Back in Singapore, Daan, although still having much confusion and disrespect for the opposite sex, and no feelings for the same sex, had made progress, although with insidious intent, towards smartening himself up. Despite his failings he had achieved a reasonable level of education and, guided by his father, now worked in the business as a junior accountant and freight shipping advisor. He had lost some weight and although not athletically built by any means was now more 'thick set' than obese. His father had bought a chic, one-bedroom apartment for him in a trendy tower block in the City and he paid the rent from his salary and lived alone.

He never got over how Mia had humiliated him, a 'girl' rejecting, ameliorating, him and he still spent hours viewing pornography related to the 'sexual abuse' of women, fantasising that the licensed and legal scenarios he watched were in fact, non-consensual on the part of the female actors.

As a known business man and model citizen, his father had received 'friendly' tip offs from local Police that they had received complaints of a 'mild' nature regarding behaviour related to Daan's 'bar fly' presence in some of the bars around the Orchard Road area. He would always be alone, had no friends to speak of, and would drink until confident enough to speak to girls, but it always ended in him becoming verbally abusive toward them. This area was widely known for its readily available offerings of prostitutes looking to fulfil all kinds of sexual fantasies for their clientele. Daan of course had tried this, but to him, someone acting and playing a role for money just did not cut it. He became frustrated with the girls, they rejected his aggressive advances even for money and having panic alarms and pimps watching for their safety and the like, had not wanted to draw attention to himself in this way.

He turned to dating sites and with the advantage for poetic license regarding his profile, not surprisingly, received some encouraging responses. His profile picture was himself and with the weight loss and blond wavy hair he appeared 'fairly attractive' to would be suitors also using this method to meet people. Daan figured some of these girls would also be shy, slightly desperate and, more for him, vulnerable.

Then, recently whilst browsing photographs on a dating site his heart almost stopped when the picture of a young woman appeared. The profile picture bore the uncanny resemblance of Mia, or 'the bitch' who remained responsible for his sexual failings and final humiliation.

He began by sending a 'flirt' and having received the same back, began messaging her with his false 'perfect gentleman' approach and received reciprocal chat regarding shared interests like nature, food, rock music and an introvert type demeanour.

After some toing and froing of messages and sharing mobile numbers, the couple arranged to meet, a date, and Daan was excited. He was also very nervous and couldn't help feeling conscious regarding the ultimate deliberation on his mind.

The girl was 23 years old and a bookkeeper. She was half Japanese, half Vietnamese, with a slight build and beautiful long, jet black hair just like Mia, he thought. Her name was Makayo and she had been brought up by her grandmother who had passed recently so, she was pretty much alone and seeking companionship.

CHAPTER 11

The couple met at a modest local Asian restaurant and, although not used to drinking alcohol, Makayo had been persuaded by Daan to take some wine.

He acted out the part having read up on dating etiquette: being a good listener, not talking about himself too much with more interest in her, making her laugh, paying compliments when he could. It was going very well for him.

She noticed how quickly he was draining his wine glass, but he countered saying he was just a little nervous, which she accepted with a smile.

They chatted for a good two hours with a bottle of wine for each hour. Daan had drunk the most but Makayo had consumed more than she would have originally intended to and, more worryingly, in excess of what she was used to and could manage.

It turned out that they both genuinely harboured a love for old vinyl rock music records, he had gotten this from his Father who had built up an extensive collection and had gifted part of it to him.

As it was time to leave the restaurant, Daan suggested that they go back to his apartment and he could play some of his music for her.

"I'm not sure about that," Makayo said, "it is our first date, we don't really know each other and no offence but, more than that, I don't really know you."

"Of course," said Daan. "I've just enjoyed your company very much and didn't want it to end so soon, we can just sit at opposite ends of my studio," he said laughing, "and listen to some rock."

Makayo had enjoyed the evening, it was nice to have met someone with, what she thought were, mutual interests and if truth be known totally sober, would not have agreed, but she did and the next thing she knew they were getting out of a taxi at the foot of his residential tower.

He paid the taxi then opened the door for her. "My lady," he said stooping regally. She got out of the taxi smiling at his over-acted show of chivalry but remained unsure and apprehensive.

"Listen," said Daan, gambling on what he was about to say. "If you really feel uncomfortable about two friends having a drink and listening to some music in a safe apartment then, I will call another taxi and you can go home, I completely understand, here," he said, "this is my business card, take a picture and send it to one of your friends, I have nothing to hide, my father is a society businessman well known with the authorities. You are perfectly safe with me."

Makayo decided it would be ok and they went up to Daan's penthouse apartment on the top floor.

The familiar security guard at the entrance had checked them in and he was surprised to see him, for the first time, accompanied by a girl. Attending local police seminars as part of his job he had become aware of some of Daan's behaviour and was a little cautious as to what he had just witnessed. However, he rightfully owned the apartment, had never caused trouble before and so he went about his business, watching the live CCTV footage covering all floors.

He observed and logged the couple enter the penthouse apartment on the top floor and went back to his coffee.

CHAPTER 12

Daan was deviously acting out the gentleman role; he took Makayo's coat and sat her down on a comfortable two-seater couch pulling up a side table for her. He opened a bottle of wine similar in characteristics to what they had been drinking and placed a poured glass for her.

"I shouldn't really," she said. "I'm already a little tipsy," she added, giggling.

"Don't worry," Daan assured her, "we will only drink and enjoy some music together."

She seemed relaxed; she curled her legs under her and waited for the music. The apartment was tastefully decorated by his mother, Lieke, stylish modern furniture without being cluttered, a large TV on the wall and a sophisticated stereo sound system: Mordant Short speakers and Bang and Olufsen record deck. They deliberated over some of their favourite artists and chose to listen to some classic Bon Jovi. Daan sat back and cranked up the volume from his remote as he sat opposite her, as promised.

The couple were lost in the music and he appeared human for once, but, as his intake of alcohol increased so did his ego and confidence. They listened to more artists whilst Daan played the perfect host, going over to refill Makayo's wine glass.

"Mind if I sit here now so we can rock together?" he quipped, imitating a drummer with air drumsticks.

She was quite tipsy by this time and said it was ok. Daan sat next to her and after a while put his hand to rest on her leg.

Makayo didn't think anything of this, after all, he had been the perfect gentleman and hadn't been disrespectful to her in any way.

Downstairs at the reception, the security guard had been alerted to excessively loud music by the resident below Daan's apartment. He had tried calling, but there had been no reply, which meant he would have to follow up physically on his next scheduled round.

Meanwhile, Daan had transmuted effortlessly from Jekyll to Hyde: his other, more sincere, side, and had moved closer to Makayo, she was nervous, but still didn't feel threatened until he leaned in and tried to kiss her.

"No!" she said commandingly. "What are you doing?" as she tried to move away from his advance.

"It's ok," he assured her, "we have had a nice evening, I like you and you like me, it's only natural."

"No!" she repeated. "This is not what I want." Bingo! His fantasy phrase, he couldn't believe she'd uttered those exact words and the real Daan revealed its abhorrent self. "You 'bitches' think you can lead me on," he snarled, "take advantage of my kindness without reward, well I'm taking it right now!" he cried.

Daan towered over her, ripping at her clothes like a man possessed, she tried to resist but was easily overpowered as she tried screaming, but, of course, the music was too loud, and her head was swimming from the wine. He pulled off his trousers and pants and, like the depraved rapist he was, supported an erection which he proceeded to force inside Makayo.

But, Daan hadn't heard the repeated banging on his apartment door and continued his lewd, disgusting act, coming quickly inside of her, at which point the music stopped as he said quietly,

"Take that Mia you fucking' bitch!" then, silence apart from the loud thumping on the door, the whimpering and desperate sobbing of a terrified young girl, an innocent victim of unquestionable rape.

Makayo realised her horrific ordeal was over. There was someone at the door, someone to help, a saviour, she thought.

"Help!" she shouted for all she was worth. "Please help me," she screamed.

Daan put his hand forcibly, over her mouth.

"What's going on in there?" shouted the security guard. "Come to the door please, sir!" he demanded.

"Err, it's fine here, everything is ok," Daan replied. "Just a misunderstanding; it's all good here, no need to bother," he shouted back unconvincingly.

"No, sir, please open the door!" he repeated. "I have called the Police and they are minutes away; you need to come to the door now!" he demanded.

Daan knew he was in trouble, he climbed off from Makayo's trembling form and just sat staring into space.

Makayo realised she was free, grabbed a throw, wrapped it around herself and fled for the door.

She burst into the corridor and flung herself at the guard,

"Help me please," she begged, "I, I have been raped," she pleaded, crying profusely.

Daan heard the word rape, it repeated in his head and he froze in stark realisation, he had really done it this time and his home city was not the place for such a crime.

The guard sat Makayo down in the corridor. "You are safe now," he said, comfortingly, and further called for an ambulance.

"Just stay here, the Police are coming, it's over," he assured her.

He went to the open door, looked inside and saw Daan just sitting as if in a dream or state of shock still gazing blankly at the wall. He decided not to engage him but just guard the only exit until the Police arrived which they did in only a matter of minutes.

Daan was arrested and taken, the apartment sealed for forensic study, and Makayo taken to hospital for examination and treatment.

CHAPTER 13

Mia was first into the Lab most days and for the past weeks had worked tirelessly with the human sperm samples she had gained from the infertility clinic in Zurich. She still had no clue where the research was leading, every scientific fact she could find pointed to a dead end or complete non-starter, but she had to persist, a burning inside saying something was going to present itself.

This day was particularly heavy going, one roadblock after another, she was overwhelmed with frustration and couldn't imagine it getting any worse, but it did.

She received a call from Lieke regarding the arrest of Daan on a charge of rape which had happened two months prior. The sentencing had just been passed by the judge.

"Oh my God, I'm so sorry to hear that," Mia said. She had no feelings for Daan and believed jail was the best place for him, but she had deep feelings for Lieke and after all it was her son. "What does it mean for him?"

She explained that the system for such crime in Singapore was swift and decisive. She went on to expound that the punishment protocol for rape was divided into bands with increasing severity based on the number of 'Aggravating' factors relating to the crime committed. So, the more aggravating factors the higher the band. Marco had hired the best lawyers and psychiatric doctors to plead his case but, despite this and his local influence, Daan received a Band one charge meaning one aggravating factor, that he took advantage of her because she was drunk. The sentence was eight years and a maximum six strokes of the cane.

Of course, Lieke was distraught, but always wondered what had happened between Mia and Daan, believing something, maybe similar, was hidden. Therefore, together with her sympathy for the young victim Makayo, she accepted his punishment. Mia did her best to console Lieke and was shocked at what she said came out at the trial.

"Mia," she said worryingly, "I find it difficult to repeat, but in the statement by the victim she said that as he had finished inside her, he said calmly 'take that Mia you fucking bitch'." There was a silence "I don't know what he meant Mia," said Lieke, "I always believed something happened between the two of you and I don't want to know now, but at least you are safe and he is in prison."

"It's ok," Mia said, rather unconvincingly, "it will be ok, I have to go now, again I'm sorry, take care and I promise to visit soon."

CHAPTER 14

Tengah Island is situated off the coast of Singapore/Malaysia, and on shipping routes between Cambodia and Thailand to Kuala Lumpur and Jakarta through the Gulf of Thailand and between Kuala Lumpur and Japan.

Vietnam had long been a haven for sexual predators and perverts especially for European men unable to find such 'treats' in their respective countries.

As a result, the prison system was overloaded with these 'unwanted' society predators and transfer of prisoners by sea from Vietnam to Malaysia and Singapore occurred at least once per month.

The supervision of these journeys fell under dubious, contracted, security companies, managed by inexperienced employees and corruption was rife. There had been many reports of prisoners failing to reach their intended destination, reported as 'lost at sea' or simply 'missing' from the manifest on arrival.

Jordan Price was a 56-year-old British citizen on the sexual offenders list in his own country and had been a regular visitor to Vietnam. He was part of a group who, worked together in a network to gain entry via other countries to Vietnam. He was thin and with weasel like features, around 60kg soaking wet through, and with receding grey hair long at the back in a Ponytail.

It had been his sixth such visit, but this time his luck had ran out. He fell victim himself caught in a joint operation between UK and Vietnamese authorities, he had been apprehended with the intention to have sex with an under-age girl.

Price had only been in the country for a few days staying in low-class accommodation in a 'recommended' target area of prostitution and trafficking reputation. The group shared information of where to go, where to stay, contacts of active 'Pimps' in a location who could provide and supply girls to

38

suit individual preferences. Price was disgusting and had a sick preference for young teens, the exploitation of which was easy with the power of the dollar in such deprived classes and communities. His previous five visits had been so 'easy', and he had grown a little complacent. The contact he had been given did not have what he was looking for and, whilst drinking in a bar, he committed the cardinal sin of making an agreement with an 'undetermined' Pimp who, himself lacked security awareness. The Pimp was under surveillance and had been for a while, but Price paid him the money deposit and received an address and a time for the following day.

The next day Price was happy again, spending it playing the fake tourist-cum-amateur photographer, taking pictures with his camera of local scenes at the markets. This was his adopted cover, he used ID from a made-up photographic agency and carried semi-professional camera equipment, striking up 'heartfelt' rapport with the local people and even rewarding them for their appearance in a shot. He was covertly tailed all day by non-uniform Police and didn't notice anything out of the ordinary, after all, he'd done this before, many times.

CHAPTER 15

Evening came around, he was dressed smartly in a Khaki, casual Linen suit, white cotton shirt and deck shoes minus socks. He knew the bars in the area and had some time, so, he took a beer sitting outside and watched the crowded streets bustling into evening life. He had developed a taste for the 'Red Label', stronger version, of the local brew 'Saigon Beer' and was supping into it slowly savouring its unique flavour. He was getting very excited now, the twisted mind of a pervert, as his meeting time grew nearer. He began to plan in his sick mind how it would go, imagining the thrill it gave him being referred to as 'Daddy', his own special brand of depraved lust.

He looked at his watch and made his way to the meeting point where he met the Pimp, paid him the remaining 50% of his fee and was handed a piece of paper with an apartment number written on it.

He made his way inside the given building, mainly of timber construction, in a row of similar buildings. It was dimly lit and there was the sound of muffled music, some shouting and a baby's crying as he headed for the top floor.

He found the door and it was slightly ajar, so, he pushed and went inside closing it behind him. The room was full of shadows cast from the dim lights outside and through a net curtain up at the open sash window. There was a musky smell, not unpleasant, but reminding him of a wooden galley or small cabin on an old ship.

Wooden furniture was sparsely arranged around the room and, the highlight, a single wood constructed bed against the wall opposite the door he had just entered through. The single orange glow light came from a small table lamp and illuminated the bed. His heart began to flutter as he gazed onto it seeing a young, innocent looking, teenage girl kneeling upright. She was pretty, long dark hair, clean and tidy and wearing only a nightgown, she stared straight at him forcing a smile from her lips, she must have been no more than 13 years old.

"What's your name?" he asked her.

"Thom," she replied shakily and with heavy accent.

"Do you know the word 'Daddy'?" he asked her

She nodded but did not speak.

He pointed to himself and said, "Daddy, ok, say Daddy," he instructed her.

There were no more words and he never got the depraved gratification he craved as the door was almost ripped from its hinges with a loud splintering of wood by the local Police crashing his planned, illicit exploit.

"On your knees now!" was what he heard next, from an armed officer, he was caught and apprehended, the girl being taken by a female officer at the same time, possibly only for now, but she was out of the situation.

There was a one to five year jail sentence for this crime, but an extradition order was put in place, and he was to be housed temporarily at the Chi Hoa Prison Centre in Ho Chi Minh City, 'temporary' as in he had already been there for 7 months awaiting his transfer.

Price was destined for Prison ship transfer to Singapore for his final extradition back to the UK to face trial, but he knew if he reached Singapore he would not get away.

He had heard of prisoners, unofficially, not completing the journey, rumours of being drowned at sea trying to escape, eaten by Sharks etc. but, he thought this a better option, especially if the network could help him. His specially placed lawyer had updated him that he should be taken to Singapore in the coming weeks so, he had to make plans.

CHAPTER 16

Mia's day never really recovered as she continued with her tenacious, self-driven attitude. She pushed herself hard at both work and play so, after the long, upsetting day, decided she needed some play time, some womanly attention.

Her early experiences of the opposite sex being all complication, self-gratification and aggression, Mia, by no means Lesbian, preferred the company of the 'gentler' sex.

She referred to the erect male penis as being like that of a loaded handgun with safety disengaged, if you touch it, it could explode at any time and make a mess. So, she steered clear of both having no need for either.

She did, however, maybe borne out of her dominance of opponents in the MMA tournaments and wanting to be in charge herself, like to be in control.

She had come across Carol, a 22-year-old research scientist who had lived around the regions, mainly in capital cities and followed her elder brother around the MMA tournament circuits. Being a relatively amateur Judo student herself, she had also, indirectly, encountered Mia AKA the 'Sleeptress' during this time.

She had been astounded in disbelief at the coincidence when she was accepted to the lab on the island having been interviewed and meeting Mia in person and they hit it off immediately with common ground and admiration on Carol's part. And admire her new Boss she did, obsessed with Mia's beauty, poise, athleticism and charm with words, the perfect submissive's play partner. Carol was of slight build, a native Australian, but brought to the region by her father who travelled with his work. She was around 150cm tall and slim build, with small breasts, hair in a 'bob' shape and a pretty, innocent looking face with pale complexion. She held almost equivalent scientific qualifications, to those of Mia and was a devout disciple to excellence and attention to detail in her work ethic. On a personal level she was easy going and laid back, sometimes to the detriment of being too trusting and under cautious, she also lacked enthusiasm when it came to remembering things that were surplus to her scientific mindset.

As Mia passed by her workstation, she caught her attention and said,

"Carol I would like to see you around 8pm in my apartment for a debrief of today."

"Yes, Miss Mia, of course I will be there," she confirmed, a tremble in her voice.

She knew what this meant, her heart began racing and she felt weak at the knees, her day was about to get amazingly exciting and she was breathless which, of course, Mia knew, smiling as she walked away.

CHAPTER 17

The two had met more 'intimately' yet, in the public area of the facilities gym where Mia was working with bag and gloves and she noticed Carol in a Judogi doing some stretches and transitioning into some solo practice 'Nage Waza' Judo (throwing techniques).

Mia recognised the art and style and quipped smiling, "Think you could throw me?"

"Of course," Carol replied rather unconvincingly. Mia knew she would outmatch her by size and weight alone but admired her spirit of not backing down.

"Shall we have a semi-competitive grapple?" Mia suggested. "It would be nice to have a 'friendly' in the flesh opponent for once, maybe we could learn from each other."

"Sure," Carol replied.

To make it fair, Mia was wearing skin- tight leggings, kick boxing boots and a training vest so, she took off her boots and socks and picked up a Judogi from the rack in the gym. As it was going to be more of a grapple, this meant both girls would be able to have a grip on each other's Judo suits.

She had every intention of being gentle with her 'tiny', in comparison, opponent as they gripped each other's Judogi jackets just above the elbow. Mia was surprised at the firm grip and stance from her opponent and even more surprised when Carol, with a much lower centre of gravity, suddenly dropped, twisting and pivoting at the hips, unbalancing and throwing her to the floor. Despite the surprise, Mia was still holding on, and her ground fighting technique skills would have been easily enough to dislodge Carol, but instead she burst out laughing.

"That will teach me," she said. "Never underestimate your opponent," she added, laughing

Carol was also laughing by now. "I knew you would go easy on me," she replied, "as I'm on top shall we go from here?"

"Why not," said Mia, rolling Carol onto her side.

They went on to have a noble, semi-competitive grapple on the floor, serious yet 'friendly' with advice on holds and techniques going both ways, Carol not being used to fighting until you can't continue rather than being called out for each submission hold.

The girls were hot and sweaty, and Mia noticed Carol didn't put up much resistance when she was on top of her, like she enjoyed it. Then, out of the blue, Carol said,

"Show me one of your 'Sleeper' holds, a basic front head scissor," she suggested.

Carol lay on her tummy with Mia seated in front of her lifting her head. Mia lay back, wrapping her thighs around Carol's neck in a straight head scissor hold and crossing her ankles.

"You must tap if you feel dizzy," Mia said, smiling.

Carol would have stayed there forever; Mia tightened her grip slowly using her toned, adductor, inner thigh muscles to constrict Carol's neck. She closed her eyes sighing and caressing the thighs around her throat.

Mia had always loved this sadistic state and felt her pussy tingling as Carol attempted to get even closer to her sex.

They both realised what was happening and knew immediately that this was a mutually pleasurable situation.

The tighter Mia squeezed the more intense feelings she was having, and Carol appeared to be in heaven and began groaning, fervently caressing Mia thighs, enjoying every moment, her own legs spread apart and grinding her womanly mound against the forgiving mats.

Mia knew she would lose consciousness as she was not going to tap, so was careful not to apply that finishing squeeze, and instead let her enjoy what was happening. And enjoy she did, in the next moment she shuddered involuntarily and orgasmed right there on the mats.

Mia released her grip and let her just lay for a while.

"I'm sorry," Carol said, "I couldn't help myself and now I feel so embarrassed." The gym had long been unoccupied except for the two of them. Mia leaned in and kissed Carol on the mouth lightly.

"Don't worry," she said, "I think we should train more often, but, in private next time," she added, smiling.

"Really?" Carol said surprised, "I would like that very much."

From that day the two met maybe twice per week in Mia's room where they developed some intimately personal role play scenarios, they mutually enjoyed and were able to explore Mia's dominant sadistic side, matching perfectly with the submissive, masochistic Carol.

CHAPTER 18

Jordan Price arose from his bunk as the 5am bell sounded, his roommate had already filled the cell with a vile smell from emptying his bowels into the enclosed toilet they shared, but, at least they had running water and a comparatively, efficient sewerage system.

There were worse prisons in the world, but conditions were still grim and regular stomach upsets were common mainly through the lack of hygiene regimes practiced in the kitchens.

The cell doors were opened and the two stood outside for roll call followed by the ceremonial march to the eating area for breakfast.

It was relatively calm, there was rarely any bother if you knew and accepted your place in the ruling gangs, and most were short term sentences awaiting transfer with no 'lifers' to worry about.

Price lived a solitary life in Bristol UK, pretty much kept himself to himself after being relocated from his birthplace in West London following his 'Minor' offence and addition to the sexual offender's register.

This was, however, his front but behind was his life of illegal pornography funded by a 'nest egg' of wealth left to him by his father, so, he wasn't short financially.

He was part of a group of similar deviants partaking in regular visits to the Far east to carry out their sordid perversions all of whom were moving in business circles and well-funded.

The group had developed a network of local contacts in most of the places they frequented, some in law enforcement where they could engage in corruption. Price's crime was attempted to be paid off but the local, corrupt, officer was outranked by the investigating officer working with the Interpol Task Force.

However, a new plan was put into place and underway to make sure he didn't reach Singapore for his final extradition to the UK.

It was visitor day and his visitor would be giving him the final details of how this was going to happen on his sea journey in the coming weeks.

How much money you had resulted in how efficient the escape would be. Price knew that some prisoners had done the same but could only pay the guards on the vessel to let them out, then turn their backs whilst they went over the side.

This was risky at best, there were riptide under-currents, sharks and often they never made land fall on one of the islands or the mainland.

His plan was better financed, in that, at a timely point in the journey he would be allowed to slip into the water with a life vest and a small craft would be positioned to pick him up and transfer him to a larger vessel, he would be reported as lost at sea.

He was looking forward to his freedom, a potential clean slate, and everything was in place, he just had to keep out of trouble and see out the next few weeks.

CHAPTER 19

Carol rang the doorbell to Mia's apartment like a nervous schoolgirl about to see the headmistress and despite this happening many times she still shook in anticipation, weak at the knees.

The meeting was always strictly pleasure time, from the first ring of the doorbell to sneaking out the following morning, no work talk, no stress, just pure unadulterated pleasure.

She was wearing a full flower, pastel coloured, patterned kimono made of silk, her dainty feet housed in comfy, furry pink slippers.

She wore little make-up but smelled of sweet jasmine as the door opened automatically.

The room was dimly, but tastefully, lit with aromatic candles and soft relaxing music. Mia's apartment was much larger than her own, very karma-like decorated and with minimal clutter of furniture.

She knew where Mia would be and still marvelled at the size of her custom-made bed which reminded her literally of a full-size wrestling ring, firm mattress and swathed in beautiful, cerise silk with pillows that swallowed your form when you lay on them.

The scenario was scripted role play with both accepting wilfully their respective roles.

Mia was kneeling upright on the bed completely naked apart from a tasteful gold waist chain rising over hips where her hands were commandingly placed. Her body glistened in the light of the candles, lightly oiled with fragrant essential oils, her jet-black hair tied in a tight, playful looking ponytail.

"What are you here for?" Mia demanded.

"I am here to surrender to your power," Carol stammered, tingling with excitement.

"What power?" Mia replied.

"To the power of your thighs, Miss Mia, and to pleasure your body in any way I can."

"Take off your robe!" Mia demanded.

Carol undid the belt around her waist and stepped out of her slippers allowing the robe to cascade elegantly to the floor.

She was completely naked and stood, hands by her side, awaiting the next instruction.

Mia looked her up and down noticing her pert nipples erect with excitement on her small round breasts.

"I approve." Mia nodded. "Come over here to the bed and lie down on your back."

She complied, lay on her back, legs slightly apart, hands by her side, eyes closed.

Mia positioned herself, knees placed either side of Carol's head facing her feet.

She reached down and began to gently pinch her pouting nipples. She sighed, squirming slightly and biting her lip.

"Tell me what you need," Mia demanded.

"Please, Miss Mia, I need to be trapped in your thighs, wrapped tightly around my neck, so I can barely breathe," she gasped.

Mia continued the fore play on her nipples, no oil, so that there was a little added, pleasurable, pain rolling them between her fingertips.

"My legs are dangerous," Mia said. "Are you sure this is what you need?".

"Yes, please, Miss Mia." As she squirmed, head trapped between Mia's knees.

Mia leaned forward, her hands at the side of Carol's hips, then, as she lifted her head, simultaneously caught her neck between her thighs, crossing her ankles, lifting herself up and squeezing the head trapped tightly between them in a classic reverse head scissor hold.

Both girls were transported, Carol closed her eyes in ecstasy caressing the thighs, glutes and perfect ass engulfing her neck. In comparison Mia's thighs were overwhelming, the small face of Carol disappearing in flesh.

Mia loved this also, her fetish for a trapped neck between her legs, the throat of her victim pulsing against her naked, completely shaved, pussy.

Carol parted her legs and Mia went down on her already wet, womanly sex immediately finding her erect clitoris.

She was in heaven, choking between Mia's perfect thighs and being licked and sucked at the same time.

Her breathing turned to panting, her heart racing, beating out of her chest. Mia expertly controlled the amount of pressure on the girl's neck again using her powerful adductors, keeping her on the edge of consciousness, right where Carol loved to be, almost dreaming.

"Can't breathe," she gasped, "please, Miss Mia, you're choking me." She gurgled.

Mia removed her mouth from Carol's slit. "This is what you came for bitch," she added then, reached back to look at the helpless face buried in her glutes and ass. She relaxed her grip, grabbing her head by the hair and pulling her almost limp form deeper into her leggy prison. Carol just moaned, accepting the new position and returning her hands to Mia's hips as she turned on the pressure once more, then buried her face back into Carol's snatch, sucking on her clitoris and tightening her deadly grip further.

Seconds later, and before Carol went completely into La La land, she bucked her hips and orgasmed, erupting like a volcano spurting love juices which Mia eagerly lapped up holding her, till the involuntary spasms subsided.

Mia released the willing prisoner from between her silky thighs and rolled over onto the bed allowing her to breathe again and recover from the intense orgasm and light-headedness induced by the choking.

Mia had always been fascinated with masochists enjoying being choked whilst reaching orgasm. She had read stories and newspaper reports where men had died (by mistake) alone, masturbating whilst choking themselves with rope. Not realising they had gone too far before it was too late, and they passed out first and then choked to death. It was said that an orgasm being choked was very intense for people who enjoyed it.

Mia wondered if in some weird way, the would-be rapist she had encountered had felt this phenomenon and why he had cum almost involuntarily and without being touched.

After a brief rest and a couple of sips of wine Mia lay back onto the silk pillows raising her knees and parting her thighs ready for her lover.

She went straight down on Mia's pouting pussy, wet from choking her, lapping up the spilled juices and then homing in on her excited clitoris which she expertly found, easily.

Mia lay back, eyes closed, whilst Carol tongued her pussy, caressing her hips as she licked and sucked.

"Eat me out completely, right there, now!" Mia demanded.

She responded, sucking hard on the clitoris trapped in her mouth, working up the perfect un-ending rhythmic cycle until Mia gripped the bed sheets and she too had a beautiful, intense orgasm.

The girls rested but the night was still young, and they had toys, taking it in turns with the vibrator working over each other's bodies: nipples, lower back, inner thighs and tingling pussies.

Then the finale for the night, Mia reached for and lubricated the double ended Dildo, both girls getting into a lesbian scissor position so that each would be fucked by the other.

Starting slowly and hands all over each other where they could reach as they were both penetrated by the hard rubber sex toy. They built up to a beautiful climax achieving an explosive orgasm simultaneously, then rolling over and falling asleep.

That was a girlie night, men not required, no complications or loaded gun.

CHAPTER 20

As was almost usual, Mia had woken from a beautiful sleep to find a small note from her lover who had creeped out and back to her room in the early morning. She showered and after last night's relief of tensions, was highly motivated to begin work on an almost impossible theory that for some reason, human sperm had something to do with being able to repair, wrinkly or scarred, damaged skin tissue.

Mia said good morning to the staff in the Lab as she made her way to the research area and noticed that Carol was already at her station or was it that she was 'glowing' at her station, she smiled to herself, but that was last night and this was now work.

She experimented with some of the sperm samples she had, straining, separating, synthesising checking reactions to stored cultures she used when developing new skin care compounds but, nothing. She was attaining absolute zero on every front and by the end of the day believed sperm was just for fertilising eggs in the right place at the right time and everything aside from that was totally inert.

She held conference calls with experts at the infertility establishment and they too could offer no leads or avenues to explore. It just seemed a dead end and yet something happened, it did, and she couldn't help but think she was missing something. What had happened that fateful night back in Kuala Lumpur that changed things?

Undeterred with physical and practical testing, Mia buried her head in search engines and her afforded access to password protected, industry professional sites and data and spent the whole week reaching dead ends. World specialists, white papers, articles even bordering on the ridiculous but nothing and then, following a search string beginning with fertility and ending up with an article entitled 'Seeds of life or death', she found something interesting. It was a short paper written by an archaeological researcher who had been involved in the original documentation and translation of murals found in some ancient caves in the Gansu province of China. It was basically an interpretation of a hand painted mural there which depicted a human seed capable of extraordinary fertility and regeneration properties at the point of, and following a pending, certain death, a one and only occurrence in a male lifetime.

Mia had no other leads but knew that part of the group had a research facility in Lanzhou, the capital of Gansu province, China.

CHAPTER 21

Pietro was on the island today and went straight to the Lab where Mia was still pondering over her notes.

He gave his special researcher a big hug, told her to call it a day as he needed a beautiful dinner companion that evening in the Italian Bistro and laughed as he told her he had booked the best table in the house.

Mia had to laugh and said, "Give me 45 minutes and I'll be with you."

"I'll be right here waiting," he quipped back.

Although, primarily, a social dinner there were additional management issues to talk about, nothing out of the ordinary, just day to day and relevant updates.

Mia mentioned she was engaged with something unique but knew she didn't have to explain as she was trusted implicitly. Her track record of developing new products based upon her knowledge and study of Aloe Vera based skin treatment for minor burns and irritating skin conditions had become a classic 'cash cow' and just went on and on with no ongoing development costs associated.

He did, however, sense that she was frustrated with something, he knew her well, more like a daughter. Mia told him that, for the first time in a long time, she had reached a dead end in something which, she knew somewhere, had answers and reason. That she had exhausted every modern, scientific, biological, chemical theories and had nothing to go on except a tenuous lead in Gansu, China.

He knew Mia and didn't even attempt to ask her what it was she was trying to discover, instinctively knowing this, was not the right approach.

"Maybe you have to go old school," he suggested.

"Old school," she replied. "What do you mean?"

"I've been in this business for many years," he said, "and some of our leading compounds and topical creams are based on old, even ancient, writings and practices and sometimes you have to begin on the ground, with proper leg work."

Mia knew he was right thinking about the successful adaptations of ancient Chinese remedies, holistic approaches and alternative therapies applied modern day in the most advanced of skin care treatments. Her own passion and study with the properties of Aloe Vera had a history of over 5000 years and all civilisations without exception had used the plant for therapeutic remedies and appeared in Chinese and Sumerian writings as early as around 3000 BC.

"I have a suggestion," said Pietro. "Visit our research centre there in Gansu province and I will arrange with someone to escort you to these caves you speak of. Talk to the local people there and," he added sarcastically, "I know they still have real life books to study!"

Mia was a scientist and, although she believed in modern research techniques using state of the art technology, knew that discoveries were still being made from the ancient writings and he was taken back when she said, "Ok, when can I go?"

"I'm leaving tomorrow," he said, "for the mainland, you can come with me and catch a connection to Hong Kong, and I will get you flown out to our facility in Gansu province."

Gansu was along the original Silk Road, an economically important province as well as culturally important transmission path. It was home to many ancient Temples and Buddhist Grottoes containing artistic and historically revealing murals dating back to the ancients.

"You can do the tourist thing as well," Pietro added, "it will do you good to get completely away for a while and you might find something."

CHAPTER 22

'Might find something' was all the motivation Mia needed, and following 48 hours of tiresome travel she arrived in Gansu and her residential apartment used normally by Pietro, housed at the facility itself.

She unpacked her things, ate a light meal prepared by the in-house staff and slept for 14 hours straight.

Mia had been assigned a dedicated host, a fellow researcher in his early thirties, highly qualified educationally and now excelling in his passion. His name was Li Jie meaning 'reason' or 'beautiful', but preferred to be called just, Li.

Mia was almost physically attracted to Li, he was tall, well proportioned, obviously a gym regular with a friendly smile and a neck she'd like to get between her thighs, she thought naughtily.

He had briefly met Mia the night before, making sure she had everything needed after her marathon journey and they met for the second time now in one of the small conference rooms.

He had arranged light snacks, some of Mia's favourite coffee and had prepared a small presentation of both the province and their facility.

She was familiar with much of the research facility part but was engrossed in the history lesson she was getting.

Gansu, she learned, was one of China's least populated and least densely populated provinces with only 26 million people. Traditionally it had been known as an area of poverty and the frequency of earthquakes and droughts with resultant famines had contributed to the economic instability and low agricultural productivity of the region. Gansu was very important in Chinese history as it was the main northern passage to the outside world and the famous 'Silk Road', the Yellow River also ran through it. There was breath-taking scenery from vast deserts, to grasslands, snowy mountains and 'Danxia' (Red coloured sandstone formations): landscapes dating back to the Cretaceous age and all showing the magic of nature. More recently, the province had become known for new plantations for growing herbs for Chinese medicine, mainly Angelica root and Rhubarb specifically developed in the province and of key interest to Pietro's skin care research and development.

"That was really informative," Mia complimented, "I have been delving back into some history, well, ancient history regarding Chinese folklore and teachings on fertility and reproduction throughout the ages and have a lead which I'd like to follow at the Maijishan caves near to here," she said.

"Sure," said Li, "we have our own library here, but I can definitely take you to the Maijishan Caves which have incredible artistic and historically revealing murals some of which remain open to personal interpretation."

"Ok," she said, "can we go there tomorrow?"

"Of course, but first take some rest because, we have arranged a dinner of local cuisine with some of our key staff as a welcome to our facility and I will make the arrangements for tomorrow and call my contact there."

"Thanks, I look forward to that," said Mia.

She felt rested, enjoyed the evening company and food consisting of Lanzhou (Province Capital) cuisine, which she looked up, referred to the roasting, steaming and braising of beef and mutton and tonight it was Jincheng Baita, Jincheng Babao and Albino Leeks with Chicken, roasted Pork and Lanzhou Beef Noodles and Niang pi zi.

Mia was the first to leave the dinner gathering, what with taking on the journey to Maijishan Grottoes the following day. She knew it was an eight hour round trip, but, had been stuck indoors for too long and wanted to make the most of it.

Li agreed, mentioning this late September day would be ideal and they arranged an early 5am start and he would bring food and drinks for the journey, together with a driver to take them there.

Despite claims by the Chinese military that the Mercedes G Wagon copy, the BJ80 Chinese 'version' was the best off road

SUV in the world, Pietro stuck to what he knew and relied on Toyota technology in the form of a V8 powered version, comfortable and easily able to cope with the, not too severe, terrain they would encounter on their journey.

They left the facility at 05:10 and headed off south towards the Grottoes.

CHAPTER 23

Daan had adjusted himself to prison life, the scars on his back and torso from his caning punishment were a memory now, although, a real awakener for a man whose childhood was more sheltered and spoilt. His cell was comfortable and in a separate wing for like offenders, as everywhere, other inmates did not approve of violence towards women and segregation protocol was followed. He was expecting more years of prison life than he cared to imagine and was determined to reduce it by way of good behaviour as much as possible. His cell was around 15m^2, the facility being quite modern, he had wash and toilet facilities, a bed, desk and small cabinet for his personal effects and a TV restricted by timings and content. The three meals per day were adequate and of good quality and he took to reading a mixture of fiction, he very much liked the mysteries and theories of Dan Brown and he also took an interest in the clandestine world of spy novels and had just finished a new book by Alma Katsu.

Daan was conditioning himself, mentally he was stronger, but physically he required some work which he was able to begin in his exercise periods, choosing the gym as his recreation allocation.

He began using his natural ability and cunning guile to divert and gain sympathy, playing the game in exactly the way the Prison authorities would wish. He had gained the trust of his internal psychological analyst during their weekly sessions. He profoundly expressed true remorse for his crime, swearing his life would be bettered by giving back to society rather than taking. The nature of the crime, rape, he had committed remained a high priority of study and the authorities had purposely selected a female as his personal counsellor. Daan was fully aware of the reasons behind this and it provided him with even more opportunity to fake his rehabilitation.

The counsellor was an American, Caucasian female in her late forties, very experienced and highly qualified in her field.

She was an attractive, very approachable, woman quite stoutly built, but making the most of her femininity. She reminded him of a school headmistress in her tightly fitted below knee length, pencil skirts, black, heavy denier stockings, patent black heeled shoes and crisp white blouses.

She always looked business like with tasteful make-up and her straight, jet black hair draped forwards over her shoulders.

He figured her shapely legs, always crossed in a relaxed pose, were meant to check his reactions and he passed every time, such was his determination to gain her trust. He knew that she could be his recommendation and ticket for early release and played every trick he could muster.

He had been the model remorseful character, he talked openly about his failings and an acceptance of what he had done, the first steps in rehabilitation.

Building on this, he put forward a unique proposal to share his experience and path towards redemption with others. Under her supervision and personal attendance, he set up the first ever inmate therapy group and chaired the meetings. Convicts guilty of similar crimes were encouraged to speak freely, to share their own thoughts with others sometimes, ending in intervention by the guard where, it became clear, some individuals could never be rehabilitated. This was expected, especially by the analyst, but she was encouraged by his endeavour and tenacity to make it work. The work was, obviously, fed back up the chain to prison administrators and Daan became known to them as physically contributing something of value to the system and society.

Oh, he was good, very good in fact, further demonstrating his Jekyll and Hyde character from his efforts in the daytime to nights where he would go over what he considered to be the changing points in his life. Like, Mia entering the family, Mia 'flaunting' around him, Mia being the model child to his mother, Mia being spoiled and sympathised with because she had been an orphan, Mia being unreceptive to him, Mia humiliating him and finally Mia driving him to commit the crime which had put him where he was. In short, yes, Mia was pretty much to blame for everything, and he was totally obsessed with this compelling reason his life had been messed up. Many nights Daan stared at the ceiling his hands in clenched fists and uttering the same words

"That fucking bitch!"

CHAPTER 24

The journey south was comfortable and relaxing, some calm driving music, efficient climate control and some Toyota luxury. This, with a few stops for refreshments prepared and served by the Driver, meant it took less than four hours to reach their destination.

Mia was always vigilant, she liked to analyse people's individual dispositions and every situation with someone new was a fresh opportunity to observe no matter how small.

During one of the rest-stop breaks she discreetly studied Li when the driver had laid out some coffee, biscuits and her favourite, cubes of Nian Gao, brown sugar cake wrapped in pastry and deep fried. The cubes were cut relatively small and on the paper plate were five pieces.

"I love these," she said smiling, devouring her second piece

"Oh, me too," replied Li and he quickly grabbed the final piece and put it whole into his mouth. "Right shall we go? He said. "Big deal today?"

No, thought Mia, but for her, Li unreservedly demonstrated his selfish side. He had already eaten two pieces just like her but had no hesitation or thought for taking the fifth piece for himself, knowing that Mia had just expressed her liking for them, and she was his guest. It was as though he just had to have it for himself with the knowledge that someone else wanted it.

'There are two of us and only one parachute' sprang to mind, she pondered, but decided it wasn't that serious.

The driver cleared up the small picnic, packed everything back into the SUV and continued their journey.

CHAPTER 25

A popular tourist attraction, it was the end of the summer season and the larger parties with coaches had all but concluded so visitors already at the site were few in number as they arrived.

Li had messaged ahead that he would be bringing a guest and was allocated a private tour guide for their visit.

After another caffeine fix, Mia was ready for the tour and the guide, a middle-aged Chinese archaeologist, introducing himself as 'call me Ken', was eager and passionate about his work and his English was perfect.

He began by explaining the history of the site in that, The Maijishan Grottoes consisted of a series of 194 caves cut into the side of the hill and contained over 7,200 Buddhist sculptures and over 1000m^2 of Murals some of which were still open to interpretation. The construction had begun in the Later Qin era (384–417 CE) and were first properly explored in 1952–53 by a team of Chinese archaeologists from Beijing.

With frequent earthquakes over the centuries, historical, constructional restoration had taken place over 12 Dynasties and the result was what could be seen today.

"Thank you for that," Mia said, "I would be very interested to see any murals depicting past beliefs, historical events and philosophies resulting in theories be it believable or verging on the imagination of the interpreter."

"I can show you many examples," said Ken. "And as your organisation help with donations towards our work here, I can show you some areas not covered by the public access, a little private viewing for you, pretty Lady," he charmed, harmlessly.

Ken took Mia and Li through the caves, mostly adequately lit, but some with dimmed, specialist lighting to reduce any damage from the radiances to some of the more delicate and susceptible ageing murals.

Mia took notes and was allowed to take pictures of some of the fascinating murals, which were of particular interest to her, but got really excited when Ken said they were going to go into an area which contained the oldest 'Hand Painted' examples. These were thought to be collections of elders of the ancients, passed down through their generations some of which depicted Chinese evolution, near extinction events and tribulations throughout the ages.

Mia was fascinated, this area was not publicly known or viewed and even to this day, there were two archaeologists examining and cataloguing some of the amazing and intricate hand painted examples of Chinese history and folklore.

Then, Mia spotted something which caught her eye, in one sense it looked barbaric and gruesome and yet salvaged with the inclusion of flowers and what appeared to be new life. This was what she had read about, this what she wanted to see.

The hand painted mural crudely showed a naked man, with a frightening Serpent like creature whose Anaconda type tail was coiled tightly around his throat, his eyes bulging from the pressure. Totally devoid from the current vista it perversely reminded her of the scene from *The Jungle Book* where the Snake, Kaa, had captured Mowgli in her deadly coils.

But, this was the adult version, his male genitals were exposed and exaggerated and there appeared to be a glowing fountain emanating from his erect penis and then, where it landed, flowers starting from shoots finishing in a full bloom and what looked like a bird appeared to be singing, its mouth open.

"Tell me about this one," Mia requested.

"This has been well studied," said Ken. "Some interesting theories, there was a time in the distant past where it was said that creatures had all but wiped out civilisation for their sins; Every life taken was a step further to annihilation. And now the intriguing and mystifying part," he added with a smile. "Theories border on the human absolute and desperate 'will' for succession, the human body instinctively taking over for survival and existence."

"Wow, very compelling and ultimate," exclaimed Mia.

"Ultimate indeed," replied Ken, "it is said that the mural depicts the ending of a life and from somewhere, who knows, the male produces its ultimate spurt of life. Not just ordinary life, but the 'final seed' emitted at the point of death like no other, so potent it will fertilise and ensure new beginnings for anything in its path. It shows the rebirth of life after near extinction," he went on passionately.

"That is one powerful and compelling theory," Mia stated.

"Yes, it is," replied Ken, "and of course there are counter arguments as to its interpretation, but it basically highlights the human nature and endeavour for ultimate survival against overwhelming odds and circumstances."

"So, the final throw of the dice in the hope that this extremely potent seed will find a way to fertilise and continue humanity?" said Mia.

"Exactly, you got it," said Ken. "Pure survival instinct."

Mia had gotten so wrapped up in the guided tour, fascinated with works that were centuries old and represented many aspects of not only Chinese but world history and evolution, she had lost her thread but, 'OMG' did it hit her with a bang! She just stood frozen to the spot and inanimate.

"Mia!" said Li. "Are you ok, are you ok?" he repeated.

"Err yes I'm fine," she stammered, "just taken in by the whole experience, it was like walking among the past generations."

"Indeed," agreed Li. "It is quite breath-taking and although I've seen some of the things before, the influence of your special visit for non-public viewing was even more intriguing for me also."

"Was there something in particular caught your imagination or area of study?" he asked.

"No nothing singularly," she lied, "as you say, so much to take in."

"But you were particularly taken by the human endeavour for survival, mural right?" added Li rather searchingly.

"It was all very interesting," she said firmly.

Li sensed more but said, "Ok I'm glad it was useful to your study."

They thanked Ken for the tour and she was pretty much silent on the drive back to the Lab, but just couldn't help looking at the pictures on her phone of the dying, desperate man involuntarily, emitting once in a lifetime, potentially, life giving seed in an attempt to continue human survival. Could it be?

CHAPTER 26

Back in Chi Hoa Prison Centre, it was visitation day and Price welcomed the sight of his fellow group member. The visitor area was physically guarded, supervised with CCTV and consisted of 20, two-seater round tables and a vending machine for refreshments.

Alex West, Price's visitor, bought coffee from the machine and they sat down opposite each other for the 30-minute allowed time.

Alex West was ex Wall Street, having retired in his late thirties, now 50, he was very comfortable with homes in the US and Malaysia and compared to Price, more refined and articulate. He was of medium height, stocky build, and kept himself fit retaining his brown, slightly greying hair and trimmed moustache. He was leader of the group, arranged all excursions and events and had corruptible contacts in many influential institutions including government and law enforcement.

West was a fellow degenerate just like his friend Price and mastermind of their sordid gang's sexually perverse, despicable activities.

They had become acquainted properly during one such activity, a party on board one of his chartered motor yacht excursions billed as a 'Bachelor Party'. West used this front often; it was a good way of diverting the attention of any authorities. He would set up the event, nominate a person to act as the groom, have on board chefs, bar personnel and on every occasion, the routine inspection by the Port authority before setting off went without a hitch. Then, once offshore, a sizeable, inflatable would rendezvous with the Yacht and deliver girls to complete the assembly. Sex, debauchery, alcohol and food would flow freely until the early hours, sometimes over a two-day period. The Yacht would rendezvous once more, and the girls were offloaded before returning the drunken groom back to Port.

They had met in the bar of a high-quality Hotel where the, then rookie, Price could be seen trying his best to secure a girl for the evening.

West watched his failed efforts and struck up a conversation finally spending the evening drinking together. He told Price that this was the wrong way and location to go about satisfying his needs and introduced him the following day to some of the other group members.

After some vetting, checking his identity and financial status, he was invited to join the 'Bachelor Party' cruise they had arranged, paying the fee in advance for the services.

He couldn't believe what was made available to him during the cruise, everything he had dreamed of, and totally safe from the authorities. He fitted right in and took part in as many events as he could, but West had been very busy and unable to plan a cruise for the past three months. Price became impatient and took it on himself to undertake a solo hunt which was where he had been caught. West felt a little responsible as they had built up a real friendship and accepted that he had let his friend down somewhat.

"Don't worry," West said reassuringly, "the final plans are in place and now you have your sea transport date everything will fall into place."

"Just what I wanted to hear," Price said, "playing with myself these lonely days, it's getting to me now," he added, winking.

"I can imagine," West replied knowingly.

The two were the pits of the male species, cunning, insidious and deviant, but like most successful organised crime groups, well-funded and connected through the sharing of their cumulative wealth and contacts.

West briefed him with details of how, on the night of the sea passage, he would be released from his cell and escorted to a secluded area of the ship. There, he would be given a life vest and helped into the water, where, a small boat would be waiting for him just out of sight to pick him up.

He would only be in the water for a short time just until the prison vessel was out of sight and then, straight away, he would be taken to a larger cruiser, with a proper shower and comfortable cabin. "Might even have a little dessert waiting for you!" West added smiling.

"That's what I'm talking about," Price replied.

So, it was all set, the money had been paid to the relevant people to make it happen and Price had just one more week to wait.

CHAPTER 27

Mia returned to Tengah in the early morning with some small gifts for her staff and after a sleep and shower went to the Lab where she arranged for Carol to visit that evening, both of them were disposed and it would be an exhausting evening, but immensely satisfying.

The next day she was refreshed and sexually sated. She had some pending work to do and some staff to organise and it was afternoon by the time she was able to refer to her notes and pictures from the excursion to China.

She looked over the theories and notes, surely the depiction was just that, of how human endeavour and the magic of the human body would attempt to overcome every catastrophe in its fight for survival and evolution; and could there be some truth in this 'Death Seed' theory? Had the man she choked to death entered this involuntary state of survival mode, his body recognising death was coming to produce what was, 'shot' on to her back? And had it been this which had repaired her scarred tissue?

It was all crazy and would she ever know? Sure, all she had to do now was choke another guy to death and help him release his 'Seed of Death'! As if that was going to happen.

Mia went back to her daily routine putting her 'Seeds of Death' research to the back of her schedule. She had more pressing, money earning work to get through, but she was looking forward to her day off, the weather was said to be good and she had planned to go to her favourite spot.

The spot was a secluded sandy cove around 30 minutes' drive along the rugged, dirt road from the Lab facility and completely deserted, nobody else ever went there, it was her personal location and the day after tomorrow it would be all hers.

It was three days by sea for Price's journey from Ho Chi Min to the Port of Singapore and he was on his way on board the privately run vessel to freedom. Housed in a squalid cell wearing nothing but shorts, trainers and a black T shirt with the word 'Squad' embellished on the back, a souvenir from one of the organised events he had been part of. His few other personal belongings were stored elsewhere but this didn't bother him at all, he had nothing to speak of and his freedom meant everything and at this moment, raging in his perverted mind, 'the dessert' he had been promised.

CHAPTER 28

By the end of her shift the following day, Mia was satisfied with her work and was looking forward to her day at the cove.

The next day she was up early eating a light breakfast with the TV on in the background and was just catching up on the local news when she came across a report that a dangerous, sexual offender had gone missing from a prison transfer ship off the coast of Malaysia. It added that this had happened before and, more often than not, the person was never seen again due to tides and sharks, however, if spotted, the person should not be approached and to call the authorities. She decided that nothing was going to spoil her day, packed up one of the facility's Suzuki Jimnys with towels, loaded cool box, sun tanning lotion, sunglasses and, as always, never being able to switch off , a small kit consisting of sample bottles, PH strips and the like. Mia felt an obligation to check the environmental condition of the waters around the island.

She headed out in the open top jeep, her hair blowing and the sun shining, what a perfect day, she thought, I'm going to have a relaxing 'me' day.

Mia parked the Jeep with a short descent to the cove, the tide was just turning, beginning its slow return from low tide ascending upwards toward the small sandy beach, perfect. She laid out her things in the secluded spot with the natural cover of an overhanging palm.

She was wearing a two-piece, black bikini thong with the bottoms having thin straps riding high and sitting on her perfect hips and the top a very simple strappy piece covering her ample breasts with maximum skin exposure. She was, however, very careful and her vast knowledge of skin and the effect UV can cause was fully oiled with high factor protection cream, she just loved the near-naked exposure to the elements and the vitamin 'C'. She lay on a towel with a small pillow and read her book beneath the rustling leaves of the palm overhead with not a single sound but the small waves falling over themselves around 50 metres from where she lay. Perfect she thought, what a way to switch off and totally unwind.

"Bottom, sand underfoot, land!" gasped Price in sheer relief.

CHAPTER 29

Price had been in the water for more than eight hours and this was not supposed to have happened.

The previous night, as was instructed, he had waited for someone to come and get him, but, when the corrupt guard arrived, he was flustered and scared.

"We have to go now!" the guard whispered, trembling. "New orders to double check prisoners has been issued and warning of a prisoner trying to escape," he added in broken English. "We must go now!"

"But are we at the correct, given coordinates?" Price enquired of him. "I have people waiting for me; are we where we should be?"

"I don't understand," the guard told him, "but, if we don't leave right now you don't go," he repeated.

Price made the decision to go in the hope they were near to the arranged meeting point coordinates.

He had entered the warm water, which turned out to be nowhere near where he was supposed to be, in the dark and had spent the last eight hours half treading water and half swimming and if it were not for the life vest he would have surely drowned. Several times he just stopped trying to swim, looking up at the incredible night sky vista. With no background light pollution, it was like nothing he had ever seen, blankets of stars disappearing to infinity and fine meteors streaked across the open sky. He wondered where he fitted in to this vast Universe, if this was his last memory, surely, he would never be found. He rallied himself finding some latent strength and belief partly being shocked back to reality as something brushed, not for the first time, against his foot. A Shark maybe, or just a fish, it didn't matter, luck was with him as he made landfall right there on a remote part of Tengah Island. He collapsed onto the sand just beyond the breaking surf, absolutely exhausted.

CHAPTER 30

Mia hadn't noticed anything, she was deep into her book and enjoying the solitude, but then, out of the corner of her eye, she saw something rise from the sand at the far extent of the sandy beach, it was a person, a man looking around and he saw her little camp there at the beach.

Mia got up from her towel and rushed to help him but, as she reached out and took his arm over her shoulder, it hit her. It was the escaped fugitive from the news, he had been washed up on her Island. She thought to drop him and run but she realised the frail and exhausted state the man was in and knew he was no danger to her at this point and in this condition.

"Do you speak English?" she asked.

"Yes, I'm British," he replied trying to speak through parched lips.

"Ok," Mia said, "I have water and some food close by," she told him comfortingly.

She led him to her little beach camp, removed the life vest and his T shirt, and sat him down. She wrapped a towel around him and gave him water which he gulped down. "That's better, thank you," he said.

"We have to get you checked over," Mia said, "I will call my people."

"That's ok," he said, "I will be fine now, just a little weary."

He went on to give her an elaborate story of how he had fallen overboard from a yacht he was cruising on with some friends and found himself stranded, but he would be able to find them. Which, of course, she knew was total fiction.

"I'm guessing this is Tengah so, why are you here?" he asked. "I thought this place had been closed for tourism for a while now."

"Yes, it has, but we have a research Laboratory and I work here on the Island, it's my day off and my jeep's just up there, I can take you," she said.

"That won't be necessary," he replied, convincingly, "I will just rest a while and be on my way," he lied.

She knew he couldn't go anywhere, there was no yacht and no way off the island without using the Lab's facilities and no one else knew he was there. She wasn't scared at all, one punch and his lights would be out, but then, something just came into her head, from where she just didn't know, like something possessed her. She gritted her teeth, slipped into role play mode and from nowhere said inquisitively, "Hope you don't mind me saying, but I have noticed the bulge in your shorts."

"Well you are a very attractive Lady and it has been sometime, in fact a long time," he added.

"Looks impressive," she lied. "Perhaps you could show me, Daddy?"

He could not believe the words just uttered to him, he had survived a night floating in the sea, been washed up on a desert island and found by a beautiful young woman referring to him as 'Daddy', was he dreaming or, already enjoying the fruits of the after-life?

His instinctive, perverted nature kicked in automatically, take advantage of any situation was his 'live-by' motto.

Still laying down he moved onto his back, reached down and pulled down his shorts to reveal the biggest human penis she had ever seen, this skinny guy with a huge erect cock.

"Wow!" she exclaimed. "Impressive, would it be ok if I touched it?"

With that, the pathetic monster smiled smugly, and lay back hands behind his head.

"Help yourself, my dear," he replied as if it were some kind of a treat for her.

Mia positioned herself to sit on his lower chest facing his feet. He was disgusting in every way right down to his oxygen wasting being, but she was totally focused.

"It's so big, Daddy," Mia said.

"See it as a popsicle, dear," he quipped back, confidently. "Be careful not to take it in all at once it may cause you to gag," he added, smiling.

Price was abhorrent and so arrogant at the same time, believing she would be interested in this ageing pervert.

Mia was absolutely disgusted and resisted the urge to throw up all over him, but she stayed in complete character. "People say I have nice legs," Mia said teasingly, "would you like to feel them so I can get closer to this beautiful cock of yours?" she suggested.

"Of course," he said, "feel free." Again, reality checking to see if he was dreaming or, by some misplaced information, died and gone to heaven instead of the hell that was impatiently waiting for him.

Mia slipped down his body sliding her thighs each side of his head. "Maybe lift your head a little," she suggested, "then I can feel your face next to me."

Of course, he lifted his head and then gurgled sharply as Mia clamped her naked, oiled thighs around his neck and crossed her legs one under the other at the ankles in a perfect straight reverse head scissor hold. The hold was perfectly executed, his neck right into her bikini crotch and her oily, muscular thighs tightening by the second.

"Hey!" he spluttered taken by surprise. "This is a bit too rough." He gargled.

"Too rough and tough, you deplorable bastard!" Mia shouted and poured on the pressure with her thighs, powerful abductors tensing on the trapped neck between them.

She raised herself on her hands to increase the pressure even more, then on one hand as she used the other to grip the base of his throbbing penis.

It didn't take long at all, within seconds his hands were tapping weakly at her glutes and ass which would be the last thing he would see, in this life anyway. Seconds later his pushing became desperate and slipped away from her oiled legs as he choked between Mia's thighs.

Then it happened, as his hands fell away completely limp, his eyeballs almost popping out of his head, at that moment, his cock pulsed and throbbed and spurted out the most unusual looking liquid she had ever seen.

She was careful to control its trajectory, milking it all out onto his belly, it was a strange almost fluorescent blue shade and there were lots of it.

I bet this would show up in the dark, she thought. Mia had studied some Marine biology and remembered bioluminescent plankton where the bioluminescence is used as a nature induced, defence mechanism to distract predators. Emitting tiny flashes of light, it disorientated and surprised the predator and these tiny organisms produced this light using a chemical called Luciferin.

She quickly climbed off his dead form, grabbed her science bag, scooped up the sperm into a sterile sample bottle and put it into the cool box with the ice.

But then it hit, what had she just done? Something had taken over her, she had thoughts of how she could get a sample of sperm from a dying person and this opportunity had presented itself and she couldn't believe she had taken it?

It was also another less degenerate male for women and children to fear, but what now?

When the tide was coming in at this point, there was a noticeable strong back current, so, Mia just simply dragged his body into the water and pushed him into the outward current. He disappeared almost immediately, and she was confident that the Sharks would do the rest, and nobody would bother to look for him anyway. Just another escaped prisoner lost at sea.

Her sample intact, Mia packed up her things grabbing his easily spotted, fluorescent life vest which she would 'lose' on the way and headed back to the lab. She had a long night ahead and had no regrets at what had just happened, in fact, she got a thrill from having a man begging for his life between her capable thighs, especially a male sexual predator.

CHAPTER 31

West had arranged a live and exuberant 'homecoming' for his friend, still feeling partly responsible for his arrest circumstances, not being able to be there with him on that ill-fated trip and no expense had been spared. He had chartered one of the largest superyachts available at the time at over 30m in length.

On board there was a select group of the membership, with extravagant spreads of Seafood prepared by the on-board chef and served by the catering staff. Champagne was flowing and of course desperate young, teenage girls had been discreetly transferred by small boat, rendezvousing with the Yacht once clear of the Port, two of them waiting in a private cabin for the delight of Jordan Price on his arrival.

Whilst the guests were already indulging in their preferred delights, West and his navigation specialist, an ex HM Navy officer, supervised the heading for the coordinates they had calculated to retrieve Price from the water.

Everything was going to plan, and they reached the designated spot ahead of time, they locked on the Yacht's automatic position adjust thrusters to remain in the same position using GPS telemetry equipment.

West re-joined his party and checked everyone was enjoying the trip, waiting for the specified rendezvous time.

He decided to board and launch the small tender early just in case as there was no AIS signal identifying the approach of the prison vessel, but this was scheduled to be disabled anyway for this period, part of the fee.

The rest of the group waited on the Yacht looking forward to the return of their friend and VIP guest.

The tender rib boat buzzed around in the darkness for more than four hours beyond the time, but they were nowhere near where Price had entered the water and West had to call the same conclusion.

With the rising of the sun, he decided there was nothing more he could do, it wasn't like they could report it to anyone so they headed back to Singapore, all except West believing their friend was probably drowned and or, eaten by Sharks. West, however, refused to accept this adversity and was determined to find out what, exactly, had happened to his friend and why everything had gone terribly wrong after such meticulous and costly planning.

CHAPTER 32

As Mia raced back to the Lab her mind was in overdrive, questions bombarding her brain like a vulnerable proton in the Hadron Collider.

Would the sperm sample be viable? What it if it had degenerated and was useless? How long would it last? Was it, indeed, any different from ordinary sperm? How could she check? What if it was full of STDs from its disgusting donor? Even that came into the equation.

She calmed herself and instinctively reverted back to her scientist state of logic and steps of evaluation and testing.

On reaching the Lab it was quiet and only skeleton staff were dotted around. She made her way to her station and couldn't wait to see what she had in her kit bag. She knew that normal, human sperm had a very short lifespan without freezing but she had a hunch about this, so many unknowns were in play and, due to the very nature of what she had obtained, she believed it would not have the normal properties of every day human sperm.

Mia was astonished when she examined the sample jar as, inside, the liquid still looked exactly, the same as when it had spurted onto his belly and she still couldn't help but notice the fluorescent glow, or was she seeing things?

The last few hours caught up with her, what was happening? She was quite a different woman, more ruthless, doing what she thought necessary to get to where she wanted to be. There was only one man she fully trusted now and that was Pietro. The others, if in her way, would be dealt with or ignored completely.

Mia went into the darkroom with the sample, closed the door and turned off the light. Or had she? Because the sample jar glowed in the dark with a beautiful florescent glow, this must surely be down to the presence of Luciferin, but she had never seen anything like this from all her studies in human biology. This was something incredible and she couldn't help but think that this was part of the 'human survival' theme she had discovered in the caves in Gansu. It was as though every natural mechanism of nature was in play to ensure and assist survival of the human species on earth. Although a very endearing story, Mia was a scientist, there were laws, periodic tables and the like and she believed in only what could be proven. She had, however, witnessed with her own eyes an occurrence she was striving to explain and potentially use as a breakthrough in skin renovation and potential rejuvenation.

She put the sample into the fridge and gowned herself up, treating the examination as a potential, low grade, biohazard.

Mia distributed the liquid into glass vials so she had many samples to work with and then tested for any STDs which, if present, would render it worthless and, to her surprise, it was totally clean. The first hurdle overcome, she thought to herself and now to work. She had studied human sperm under a microscope many times and viewed the sample at 400x it was incredible, like nothing she had seen. It reminded her of the night sky with no artificial light pollution, it was beautiful and absolutely brimming with life.

CHAPTER 33

Pietro Allard, like Mia and one of the reasons he had such an affliction with her, also grew up an orphan in the rougher suburbs of Paris, his single, penniless, mother giving him up as a baby and street life became the norm for him.

From an early age he ran small, minor criminal, businesses, stealing and reselling anything from cigarettes to jewellery and gained quite a reputation as a budding child entrepreneur. He pursued his skill of making things happen, turning lost causes into money making opportunities. As maturity developed, he became aware of the value and intensity of prostitution in the 'city of romance' but not the average 'quick fix' for frustrated or wayward husbands. In his early adult years, he began to focus on high end activities moving gold and diamond jewellery through his acquired network of fences and thieves. Like many, eventually successful, business entrepreneurs he had to work his way up.

He diversified and began to engage in the business of providing high class courtesans to rich and influential clients, effectively an elite Pimp. He offered his clients total anonymity and security, essential to men with valuable careers and even political positions to think about. In conjunction he built up a reputation for fairness and safety with the girls he used, and they stuck with him knowing there would be regular income and the clients were wealthy, discreet and secure.

From this circle of operation, he recognised an opportunity for making custom movies, strictly in the sex industry, but with very select and highly vetted, wealthy clients. The movies were high quality productions, the actors were professionals and all health and safety protocols were employed and with absolute discretion.

He soon learned that people with exorbitant amounts of money could 'buy' whatever they wanted if there was a supplier to suit their needs. He also discovered that there were no suppliers in some areas of this industry and to him this was a 'gap' in the market, one he intended to exploit.

A regular, very wealthy, purchaser of his custom 'female domination genre' movies approached him and asked if he could produce a 'snuff' video or event. He had heard this phrase before but, until now, had never it appeared on his scope of supply so, he delved deeper, investigating this new genre.

He found that 'snuff Videos' were essentially a staged event where a person was murdered for the entertainment of a jaded few in a sexual scenario. This was a different ball game, he was surprised when he discovered that there existed, a significant number of people wishing to indulge, in this degree, the actual murder of a person for discerning pleasure of the viewer. He saw the lucrative potential, this was not for the average person paying a few hundred dollars for a custom video scenario, this was sheer wealth indulgence and he decided to cultivate it. However, as he carefully developed the network, he found the few were many and began making thousands of dollars arranging live, intimate shows. Then, with technological advances in IT, the advent of high-speed internet and streaming feeds, he could arrange worldwide subscription paying, select audiences and remain completely undetectable. With this advancement in systems, his exploits and reputation cloaked in secrecy, moved from thousands of dollars to hundreds of thousand dollars to millions of dollars, such was the calibre of his worldwide audiences.

Pietro realised the opportunity of exploiting not only the paying viewer but, unbelievably, actual disposed victims willing to participate in personalised custom 'snuff' events where they chose the scenario and ending based on individual fantasy with a certain type of death, gunshot, stabbing, strangling etc.

Some requested it as a real-life ending situation and others believed they were playing out a fantasy role play with respected limits. The latter, Pietro found, were more entertaining to the enriched, lucrative audiences because every act was against the actual will of the client or victim and very real.

He had to carefully select victims which he did through a real-life, but retired, dominatrix who placed ads all over the world offering punishment services, then carefully vetting the single, unattached submissive men offering them a chance to take part in a production with a beautiful girl or two girls without knowing how it would end. They would end up as just another 'missing person' and that's if they were ever reported missing as many of these men had little or no ties to anyone, virtual recluses.

He developed a highly efficient and discreet clean up regime where the bodies were disposed of, it was costly, but worth the peace of mind. The girls were also highly vetted and well paid, mostly Female Dominants skilled in sexual torture techniques. Physical beatdowns, physical domination, breath play, asphyxiation techniques, CBT and other role play scenarios were requested and very sadistic so, they enjoyed their work with 100% job satisfaction.

Although this revenue activity had retracted as a major income stream, since gambling on the purchase of a small skin care enterprise and growing it to the huge set up he had today. Pietro was still asked to arrange these events for the wealthy and was able to be very selective and had a list of requests and pledges of money to stage them. How could anyone resist such huge paydays? There was demand, so he provided the supply, basic marketing to him.

CHAPTER 34

Mia was aware of Pietro's, highly ethically questionable, extracurricular activities. He had been very open and trusting with her from day one. He appreciated and sensed Mia's sadistic side, a trait which he had just learned to recognise naturally.

The previous year she had, in fact, watched, with him, an arranged snuff event, one where death would be by strangulation and choking and although very brutal it made her, surprisingly wet. She remembered asking him, "Pietro are people actually killed in your movies?" To which, he replied, smiling, "I can't really confirm or deny that."

The event location was, of course, secret but he told her this one was in California with no physically present audience, just the participants and an audio-visual specialist ensuring the live feeds to private, paying, viewers around the world. Externally and based in Singapore, an IT specialist was arranging highly technical VPN systems, switching seamlessly to avoid detection and locations. It was all very efficient and well organised.

The scene was set. The victim was a single, male submissive from Western Europe, very lean build, in his late forties who believed he was going to be filmed being sexually tortured in a dungeon style setting by two Dominatrices.

He was placed, naked, in the dungeon with furniture of a bench, wooden cross and various equipment like chains, nooses, collars, CBT equipment, whips and canes. He was visibly excited and yet exposed as he looked around in nervous anticipation.

The room was rigged with 26 UHD cameras able to catch every part and from every angle, the spectacle about to take place and the select audience had the ability to switch to the camera that best suited individual interests.

The two girls entered the room, both tall, statuesque, long legs, voluptuous bodies, and identical swept back hair in tight ponytails. One blond and one brunette, both in their late twenties. They wore thigh high, stiletto PVC shiny boots, shiny PVC corsets laced at the front but with their very large breasts exposed. PVC elbow length gloves and PVC eye masks completed the outfits as they paraded their imposing feminine forms around the room.

"We have 20 select viewers right now," Pietro told her, "each paying $250,000 and during the scene they are able to transfer money for something 'extra' they would personally, like to see."

The 'slave' looked up, he couldn't believe what was happening, it was a fantasy harboured for a long time. The lead brunette received the go ahead from her earpiece and acknowledged via the

mouthpiece with the words, "Yes sir, understood." By communicating directly, any instructions could be given to maximise the instantly transferred funds for an individual request. "What you will see happen is at the request of what our clients wish to see as extra, although, the ending in this is always fixed as billed or, should I say, how it ends," Pietro explained.

CHAPTER 35

"Don't you dare look at me!" she barked at the slave. "You are not worthy to look at me, look at the floor!" the Blond shouted at him.

He responded without question looking down at the floor. She moved in, landing a fierce kick directly up and crashing into his exposed ball sack. He collapsed to the floor in agony both hands trying to protect his genitals from further punishment.

The girls pounced on his foetus-like, crumpled form, a leather collar with chain leash was fitted tightly around his neck, he was helpless, and the girls were already receiving instructions.

Together, they dragged him across the floor by his throat as he tried to grab the collar to relieve pressure, he thought it a little extreme. He had no idea of how extreme it was going to be and from the outset there was going to be no mercy. This wasn't an act, it was real, and there would be tangible suffering. They towed him to the crucifix where they took his arms and lifted him up, fixing him spread-eagled to the cross.

"This is what you want, right?" the blond whispered in his ear and the other began working his nipples, pinching them with her gloved fingers. He moaned with pleasure as the torture began.

The girls worked as a team perfectly, his bruised genitals were fitted with tight steel retaining rings after which, his cock rose to erection and strained against the unforgiving restraints. Lubricant was applied and the blond just stood, one hand on her hip, and the other grasped around the base of his cock but this was not going to be intimate or pleasurable. She nonchalantly wanked his cock non-stop until he came all over the floor, groaning with a mixture of pleasure and pain. She squatted down, scooping the warm sticky goo into the palm of her gloved hand and fed it to him. Then, she went back to work on his cock the same, no words, no expression, just a matter of fact male milking a second load out of him which, again, he was forced to eat. His cock began to wane, but she repeated the process and, even though almost flaccid, managed to tease more liquid from the depths of his aching balls. A request, it later transpired, from a lady viewer wanting to see him totally milked out of his 'male filth' as she put it and Mia began to understand how it all worked.

He was sexually, completely spent, drained of any testosterone power he had and very much weakened by the forced extraction.

Receiving instructions all the time the Brunette set to, repeatedly aiming kicks to his defenceless cock and balls. He was screaming in agony, but she continued, there was blood from his penis, but she just smiled. "Pig!" she exclaimed.

He couldn't stand by himself now, he hung from the cross and begged them to stop, that the punishment was too severe, and he wanted to leave. But it didn't matter what he wanted; it was what the paying audience wanted.

Pietro had long since left the small booth he was watching in with Mia, not really his thing, but she was fascinated and wanted to see what happened next and it was extremely brutal.

The girls used the collar to hold up his head securing it around the back of the wooden support.

Then, taking a turn each, they began punching him in his gut with some 'side kicks' thrown in. He was screaming with agony, begging for them to stop, his ribs either broken or fractured, but not enough to puncture his lungs as this was not how it was supposed to end.

The girls were putting everything into the slaughter and, after taking a rehydration break, they returned to his groaning form, his head still held up by the collar and began punching him in the face.

The blond was well built and with a striking punch across his jaw he was out, unconscious, relief at last.

The girls were covered in blood from his bleeding mouth and nose, he had cuts above and below his almost closed eyes, it was like a scene from a horror movie.

They received final instructions and threw water on his face to wake him up; they didn't want him asleep and not feeling the pain.

It was instructed that the Brunette would complete the execution and the girls were genuinely excited as one encouraged the other.

She began with more straight punches to his face but not enough to knock him out again.

She kneed him in the gut again and again and he weakly twitched but remained conscious.

Then, as the blond encouraged her to 'finish him', she simply stated, "Time to end your suffering, Pig!"

She stood in front of him, feet apart, her shiny boots taught around her powerful thighs. The blond went around the back of him, released the collar and then drew up a chair just to the side of her fellow executioner. Then, she removed the tied G string from her waist and sat laid back on the chair, spreading her legs wide and revealing her completely shaven pussy. She removed the glove from one hand revealing her black perfectly manicured nails and began rubbing herself. She found her swollen clitoris and began teasing it between her fingers, working herself up. She nodded instruction to her partner to begin.

The Brunette leaned in at an angle clasping her hands tightly around his neck adjusting her stance for maximum effect. Then, she tightened the grip around his throat, he gurgled helplessly, blood oozing from his mouth. She pressed her thumbs deep into his larynx, crushing his windpipe whilst her fingers dug into the carotid arteries in the side of his neck creating a simultaneous air and blood choke. He was totally unresistant, much too weak.

The blond didn't take her eyes from the scene, it was a huge turn on and she began to moan and increased the tempo on her excited clitoris.

The choke was lethal, he began to splutter, blood spurting from his mouth on to her huge breasts trickling down over her erect, excited nipples, the overhead camera catching every last breath as the girl looked up, eyes closed in ecstasy as he twitched finally, and went limp just as her partner reached an intense, audibly loud orgasm. She continued the choking for at least a further minute, making sure he was dead, then releasing him from her grip. Head slumped onto his chest, he just hung by his arms from the cross, choked to death for a live audience, blood dripping from his mouth but, what Mia didn't notice at the time, a fresh puddle of strangely glowing liquid on the floor and on the shiny PVC boots of his killer which went unnoticed by anyone amidst the mess that was already there.

But it wasn't over just yet. "Yes, sir!" As a message was relayed to the girls. They undid the restraints and his beaten body fell to the floor. Arranging him face up, both took a turn squatting down over him to relieve themselves, urinating over his face whilst the other stooped down to kiss the other, diluted blood washing over the floor and, when sated, left the room and the lights went dark

A very dollar successful event Pietro told her later.

CHAPTER 36

Mia was irritated, she could spend copious and costly Lab time hours and equipment attempting to refine or synthesise the samples she had but was there anything to discover? Was it all just coincidence?

She decided to cut to the chase, after all, if it really was the sperm, it had worked in its raw state on her and she had an idea to confirm once and for all.

Mia knew that Carol had a small scar on her leg which she collected when nine years old following paddling in a brook close to her home trying to catch the small crayfish there, to put in her little bucket and show her father when he came home from work. She had stumbled over loose rocks and cut her leg just below the knee on a shard of glass protruding upright, unseen, laying on the bottom.

She ran all the way home, her leg bleeding, but, on examination, her mother decided there was no need to go into town for stitches. She washed and bandaged it and within a few days it had healed. However, when the scab eventually peeled off it did leave a small scar which, over the years, faded but remained indented into her otherwise flawless skin with a shiny, gossamer looking appearance.

It was past normal working hours, but Mia knew that Carol would just be relaxing in her apartment and went there.

Carol was surprised to see her. "We hadn't arranged anything?" she enquired, smiling.

"No, not tonight," Mia assured her laughing at the thought. "Do you have a moment? There's something I'd like to try on you, just an application of, well, a gel, don't worry it's not painful," she added, winking.

"Sure, anything for the advancement of science," she answered, smiling.

"Not sure if this is even science," Mia quipped.

She didn't give Carol any detailed information, just that she had formulated a sample for testing that she believed could repair scar tissue. However, she needed a 'live' test, the compound was harmless and just natural, and could she apply it to the scar on her leg?

Carol agreed, eagerly saying she would love to be rid of it but couldn't imagine any topical application capable of having such effect on her age-old scar.

She sat on a chair exposing her leg and the scar, Mia had brought a tiny sample of the strange looking glue-like substance and simply applied it with her finger to the scarred area and then stood back.

The pair looked at each other, then at the scar, back to each other and back to the scar as if something was going to happen immediately but it didn't. It was getting late and Mia left, just asking Carol not to wash the area that night which she agreed to.

CHAPTER 37

Mia was woken from a lovely dream; she was personally carrying out a list of executions of death-row rapists. They had been customarily sedated and the one choking slowly between her thighs was unrepentant to the last as he mumbled, "It was what women were born for", but not this woman as he surrendered to the pressure and began to fade away. But then, what was the alarm signal? Did she have to stop? All the papers were signed off, it couldn't be a reprieve but the constant alarm? She opened her eyes and realised it was her doorbell being rung constantly, what the fuck? What time was it? She looked at her phone it was 5:32am. She slept naked now, knowing there would never be anyone to bother her where she was, got out of bed, pulled on a silk robe and looked through the sight glass on the door.

It was Carol and she was literally dancing around on the spot looking like she was about to pee herself.

Mia opened the door and Carol just blurted out, "It's gone."

"What has?" Mia replied, rubbing her eyes trying to make sense of the sudden wake up call.

"My scar," said Carol excitedly, "my scar, what was it? What did you put on it? It's gone without trace, I've had it for years and it's disappeared overnight," she went on.

"Come inside and slow down," Mia told her, "smell the flowers, blow out the candles, breathe."

Carol collected herself and elatedly went on to show Mia where her scar had been and there was absolutely no trace just like had happened with Mia's.

"It's incredible," said Carol, "what did you put on it?"

"Just something I'm working with," replied Mia.

"Just working with, just working with?" she screamed. "This must be the skin care breakthrough of all time; this is industry award stuff," she cried.

"Listen, Carol," Mia said, "let's not get carried away, it's just experimental right now and I don't know if I can even replicate or compound it. And the key ingredient is virtually impossible to reobtain, please just keep it to yourself for now and I promise to update you as I try to develop it."

Carol agreed that something so potentially prolific warranted careful work, patience and understanding but, for now, was very happy she had been the initial guinea pig.

Mia now knew, without doubt, that this strange liquid, the 'Death Seed' or 'Seeds of Death', really had regeneration and healing properties and the potential applications and treatments were phenomenal and, quite frankly, mind-blowingly unbelievable. She imagined how the scientists felt when discoveries such as Genome Editing, RNA-sequencing, Molecular structure of DNA and even way back to Penicillin, were discovered. It also seemed that, even outside of the refrigerator, the seed had incredible longevity of life, again, fitting into the 'Last resort' theory.

She tried to stop her mind racing at the implications the discovery could have and straight away, whatever she could develop, the key ingredient could only be gained with the taking of a life. How could she do this and with quantities required to produce it on a commercially viable scale? Or did she need large quantities, was it even possible to formulate something from human bodily fluids?

Her head was spinning. She needed to de-stress so she headed for the gym and would make a plan of action the next day.

CHAPTER 38

Daan was coping well with his new, enforced, lifestyle, finding an inner strength and focus, that focus being Mia. He was obsessed, she was the root of all his problems and circumstances and every time he was at a low ebb, he would think of her and what she would face from him as consequence.

It was his main driving force, he pushed himself in the gym and was no longer the sloth-like figure he used to be. He had periodic reviews with the board of governors and authority representatives checking his mental state, attitude, remorse, state of reformation etc. How he might react when introduced back into society, which would eventually happen even if he served the full term. He carefully prepared for each meeting, giving them the answers, they wanted to hear and with such conviction and false honesty. The Board were continuously impressed with his attitude and evolvement, if only they knew the driving force behind his encouraging progression.

Back in the office in KL, Malaysia, above a very inconspicuous Print and Copy shop, Alex West was reading an e-mail from one of his informants. He had retained this cover for the past five years and used it as a front to hide his other activities. From here, West arranged the visits and events to selected locations and countries for wealthy perverts from all over the world. He utilised sites on the 'dark web', a part of the internet not visible to search engines using 'anonymising' browsers and sophisticated, anti-detection and tracing software.

His network was costly to maintain as he needed to hire a very proficient hacker and the same IT guru had been with him for the past two years and the whole set up very efficient.

West had affectively received a report of events from the night his friend had left the prison transfer ship and it was obvious why they were unable to find him. From the information, Price was nowhere near the arranged rendezvous point when he was told he had to leave, but there was landfall, albeit a long shot, in the form of Tengah island. West knew Price was a survivor and given the chance would not have given up easily. He had a lead but, with no physical body recovered, didn't have much more to go on.

CHAPTER 39

Mia had frozen most of the 'death seed' samples for longevity but retained adequate quantities to work with immediately.

She knew the time and resource needed to research what she had discovered would be out of her daily available time, so her first task was to arrange a video call with Pietro.

"My favourite girl!" he exclaimed as she came into view on his Zoom screen. "To what do I owe this pleasure and love the background, that's your hideaway cove on the island, right?" he quizzed.

"Yes it is," she laughed, "well spotted, but, I have something new I wish to discuss with you, and the reason for the call is that it is going to take extraordinary time and resource, I need to dedicate myself, and an assistant, full time."

"Wow this must be something enormous," he said seriously.

"I believe it could be immense and with vast repercussions," she replied.

Pietro trusted Mia implicitly and didn't even question her request or delve into the detail. He knew that, if she requested something like this, then it would be a risk worth taking.

He went on to tell her that the timing was good because, as part of his worldwide philosophy and training programme, he wanted employees within the organisation to work in different locations and on varying projects. There was a researcher and his assistant that were due to be seconded from their usual base and that person was Li Jie from the Lanzhou facility whom she had met with recently.

It fitted perfectly, Mia said she wanted Carol to work with her and the Lab would still be staffed correctly with the addition of Li and his assistant Victoria.

"Have you finished with me now?" Pietro asked, smiling. "I have one of my 'special events' to arrange and a big pay day coming with it, maybe you'd like to watch," he winked.

"I'll let you know," she said. "Right now, this is my focus, you be careful."

"Always, you know me," he replied, and they ended the zoom call. The new arrangement could be set and implemented immediately so Mia was able to meet with Carol and explain that, from the beginning of the following week, they would work together exclusively on her new project. Carol was excited and humbled that she had chosen her for the project knowing Mia kept personal and work separate and, that she had been chosen on her merit and not for her bedroom orientated oral skills, she thought, smiling. Although, she was very good!

CHAPTER 40

Pietro had recently invested a considerable sum of money on the acquisition of another skin care SME to add to his portfolio, he was a firm disciple of the philosophy 'Cash is King'. Through his researcher, he had received a lead to set up one of the live 'snuff' events one which, dollar wise, he couldn't ignore.

This would provide him with some real cash reinjection, it meant a complex production, but he believed it could be arranged quite quickly. The lead researcher answered an ad recently, she had followed up with the enquirer who had a specific, fantasy scenario. He requested to be set up as the leader of a marauding band of white men infiltrating a fictitious African kingdom inhabited by black Nubian Amazon type women, stealing its diamond treasures.

His band had been overpowered and killed by the women and he was brought, shackled with chains and a yoke, before the Queen, sat on her throne, for his sentence. "Takes all sorts!" she thought, but the victim had, so far, passed all security and background checks. A loner willing to stump up the money for such a meeting, being made aware that the girl would be a skilled actor and that the production would be his to keep after the event. Everything checked out. Pietro had a very beautiful girl originating from the Chopi people of Mozambique, one of the darkest skinned people in the world, he had used before. He wasn't going to be too specific this time about the ending but would bill the title as 'Surrender to the Nubian Queen'. He knew this would attract attention from his list of clienteles and the researcher had begun the process of vetting and making initial contact. He boarded a flight to O'Hare international to meet with his stage production team and IT experts, events such as this had to be meticulously planned with total anonymity and secrecy. Pietro avoided staging his shoots in major cities, so, he planned to hold this one on the outskirts of Charles City in Iowa. Iowa treated by Americans as a 'Fly Over State' and where he had a remote warehouse facility used to store corn for one of his production factories. No outsiders bothered with the State since Universal Pictures built a Baseball Diamond on the outskirts of Dyersville for the shooting of the 1988 film *Field of Dreams* and the visitor centre shut down through lack of tourists.

He would arrange for stage fitters to create a 'false' jungle clearing with a large throne complete with plants and sound effects, the more realistic the more his selected audience would buy into the created scenario and it wouldn't just be male interest either.

Everything went to plan, he gave the team the go ahead, a date was set, and everyone knew what they had to do to make it happen.

The 'victim' received confirmation of the process and proceedings and would begin once he had wired the full amount to one of Pietro's 'hidden' sub accounts, he didn't know it but was basically paying for his own death thinking he would be acting out his role play fantasy, being executed by a Nubian Queen.

CHAPTER 41

Arusi received notification that her 'special' services would be required and a brief highlighting the scenario. She was a regular 'actress' for a video company based in Rio de Janeiro. The company specialised in dominant women and there was no shortage of willing, masochistic men to play victims. Everything here was legitimate, registered actors, disclaimers, certificates everything was above board.

She was only 21 years old, a college student around 160cm tall weighing 54kg with a toned, athletic physique, very attractive, flawless jet black, with an almost blue tinge, skin and a disarming smile. Her best feature, below her slender hips and washboard tummy with pierced button, was her beautifully rounded, firm to the touch, voluptuous, 'bubble-butt' ass. She took great care of this feature with regular massage therapy and oils, after all it was what made her popular for the work she did. In comparison, her breasts were small but rounded and firm with nipples seemingly constantly begging for attention.

She had just finished shooting of a video entitled *Suffer under Nubian Black Ass* where she applied long, intense, front and rear face sitting with forced ass and pussy licking on one of the hired actors and he was genuinely gasping for breath when she finally let him up.

Even under these controlled sessions they had some actors becoming so 'lost' in the moment, so intoxicated by the soft, warm, fleshy female form engulfing their faces, they passed out under the goddesses. The girls watched for this, they knew their power over weak men and instantly released them at the first sign of inactivity or limpness.

Arusi had been adopted as a baby and taken to Brazil by a 'performing arts', freelance Portuguese couple and grew up around glitter, make-up, costumes and acting and she loved it. From the age of five she would often be found, strutting around in oversize heels and elaborate dresses hanging from her undersized frame but she didn't care, she was a natural and took every chance to dress up and be a different character in her own mind. The dressing up gave her confidence, a feeling of dominance, able to be anyone she wanted to be, and quickly learned the power of beauty and more importantly, femininity, especially over the male of the species. Her adoptive parents managed to pass her through college and, naturally developing an instinctive, dominant tendency where men were concerned, she continued and thrived. She found there was no shortage of victims to meet her sexual desires and fantasies but, not to the point of finishing them off!

She had worked with Pietro before, knew the prerequisites and it suited her, she was very sadistic, enjoying men suffering under her control, wishing almost every time she could finish the victim off for good. The feeling from her first kill gave her a sense of absolute power and control and she craved for more, especially if they were white Caucasian males, it gave her that extra special position of undeniable dominance and feeling of ancient, reversed slavery. She would also be very well paid and was looking forward to the event. Her work here providing a reasonable, legally acceptable, solution and alternative to her sadistically dark tendencies.

CHAPTER 42

Mia and Carol were early into the Lab on the Monday morning, both excited yet realistic about the task in hand. Mia had taken the decision to be open with Carol about the nature of the samples they would be working with but not, initially of course, how they were obtained. She had told her that they had come from the infertility clinic but from a certain group of donors with unique characteristics.

Carol was intrigued, especially how just a tiny smear of the raw, unrefined substance had produced such a phenomenal reaction to her age-old scar.

For the whole morning they were locked in a private meeting room discussing, debating, even arguing, a plan of action.

The world over, animal rights and associated groups continued to demonstrate against certain ingredients used within the cosmetics industry, particularly the use of live animals for testing and Skintakt had a policy of non-animal experimentation. The PR for Skintakt made this clear on all packaging although certain ingredients were animal derived, as no known alternatives gave the same effects. Most of the skincare cosmetics there used natural extracts but this one had to be different and it wasn't, exactly, animal derived.

Mia had chosen Carol to work on the new project based on her specialist areas of development. Carol had worked with and was the lead for working with Arachidonic Acids, liquid unsaturated fatty acid found in liver, brain, glands and fat of animals and humans, generally isolated from animal liver and used in skin care creams for soothing eczema and rashes. Mia believed this work could be useful in their attempt to develop a topical cream with the potential of being liquid gold.

The key would be finding the active ingredient, the component responsible for the miraculous healing ability within the 'Seeds of Death' sample, isolating it, and synthesising it into a useful and applicable ingredient for a skin care cream and, of course, determining the quantities required for a commercially viable proposition. One step at a time, they both agreed, assigning each other a place to begin.

The day before, Li and Victoria arrived from Lanzhou and had been settled into their accommodation and were being given a tour of the Lab and briefing of their project portfolio to begin the next day. As in Lanzhou though, the evening would be a get together meal in the Italian Bistro with all invited.

They were introduced formally and then informally around the table where they were warmly accepted into the group.

The next day, following his induction, Li found Mia at a break in her schedule to say 'Hi' and the pair exchanged memories of their trip to the grottoes together, Li exchanging some noticeable glances in Mia's general direction which she noticed but did not return. She did, however, feel obliged to make sure that Li had everything he needed just as he did with her in Lanzhou.

"So, our trip was useful for your project, Mia, I guess, otherwise we wouldn't have been able to come and work here on this beautiful Island, I hope you will find the time to show me around the Lab projects areas in more depth, personally, one day," Li suggested.

"Err yes of course," Mia stuttered, uncharacteristically. "I would be happy to, although, my new research is very urgent and time consuming but, whilst you have a few minutes, I will get Carol to give you the 5 cents Lab tour," she proposed.

"That's great, thanks," he added.

Carol escorted Li on a whistle-stop tour around the Lab explaining 'who was who' and what areas they specialised in. She found him to be very interested if not over interested in everything going on, either he was very thorough and dedicated or just plain nosy! She smiled to herself.

"One thing really new to me is the strict security even at my level and we have all been vetted, signing strict NDA agreements, so why the extra levels?" Li asked Carol.

"It's just protocol here," she replied. "I've worked with more and less security but, it enables accountability during our project work, you'll get used to it."

"There are so many passwords and PINs to remember," he said, shaking his head and rolling his eyes.

Carol just waved her phone, laughing, and said, "Yes, I agree, not my strong point either but it's all about contacts and numbers for me, being a little forgetful." She laughed.

With that, the two of them went their separate ways, Li thanking Carol for her time.

CHAPTER 43

"So, we can arrange a search around Tengah Island then?" West asked the Police commissioner.

"I believe so, I have filed a missing person report which has to be followed up in the absence of a body," he confirmed.

West was in the office of the local Police commissioner in the town of Mersing, a coastal town of South East Malaysia known for its Ferries to offshore Islands like Pulau Tioman and Pulau Rawa and the closest place to Tengah Island. West had not given up on his friend even if just to establish what had happened to him, knowing that a few escaped prisoners had survived the same journey. He had found the coordinates where he believed Price was last seen and discovered that the nearest landfall would have been Tengah.

The commissioner had much better things to do but the money he received from West was enough to even follow up what he believed to be a lost cause.

He was a wily character known as Chan, been around the block, worked in the bigger cities but, now had his posting in the relative peace and quiet of Mersing for the past five years. He knew everyone, everyone knew him, and things were pretty low key with nothing much to deal with other than petty crime. This suited him, he was in his sixties with retirement in sight, a wife and six grandchildren kept him busy. He was still in good shape and could be found running at least two to three times per week. Native Malaysian around 170cm tall and 70kg, grey hair and sun-worn features, a family man but open to earning extra money when coming from a trusted source such as West, who he had known for the past two years.

"Who owns this Island, I heard it's not for tourists anymore?" West asked.

"The Island is now wholly owned by Pietro Allard, a French national, multi-millionaire businessman, he operates a 100%

legitimate and registered skin care research facility there," Chan told him.

"Do we have to gain permission to visit?" he asked him.

"No, this is a missing person investigation and we believe Tengah to be the closest landfall from where he went missing, but out of courtesy, I will seek his permission first and if refused I will arrange an official warrant. However, I have dealt with Mr Allard before and he is a very amicable and straightforward person, I cannot see any objection at all."

"So, you can arrange this and let me know, I'm staying at Maylay Lodge Resort Hotel, you can reach me there when you get an answer," said West.

"Yes of course," replied the commissioner. "I will be in touch."

West went back to his Hotel, he'd booked for a few nights enjoying the comforts of the resorts facilities, he felt he needed a break, but, when he had a hold of something he was like a terrier with a bone, wouldn't let it go until there was nothing to hang on to. He was determined to find out what had happened to Jordan Price even though all indications were that he would have drowned or been devoured by Sharks.

Pietro's overwhelming front was the model businessman and upstanding citizen, always willing to help, especially the authorities, keeping all but one of his enterprises completely transparent so when he received a call from the Police commissioner seeking permission to visit the Island as part of a missing person investigation, he was only too willing to assist.

He would arrange for his chief of security to meet the visitors to the Island the following day in his absence.

The Police commissioner had expected such a response with relationships maintained on a friendly basis, and he informed West that he would be picked up the next day and they would travel by boat to Tengah.

CHAPTER 44

The next day West was collected by one of the commissioner's officers and they met at the quay in Mersing. The journey by speedboat was only 30 minutes maximum and in good weather like they had today, around 20 minutes so; they would have plenty of daylight hours.

Until now, no one had conducted any kind of search on or around the Island for a missing person so any trace of Price's presence on the Island would be virgin ground.

The three visitors arrived at the private Jetty, capable of receiving a sizeable supply ship but this time just a small speedboat, and were met by Skintakt's security officer, Thomas 'Tom' Wisetzki, of Polish descent, ex-military European special forces and long serving employee of Pietro. Indeed, the two of them had been in some real scrapes during their association together.

He welcomed the two men to the Island and escorted them to the reception area of the facility where he had laid on some coffee and doughnuts freshly made from the kitchen.

Chan explained that a relatively low risk convict had recently gone missing from a prison transfer vessel off the coast and with what they knew, the nearest landfall position was the Island. He introduced West as a close friend of the missing person and said that he believed his buddy was a survivor and not ready to accept he was dead under such circumstances. An official missing person report had been filed and it was his duty to follow up any lead no matter how small.

"We have had reports of prisoners from these ships before," Wisetzki said, "but nothing has ever been found here, having said that, I can escort you wherever it is possible to reach," he offered.

"That's kind," replied Chan, "Mr West here would like to accompany us, if that is ok?"

"Of course," Wisetzki replied, "there are some passable roads around the place from the days of tourism and we can go to the most westerly points where, if anywhere, someone may have been able to make land."

At that moment, Mia, wanting to clear her head with some fresh air came into the reception area as she headed for the outside doors. "And who might this divine creature be?" piped up West, his natural instincts taking over.

"This creature, as you refer to her," scowled Wisetzki, "is one of our lead researchers, Mia."

"Apologies," he replied, hand on heart, "it's just when I see beauty, it comes out wrong, please forgive me, Madam." Mia just gave the death stare and continued on her way out of the door to the outside steps and fresh air.

"If you'll excuse me, gentlemen," said Wisetzki. "I will bring the Jeep around the front and we can be on our way."

As he headed outside Mia asked who the visitors were, and he explained what they were doing there and that he was going to do a search with them on the Western side of the Island.

Mia froze for a second, they were looking for the man she had killed and would, undoubtedly, find her cove, there may be evidence of her recent visit there although she was meticulous not to leave any kind of rubbish so what could they find? Certainly not a body; that would be gone by now. Then her mind flashed back, she had taken the trouble to remove and dispose of the fluorescent life vest but, then it hit her. The T shirt, what had she done with the T shirt? Where was it? She knew she removed it from him but could not recall what had happened to it. She felt sick to her stomach, what if they found it and somehow linked it to her? Certain people knew where she went to relax and that would lead them to her.

Stay calm she decided.

The trio headed off, following the dirt roads towards the Island's westerly coastline and stopping at any point they felt a weary swimmer may have been able to make land.

"Tell me, Wisetzki," quizzed West, "you seem to have this place secure, you must have a good contingent of staff, my friend?"

"The work here is low risk and, being an Island, we don't really get many intruders and if we do it's usually by accident," he answered. "We use technology rather than physical bodies and have a control centre monitoring cameras and alarms etc. but, like I said, we don't have anything to attract criminal attention."

"I understand," replied West, "so mainly the Lab facility is the only risk from sneaky competitors no doubt," he added laughing.

"That's about it," replied Wisetzki, "but, myself and my colleague are both ex-military and have the necessary equipment and knowledge to use it if called upon," he added with a warning tone to his voice.

After around two hours of stop/start they reached an elevated point with a beautiful sandy beach and Palm tree below, it was Mia's private cove.

Chan took out his binoculars and began scanning the area with a left to right sweep across the beach area and then he stopped, focusing the instrument closer.

"What's that?" he exclaimed, "I can see something black, looks like an item of clothing, we have to go down there!"

CHAPTER 45

Mia returned to the Lab where she had left Carol occupied with one of the samples they had been working with.

"Are you ok?" Carol asked when she saw Mia. "It looks like you've seen a ghost."

"I'm ok," Mia replied, "how are you getting on?"

"Not just getting on, got on!" she cried. "During your break outside, after what you told me to try before you left, we—!" exclaimed Carol with a deliberate pause, "we have just isolated our active ingredient from the sample."

"You are teasing me," Mia gasped, "my theory method has worked?"

"100%!" said Carol. "We now have our active ingredient, stripped away from the usual components we would expect to find, your supernatural element, the only 'unnatural' presence, it just has to be it." She smiled.

They hugged each other and Mia forgot about the search going on for Price and neither of them noticed the partially hidden figure taking in the physically animated merriment, Li Jie.

CHAPTER 46

Li Jie had grown up in the Gansu province of China as one of nine children born to his mother and father, six boys and three girls, he was the youngest out of the brood. His parents worked every hour God sent to feed, clothe and house them all in poverty but relative comfort and safety.

Being the youngest sibling meant that he was always down in the pecking order and learnt quickly to accept opportunities as and whenever they presented themselves. He became quite the stealth agent, finding the stashes of his brothers and sisters, treats like candy, but never personal belongings or money. He carefully calculated every time, smiling when he heard one say, "I'm sure I had more sweets left than this, but I must have eaten them, have you seen them Li?" Of course, he would always say he didn't know what they were talking about.

His trait continued as he managed to gain a scholarship out of his village to college in Lanzhou studying chemistry and biology after 'somehow' managing to see, the day before, the following day's test papers.

He knew the professor had received the test papers and would be setting up the classroom ready to host his class as the invigilator the following day.

The professor was in his sixties, still very competent, and indeed ranked highly for his pass rate for chemistry students within the province. However, he was very trusting, borne out of the fact that most of his students were very honest, feeding from generations of honourable parents he knew personally and had taught. But, in comparison, Li was different gravy, he had gained entry, yes, through natural, academic study, but, his profound talent was that he could remember large amounts of text or data after only a brief viewing time, all in all a photographic memory.

He had offered to stay behind after class, to help the professor move some of the heavier furniture to create an examination type setting for the next day. He was grateful for this but, in all the moving and shifting and going back and forth checking and rechecking, Li somehow gained the opportunity to view the test papers. Glancing over them was enough for him to check the subject matter to be tested and he spent the whole evening preparing his advantage.

Although a gainful opportunity at the time, he knew it would be different going forward and studied hard finally becoming qualified enough to gain a position in Pietro's facility in Lanzhou. He was, however, very selfish; he always put himself first and was readily prepared to step on others if there was any chance of making something for himself.

CHAPTER 47

It was late afternoon by the time the 'search party' arrived back at the facility with West clutching what turned out to be a black T shirt they had found at the cove. However, it wasn't just any T Shirt and, though void of any forensic traces due to its exposure and conditions, the remains of a ghosted word once emblazoned on the back, 'Squad', could still be made out. He confirmed that he had one just the same together with three other people from a 'guys' trip, as he called it, the previous year. It didn't, however, prove that it belonged specifically to Price but, West was absolutely convinced it was his friend's T shirt.

Mia and Carol had secured their work for the day and were having a coffee in the cafeteria, discussing next steps when Wisetzki, alone, came to the table.

"Everything ok?" Mia asked.

"Yes, fine," he replied, "but this West character is convinced they have found a T shirt belonging to the guy they are searching for at the Cove where you go to relax."

It was no secret where Mia went, it had become known as 'her' place, a place the others avoided going to, respecting her privacy. It did, however, mean that, Mia was the only person who may have seen something.

"Can I ask when you last went there?" asked Wisetzki.

Mia kept calm and replied, "Yes, of course, it would have been on my last off duty, whenever that was, I can't remember the exact day, it seems so long since I had a break but, everyone knows I go there it's not a secret."

"It's ok," Wisetzki assured her, "I can check the off-duty roster for the exact date, but did you notice anything unusual or see anyone else that particular day?"

She knew this would place her at the cove at the time when Price may have been stranded there but she remained nonchalant. "No, nothing from the usual," Mia stated strongly. "Same as any other day I have been there: sun, gently lapping waves, my palm tree and book, that's it." She smiled, "Is it important?"

"It's a long shot," Wisetzki replied, "but there is a possibility that, if the convict made land, he may be somewhere on the Island, dead I would guess but, we will search the area just in case. He may also have decided to try to swim further around the coast and died that way but, if he was alive, I think he would have been discovered or made himself known by now, not to worry, Miss Mia."

Based on the findings and the report given by Wisetzki they agreed that Chan and West would return the following day, with a diver and dogs to search the waters and area around the cove.

Mia was concerned but, having gone through everything in her head, there was no way of connecting her to Price's disappearance. She knew they would never find the lifejacket as she had decided not to throw it anywhere on her way back but had incinerated it in the Lab's furnace.

CHAPTER 48

The following day, the search party returned to the Island again, hosted by Wisetzki who had updated Pietro on proceedings the night before. He wasn't overly concerned but, always cautious especially with police, possibly corrupt Police, sniffing around, he knew Tengah was completely clean. However, he told Wisetzki, who he trusted with his life and had done so on more than the odd occasion, to be cooperative and see it to the end yet without offering any more than they asked for.

He acknowledged and understood fully his first charge being undying loyalty to his long-time friend and employer.

This time a larger piloted boat materialised complete with diver, a handler with two German Shepherd sniffer dogs, West and Chan. After dropping off West, Chan and the dogs with the handler at the jetty the boat's pilot ferried the diver directly to anchor in the cove itself to be able to cover more area in the time they had. The waters were shallow so many dives could be carried out without the Diver having to pressurise and they had planned an all-day search mission.

Wisetzki had organised the small open backed pick-up truck usually employed to transport the Aloe Vera from the fields which was ideal for the dogs whilst they led in one of the Suzuki Jimnys like the day before.

By the time they reached the cove, the boat was already moored and the diver foraging around in a patterned sweep in the water.

They concentrated on the land search around the cove and then up onto the road where they had parked the jeep and the surrounding areas.

After searching all day with no lead or trace at all, West said to Chan, "I know he was here, I just know it."

Chan was emotionally unattached and spelt out the hardened facts to him. They had searched the waters, no sign, the dogs hadn't picked up anything at all and if there had been a rotting corpse on land, they would have, he assured him. He went on to say that if Price had indeed made land at the cove he would probably have decided, believing the island was uninhabited at this place, to venture back into the water in an attempt to swim around the headland in the shallower water but been dragged back into the current and gotten into trouble or attacked by Sharks. "There's no sign of him other than this T shirt which we cannot say for sure belonged to your friend," he concluded.

"It is his shirt!" West proclaimed angrily, "and I don't believe everything is innocent here, I want to speak directly to the person who Wisetzki says uses this beach sometimes."

This being, of course, Mia.

Wisetzki agreed to take them back to the Lab and, if Mia was available, they would ask her in person whether she had seen anything. However, he stressed it was out of courtesy and nothing else which Chan agreed would be the scenario as there was nothing at all to go on unless she could help in any way.

They arrived back at the facility. Wisetzki left the two of them in the cafeteria with refreshments and went to find Mia who was in the Lab with Carol.

He explained what had happened, but the friend of the missing man just wanted to ask her again if she had remembered anything.

Mia agreed and followed him to the cafeteria where the two men sat, both standing when she reached the table.

"It's you, my dear," West said smiling. "What a pleasure again."

"Creature if I recall!" Mia returned, smiling.

"Just a figure of speech, my dear," he said. "No offence meant."

"None taken," Mia replied sarcastically, "how do you believe I can help?"

Chan led the conversation explaining he believed she may have been at the location where the T shirt was found at the time when Price may have been stranded there or thereabouts.

Mia explained that, this was her special place, she went there for solitude and her last visit was exactly that, nothing out of the ordinary, just a winding down day of relaxation. She added that she took care of the environment so always checked the beach for any plastics and anything other than natural driftwood, if there was a T shirt on the beach at that time, she would have found it and she hadn't.

There wasn't much else to say, she was straight to the point and covered everything. Chan was convinced that Mia didn't know anything, and he couldn't press for anything further especially when the prisoner had been sprung illegally in the first place and that he himself was on dodgy ground together with West.

"We will leave you to your research then," Chan wrapped up, "thank you all for your hospitality and cooperation, I believe we cannot do anymore here, thank you." As he turned to West, knowing he wasn't finished somehow.

They left the Island, Wisetzki reported back to Pietro and Mia went back to Carol in the Lab, an early finish and a late night she thought, I need some relief!!

CHAPTER 49

Back at Chan's office in Mersing, he and West were reflecting on the trip to Tengah and what they had found or hadn't as far as West was concerned.

"Somebody there knows something!" said West. "I am convinced and that researcher, the stunning one, she knows something, I just know she does," he added physically clenching his fist.

"Look Alex, there is nothing to be found," Chan stated, "no leads, no trail and certainly no evidence, the only thing we have is a T shirt which is nothing more than circumstantial."

"You look here," said West, "anyone else other than Jordan and I would agree but, I know him, he's a survivor and I know he wouldn't have given up and if he managed to get to the Island why would he just disappear? No, something is missing, and I want to find out, do you have anyone with any connection to the Island facility?"

Chan wasn't happy with West but went on to tell him that the reason he had developed a working relationship with Pietro was that his wife's cousin had a son who had been looking for work, he wasn't really skilled in anything, just manual work. He had noticed an advert for a labourer to work on the Island as a second mate to the agricultural specialist responsible for the Aloe Vera crop. He'd known Pietro through some legal and licensing paperwork, so contacted him directly, vouching for the teenager. He gave the boy the job and he had been on the Island now for over two years and enjoyed what he did.

"I don't want to cause any problems there," Chan said. "It's family and he is just a good boy, he works hard and is innocent of any wrong doings and I want to keep it that way, Pietro gave him a job despite his autistic disabilities and I'm grateful for that."

"Ok," said West, "I get it, but when is the boy next due to be here? Just a chat, with you present, just to see if he's noticed anything unusual, that can't hurt can it?"

"I guess not," Chan replied. "He will be here on Saturday; we have a family birthday and we will all be getting together for that."

"That's great," he replied, "I will extend my stay a little longer, I have nothing pressing back at my print shop, any chance you could fix me up in the meantime?" he added, smirking.

"Let's keep everything here above board," replied Chan, "we don't need complications around here."

"Sure," said West, "I understand, let me know when we can meet with the boy."

CHAPTER 50

The young man was 19 years old, a little slow initiative-wise which was put down to complications at birth where he went for too long without breathing. As a result, he contracted autistic tendencies but, was hardworking, took instruction well and was very diligent and precise when given a task to carry out. He made the ideal labourer for the work required and nobody complained about him. Everyone knew him and called him fondly, 'sparkplug', because, he had fixed one of the petrol mowers when everyone else had discounted the fact that the spark plug was missing from the engine block and the reason it wouldn't fire up.

Sparkplug worked with Joe, a 60-year-old African American from the Mid-west with a wealth of agricultural knowledge from years working with various crops and cultivation techniques. He was responsible for the Aloe Vera crop they used for experimentation purposes rather than production quantities and produced prime samples every time. The two of them were outside, general handymen around the place and responsible for maintaining the landscaped garden at the facility as well as refuse control and disposal and any other tasks not mentioned.

Sparkplug had been looking forward to his weekend with the family but, had made sure everything was left in the best possible state before he left, he hated anything to be out of place when he wasn't there.

He had boarded the launch with his small overnight bag together with the three others taking their two-day break from the Island and they were in Mersing by 10:00 hrs.

He was surprised when he was met by his uncle Chan at the quay but, was always happy to see him. Sparkplug looked up to his Uncle Chan, he was the most respected in the family and he would let him hold the unloaded revolver he carried when he was younger.

"I'm here to collect you," Chan told Sparkplug, "and take you to your mother, but, I just need you to see someone with me, a friend, just for a few minutes on the way, would that be ok? I think he will treat you as well."

"Of course, that's fine," answered Sparkplug, "is he Police like you, Uncle?" he asked, enthusiastically.

"Err no, not quite, but he's an old friend," answered Chan, "let's go."

Chan took Sparkplug to West's Hotel where he was waiting in the lounge area of the Lobby.

He introduced himself as Alex and arranged a large mocktail with an umbrella for sparkplug which he thought was amazing and very generous.

"Sparkplug," West said, "I can call you sparkplug?"

"Sure," he replied, "everyone does, I fixed the petrol mower," he bragged sticking his thumb up.

"So, I heard, you are famous on the Island," he said, building his confidence.

"Now listen," he went on, "I do security as my job and I'm looking at making a proposal for some additional security cameras at your workplace Laboratory and, you being on the inside and in the know, would you happen to be able to help suggest where these might be needed?"

"I don't really go inside that much, Mr Alex, mostly wearing overalls and all," Sparkplug replied.

"Ok," said West, "have you noticed anything different or strange happening over the past couple of weeks, things you would spot being an undercover Policeman?" he laughed.

"Not really," sparkplug replied, grinning. "Miss Mia and Miss Carol came recently, to see us personally, to check when they could have more Aloe Vera leaves, they use it for testing you know, said they needed more than usual, but, other than that and Miss Mia using the furnace which is 'my job'." He tutted, shaking his head. "Nothing."

"Using the furnace?" West quizzed. "Using the furnace for what and who is this Miss Mia?"

"The girl you referred to as creature," Chan piped up laughing sarcastically.

West had visons of the two women heaving a body into the furnace, but Sparkplug explained that Mia just threw in something quite small in a brown paper bag. "Nothing," he added, "she just said it was something from the Lab, not dangerous just an old shawl she found a cat had been sleeping on outside."

"I think that is enough for now, Mr West," said Chan, "he is itching to see his mother and cousins."

"Sure, and thanks, Sparkplug," he replied holding out his hand.

Sparkplug shook his hand, thanked him for the drink, and with that, Chan took him off to meet with his mother ready for the birthday celebrations.

A furnace, West thought, what was she really throwing in and if it was just a shawl why did it have to be in a bag and why did she keep coming up at every turn? He didn't think Price was alive anymore, but he was convinced there was more to his disappearance and this Mia knew something about it, he was sure of that, but what could he do next?

CHAPTER 51

"Can I ask you what you are doing alone in here?" Mia asked Li, whom she had found reading notes in her Laboratory when she came back from getting coffees for herself and Carol who had just gone to the bathroom.

"I came looking for you," he answered nervously.

"But you could see through the glass that I was not in here," she replied, "and you came in anyway?"

Li played the ignorant with an air of sarcasm. "Oh, I'm sorry I didn't realise this was a restricted area with sensitive information," he joked, "and the door wasn't closed."

"You know it isn't within the confines of the Lab," replied Mia, "but you also know that I'm working on a dedicated project which isn't ready for any kind of public broadcast."

"Oh, I'm just public, now am I?" responded Li sarcastically.

Mia was angry and he knew it. "Be careful Li Jie, you know full well what I meant, and you also know our protocols, if you need to speak to me then wait until I'm available, is that clear?" she added commandingly, reminding him of her position in the process.

"Crystal!" he replied.

"So, what was it you needed me for?" asked Mia.

"Oh!" he replied. "I was wondering if you would like to have something to eat later in the Bistro with me and a glass of wine maybe?" he charmed.

Mia knew he had just made up the social gesture and thought about it but said, "Maybe another time, Li, I have a lot on with this project and you have your own assignment with Victoria so please go back to your station," she instructed.

He left without another word but knew she was angry and maybe suspicious of his true intentions, he wanted to know what she was working on; it must have been linked to something she found in the grottoes they had visited, something big, something in it for him, possibly?

Mia checked around the Lab and told Carol what had happened, there didn't appear to be anything missing but both concluded that their respective notes had been rearranged from how each had left them. There was, thankfully, nothing sensitive left around as, at the end of each day, all major updates and findings were recorded electronically and securely with password protection. They did, however, agree to watch out for Li as Carol mentioned for the first time that, she hadn't liked him from the first day she had been introduced, an instinct, she added. "I agree," said Mia, "and with him lurking around I suggest we always make sure our Lab door is secure even during the day and even if for a short absence."

"Agreed," she replied.

They remained in the Lab till late despite an early start, Mia and Carol were ruthless in their dedication to the project in hand, both excited at the prospect of what could be achieved. The actual carrier or base cream for this potentially amazing formulation was not the issue, they had stock product already formulated, oil in water and water in oil emulsions with Aloe Vera extract. Within the beauty industry, many off the shelf items contained human products such as baby foreskin cells and urine. Therefore, the addition of their 'magic element' was not the issue, they had to determine how much was required to make the cream active and how that correlated back, to how much of the 'special' sperm was needed for it to be commercially viable and, more importantly, how they could obtain it.

CHAPTER 52

The sun had just set on the Island as the dark figure of Alex West slipped discreetly from the small rib boat into the calm shallows of a cove close by to the Lab facility on Tengah Island. He had paid the Captain of a fishing boat to take him just offshore from the Island, await his return and then take him back. He wore a black, military style jumpsuit and combat boots with a black beanie style hat. Under the light of a New Moon, he had decided to do a search of his own in complete defiance of the Police commissioner who had demanded no further action into the disappearance of Jordan Price. Security was over adequate, based on the risk factors, for the Lab facility and main personnel quarters but not so in some of the old converted outbuildings and stables adjacent to it. These buildings consisted of storage for farm equipment and tools, storage and processing of the Aloe Vera crop, furnace and recycling compression unit and what could only be described as a small cottage. Here, Joe preferred to live together with his apprentice Sparkplug, it was almost like a Father/Son relationship and the relative isolation suited both. The cottage used to be a massage spa in its tourist days and had been completely refurbished with every facility and the two were very happy to be away from the main Lab and amongst the equipment they both loved to work with. The furnace was an important part of the waste disposal facility and was only fired on certain days of the week or if there was a specific demand request. This was West's target of interest. He just had to see for himself its location, size etc. following his chat with Sparkplug.

West had discreetly photographed a site safety evacuation, fire escape map on the wall of the reception when he visited and knew that the utility buildings were adjacent to, and set back from, the main Lab facility, so he made his way keeping a safe distance from detection to his area of intent.

"Carol, I think we should call it a day now, agreed?" Mia suggested.

"Yes, Mia," she replied, "I have gathered up all of our physical, handwritten notes and it's a lot," she added holding up the huge sack full of the papers. "Everything so far, is now documented and secured electronically and after our experience with Li, I know the furnace is lit today so, I'm going to go there and dispose of everything personally, it's done then," she added.

"It's dimly lit across the yard at this time," Mia warned, "could leave it until tomorrow."

"Its fine," said Carol, "done it many times, and anyway the furnace won't be lit tomorrow, and I don't want this paper trail laying around here any longer, I'll be ok, there's no one here going to harm me."

"Ok, but watch out for the bogey men," Mia said, "I'll see you tomorrow."

"Will do, good night, Mia, good day's work." She added.

The pair locked up, Mia headed back to her rooms and Carol made her way to the outbuildings.

CHAPTER 53

West had reached another dead end, he had located the furnace, which was in operation despite no obvious physical smells or sound more than that of a hair dryer. The furnace was high-tech, run on LPG with the already low emissions, exhausted through complex scrubbers, making the resulting expulsion to the atmosphere 99% clean. Pietro wanted his facilities to be a model example in every way he could and all of them boasted ISO 14001 environmental certification.

It was located in its own spacious barn with room around, a sophisticated control panel, fire safety equipment and the area around was lit, but only by low level, yellow-tinged lighting.

He began to wonder what he thought he could have possibly found there but had been overwhelmed with his deeply rooted thoughts that something more sinister than a failed escape attempt had ended the life of his friend.

Anyway, his curiosity was satisfied for that part and he decided it was time to get back to his boat. He had done what he set out to do and didn't want to take any further risks so, he headed for the door, but stopped dead in his tracks. "What on earth is that?" he said out loud, dodging quickly behind some wooden crates.

He recognised the song, someone singing 'Waterloo' by Abba at the top of their voice!

It was Carol, armed with air-pods listening to one of her favourite bands and was joyfully singing along at the top of her voice as she entered the furnace room.

On reaching the plant she removed her air-pods, the furnace had a separate chute to deposit material and relied on indicator lights and bleeps as the steps for disposal were followed and completed, it was a safety system requiring all of her senses.

West had thought about running but he would be seen, so he decided to wait it out after all, it wouldn't take long for her to do what she had to do.

Carol deposited the material safely into the dedicated chute on the furnace and was about to leave when she found her airpods had become disconnected from her iPhone. "Damn!" she said out loud. "I think I've worn these ones out, need to get new ones." This had happened before and she needed to restart her phone which was her life, it had everything in there, so she took a seat on one of the crates right in front of where West was hiding and began the process.

But then, she froze, she literally sensed someone was directly behind her, she slowly stood to her feet, about to turn around but he moved quickly, grabbing her from behind, one arm around her waist and the other hand over her mouth.

He knew she hadn't seen him and if he could keep it that way there was no need to do anything more than maybe tie her up and gag her.

'Tie-up'? 'gag'? 'Carol'? Not belonging in the same sentence!

She gripped the forearm of the hand over her mouth, dropped her hips and spun him to the ground in a Judo type throw channelling his grip and applied force of direction against him. Unfortunately, he kept his grip on her waist with his other hand and they both ended up on the floor. Carol was winded and he managed to get up first and stood over her, she had seen his face, he drew his arm back ready to punch her in the jaw and hopefully silence her so he could get away.

She closed her eyes, waiting for the blow and the cracking sound, which came and was very loud but, to her absolute surprise, no feeling.

She opened her eyes, slowly squinting, then into full focus and to her surprise and delight, her attacker was laid out on the floor and, stood up over him, a familiar face.

"Sparkplug!" she cried. "Thank God, you little saviour, but how did you know?"

"Are you alright, Miss Carol?" he said helping her to her feet and putting down the baseball bat he had just used to despatch consciousness from West.

"I was just sitting out in the yard, Mr Joe and me had been practicing baseball till the sun went down when I heard you singing Abba, I knew that it was you and thought I'd come and see what you were up to, if you needed me for anything."

"Thank goodness you did, Sparkplug," she said, hugging him, "but, who is this?"

"I don't know," he replied, "but you go and get Mr Wisetzki and I will make sure he doesn't go anywhere until you get back, ok?"

"Ok," she replied and hurried off.

Mia was alerted also and found Carol a little shaken but totally unharmed.

She was, however, alerted to the fact that she may not have seen the last of Alex West.

Wisetzki recognised the intruder and secured the area, convinced he was alone, he decided to detain him there, on the Island, until the following day when the Police commissioner would come to collect him.

The next day he filed the necessary complaints with the commissioner but, had the feeling there was something more between them than appeared and didn't expect much more than a sob story and apology. However, he was determined punishment be handed out for the assault on Carol which again, he knew, would probably be a ticking off and a fine which he could easily afford.

He made his report back to Pietro and asked for authorisation to install some CCTV in the furnace area which, was agreed and noted.

CHAPTER 54

The following day, Mia had a secure video call with Pietro.

"Why secure today?" she asked him, "because of last night?"

"No, I don't think there is any real security threat, just some guy with notions of being a detective. I wanted to have our routine catch up but, with an invite," he replied excitedly.

They went through updates regarding her project and she informed him that her initial work with the new substance acquired was primarily for a new skin care product but could, after further investigation, be a breakthrough in the effectiveness of fertility treatment and have potential value to the Infertility Clinics within his portfolio.

She requested further time, to which, he told her to take as much as she needed.

"So, what is the invite?" she asked curiously.

"Oh yes," he said, "I recently had an opportunity to fill up the cash coffers, always a good thing," he added, rubbing his hands together.

He went on, "I have one of my live special events and wondered if you would like a link to watch, it's next Saturday, you know the routine, man suffering at the hands or other parts of the superior race!" he quipped, smiling.

He knew full well the stirring this would have on Mia and wasn't really surprised when she said she would like to watch.

He agreed to have her furnished with the necessary passwords and secured links and apologised that he couldn't watch with her on this occasion.

Mia was always excited and sexually aroused by the thought of the male demise by a woman and planned her Saturday around the event, it would be around 2am her time, so she could relax, take a long bath and open a bottle of wine before sitting in front of her 55" 5K TV.

CHAPTER 55

"Can I have your attention please, so, with everyone gathered here tonight," announced Wisetzki over the microphone.

He had arranged an assembly in the main canteen area the next day, following the handover of West to the Police commissioner, where he commended Sparkplug for his bravery and quick thinking coming to the aid of Carol the day before.

At the end of his greeting the Chef appeared with a hand-made cake, decorated with an icing sugar Sparkplug in a cape.

He was visibly embarrassed but enjoyed the applause and gratitude even though everyone loved him anyway. He received pats on the back, handshakes and, of course, hugs from Carol and Mia; it was like a birthday for him and he struggled to erase the huge grin from his cheeky face.

Li was there, but away from the group watching from a distance. To him there was something more going on, was this incursion something to do with the project Mia was working on, was it linked somehow? He was convinced it was and determined to find out more for himself.

West had been collected by the Police commissioner, who apologised to Wisetzki for the intrusion, but could vouch for the perpetrator, in that, he wasn't a violent person, he had been scared and didn't know what to do when he had been discovered. He explained that West was grieving for his friend but he would be formerly charged and give an official apology to Pietro Allard.

Few words were spoken between the men the whole journey back to the commissioner's office in Mersing but he was seething as they sat in his office.

"Why, Alex?" he yelled. "Why? I got you to the Island, we searched, we found nothing, no trace, I'm sorry for the loss of your friend, he's dead and there are no suspicious circumstances, he was an escaped prisoner for God's sake!" He went on, "You have placed me in an awkward position, I have a good relationship with the owner of the Island, Mr Allard, we don't have any issues there and I want it to stay that way, do you understand me? We will probably be able to get away with an apology, but you assaulted one of his employees and Mr Allard has every right to take it further, what were you thinking?"

West acted totally repentant, "I just had to see if I could find something, that researcher, she knows something I'm sure, but I never meant to physically harm anyone and I'm the one with the big headache from that relative of yours!"

"Just drop it. ok?" the Police commissioner concluded. "I will see what I can do but, you must never go there again and don't think for one moment that I wasn't aware of how you got there, it's my town and I don't miss anything, remember that."

"I won't," agreed West. "It was foolish, I won't go there again, and I will donate to their named charity if that will help?"

CHAPTER 56

Carol and Mia continued to progress with their work on formulising a 'miracle' cream from the sperm sample. They had found that the active ingredient was in abundance within each droplet and contained more than enough for their initial tests. They formulated a carrier in the form of a gel using a traditional skin cream formula and had samples ready for testing. Mia worked with a Boston based company specialising in the growth of human skin in their laboratories formed into 'dime' size pieces for testing and research. The alternative would have been to test on animals, normally rabbits shaved to expose patches of naked skin, but Skintakt did not utilise animal testing so these human skin samples were important to their testing procedures.

The skin samples had to be kept at a constantly cool 39 degrees and she had arranged a new batch for the following week.

Mia had also been speaking to her counterparts at Pietro's main infertility research and clinic facility in Zurich. She knew that successful IVF treatments was the only way couples, with male infertility issues, could have a child of their own and the rates of success dwindled as the age of the woman advanced. If her theories were correct, then this 'death seed' she had frozen could have other benefits if it was as potent as it appeared to be.

Her only reservation was the man the sample came from, the last thing she wanted was a cloned army of rapists or depraved sex offenders, however, studies had shown that there was no evidence of a 'sex offending gene' it was more likely due to factors such as education, upbringing etc.

She was informed that the clinic possessed an abundance of female eggs which could be frozen from 5–10 years. Many patients agreed that any surplus eggs harvested beyond successful fertilisation could be donated and used for research.

Mia arranged for a small sample of the frozen sperm to be sent for testing to the Lab in Zurich and that was that for the week, it was Friday and she had arranged an evening with Carol which they were both looking forward to and the next day was Pietro's live event, a promising weekend, she thought.

CHAPTER 57

Meanwhile in Iowa, the project manager responsible for the stage setting of the live event was escorting the 'victim', wanting to be known as Bula Matari ('Breaker of Rocks', the nickname given to Henry Morton Stanley, one of the cruel, early exploiters of African people and territories) around the set they had manufactured.

Staying in character. "What are your thoughts, Mr Matari, about our African Kingdom set up?" he asked.

"It is absolutely outstanding!" Matari replied. "Just how I imagined and hoped it would be, perfect!"

The set was spectacular, a stone looking façade reminiscent of the entrance to an ancient Temple behind an authentic looking, majestic stone-like throne reached by steps. In front, a rough, real grassy area with authentic palms and bushes forming a jungle type clearing where he would be brought before the queen to pay for his sins.

"Glad everything is to your liking and approval," he stated, "you have instructions and we will collect you tomorrow for your filmed adventure."

"Perfect, I can't wait," replied 'Matari'.

The scene was set, Pietro had an audience of 10 selected individuals all paying $300,000 each, as there would be no extra requests during this viewing. It was an equal mix of men and women but, you could separate easily as five masochistic men and five sadistic women who, on this occasion were all but one, black. Pietro concluded he had reached out to a more discerningly racial, female audience with the scenario format this time, one for the future perhaps?

In the gym, Mia had worked out hard in the afternoon following a night of lust with Carol, then had a lazy evening with an aromatic herb and oil bath soak. She had positioned her chaise longue with a small side table supporting a beautiful crystal decanter of her favourite South African Pinotage and a glass in front of her TV. She wore her silk kimono and, with TV remote in one hand and wine in the other, she pressed the buttons for the live broadcast about to happen in Iowa.

CHAPTER 58

The crystal clear picture filled her TV screen and she was astonished as she switched from one camera view to another, the setting was unbelievable, you could have actually been in a jungle clearing at the foot of an ancient Temple and then the throne.

She gasped; thankful she hadn't taken a sip of wine at that point for, sat, legs crossed, majestically on the stone throne was the most beautiful creature she had ever seen in her life. Arusi, a stunning Nubian black goddess, completely naked apart from jewellery and accessories consisting of a series of layered gold neck rings, huge gold hoop earrings, coloured wrist and ankle beads and heavy gold chain adorning her beautiful waist, riding high on her womanly hips. Her head was completely shaven, and her flawless black skin was shining from the stage lights above, anointed with oil.

'Matari' wanted the full scenario, he was dressed in pre-muddied khakis, shorts and shirt, Pith helmet, boots and socks and he was being led, held each side, onto the set by two African Amazon warrior-dressed young girls with spears.

The two additional actresses had been told that this was a fantasy scenario and they were to bring him before the queen, throw him to the floor and leave. This way there would only be Arusi as witness to the proceeding events.

However, in true African, jungle type, scenarios no one saw Matari flinch as a red flighted dart penetrated his buttock, shot from an airgun by one of Pietro's stagehands and loaded with the Neuromuscular blockading drug Succinylcholine. This scene was one man and one woman, and they couldn't risk a fightback by the intended victim so, he would be like putty in her hands.

"We have brought this marauding white man before you, Queen Goddess, for the death sentence for his crimes against our people," said one of the warrior women, throwing him to his knees.

"Very well!" proclaimed the Queen commandingly. "You have done well, and you will be rewarded but, may leave now," she added, and the two warriors left the set.

The drug was taking effect on Matari, he was weakened and was a little bleary eyed and groggy as he looked up at the Queen, straining from the wooden yoke around his neck, restricting his hands tied to it.

The queen shuffled forward on her throne, uncrossing her legs and parting her shiny black thighs for a glimpse of her perfectly shaven and small gold ring, pierced pussy.

Matari was totally stricken and weakened further by the beautiful black goddess in front of him, she was incredible, the Goddess of his dreams; he would do anything she asked of him.

"You know why you are here?" she barked

Matari was sweating profusely, his heart racing with a percussion type pulse as he gazed at the goddess above him. He knew he had been shot with something, a dart maybe, but he thought it part of the scenario and played along. "Yes," he stammered, "I beg mercy!"

"No mercy!" she replied standing up and approaching his crouched form below her.

"Please?" he begged.

Arusi was lost in the scene, totally playing out the story, power oozing from her body, wicked thoughts whizzing through her mind. He was hers totally, she could inflict whatever she wanted over the piece of white, marauding trash before her and she was incensed.

Mia watched in amazement and, for a switching, was half wishing she could be before the queen but, not under these circumstances of course, she thought.

The queen placed the sole of her foot on Matari's face and extended her leg outwards, pushing him harshly onto his back, knocking his loosely strapped Pith helmet from his head, completely immobilised, his breathing faculties totally vulnerable and facing upwards.

She strutted over to him looking down at his prostate body. "You know the sentence is death?" she enquired.

"Yes, queen," he replied squinting from the artificial sunlight beating down on him, "but please show mercy?"

He wasn't sure about the acting now; couldn't grasp why he was partly paralysed and if this was how it was meant to go. However, he had been warned of realistic circumstances so decided not to question the professionalism of the production but to keep playing and that his video would be a very true reflection on his life-long fantasy.

Arusi got down on all fours and began crawling, circling her prey like a lioness, her head held high and forcing her shiny buttocks upwards as she made the way towards her target area.

She knew that she could simply pinch his nose with one hand and cover his mouth with the other but, that wouldn't satisfy her at all, wouldn't satisfy the tingling between her legs and erect nipples or the discerning, paying audience.

Time was in slow motion, the drug would last at least two hours, not that much time needed, but she wanted it slow and sensual.

She casually crouched over his face and then lay down, his face smothering in her belly. The effect was of course instant, he couldn't breath and with the limited movement he had left just managed to kick his legs weakly and open and close the fingers of his trapped hands.

Arusi smiled, her diamond white teeth flashing between her sumptuous lips. She didn't want him to suffocate there, not yet anyway, she rolled to the side, off his face, to gasps and splutters and caressed her perfect belly. Then back down again putting him under once more. She repeated this several times and each time Matari was becoming more and more desperate with his pleading for her to stop, that he had taken enough and wanted the story to end, it was too much for him.

This was, however, just what she wanted to hear from him, genuine desperate pleading, the tingling between her legs increasing and a warm wetness developing there.

Matari was becoming weaker, the constant lack of breath with small amounts of recovery time between were taking their deadly toll on him.

Arusi switched weapons and target, she was confident enough by his weakened and drugged state to remove the restraining yoke from his neck and wrists, lack of oxygen was going to be replaced by lack of blood to the brain as she coiled her beautiful, black, shiny thighs around his throat and tightened her grip, like a jungle Anaconda despatching its helpless prey.

His hands, now free, clutched weakly at her sinew straining thighs but, with no effect whatsoever, he was helpless, and she piled on the pressure tensing her deadly, inner thigh, abductor muscles.

He began to twitch violently, the sign that he was about to lose consciousness, she relieved the pressure and looked into his glazed eyes knowing he wasn't sure what day or where he was.

"White men were born to be punished by black goddesses," she hissed, "do you understand?"

He could only weakly nod in compliance and when she thought he had recovered sufficiently from her first choking she repeated it again only stopping when he began to twitch involuntarily, but this wasn't her plan, to choke him to death, just to weaken him so much that his physical resistance would be non-existent.

CHAPTER 59

On both occasions, Mia had switched camera view to his crotch area trying to catch a glimpse of the 'seeds of death', he would hopefully ejaculate on his passing.

Arusi knew how she would finish him, a normal desperate, but physically abled, person would do anything, kick, bite, scratch to avoid the inevitable, but she was confident that this white man was already done.

She finally stood over him feet either side of his head and facing his feet, she had a bottle of coconut oil which she applied to her already shiny body, her beautiful breasts and erect nipples, her flat belly and pronounced hips, her prized asset sumptuous firm ass and toned thighs. Then back to the matter of a real execution, her heart racing in delirious excitement and pumped adrenalin.

The helpless, hapless face just stared up at her. "No more," he muttered in complete submission.

"Absolute surrender," she whispered, "white slave to a black Goddess!" She slowly lowered herself over his face, she reached behind parting her ass cheeks with her hands and releasing them as she settled herself onto his face creating the perfect seal. She adjusted herself slightly, there was no resistance at all, easing her feet under the back of his head and creating an inescapable position.

Fully seated and with full weight bearing down on his face she settled both hands on her hips and stared, remorselessly ahead. Matari was almost senseless with no power to resist what was happening to him. For a brief, moment he remembered squinting from the bright lights above and then warm, wet darkness as he was engulfed in her flesh, his mouth sealed by her soft, fleshy vulva and his nose buried deep in her shiny black ass. There was just weak movement under her now, mainly his legs and feet squirming desperately, but she nonchalantly ignored everything, slowly gyrating her hips, working his face deeper into her soft, wet, suffocating flesh, sealing every possible airway.

Mia was transfixed, mesmerised by the beautiful but ultimately deadly scene taking place live in front of her. This beautiful black Goddess suffocating a white male to death beneath her was exhilarating and an immense turn on, she was wet between her own legs, tempted to touch herself such was the spectacle.

Matari was into the final seconds of his life on earth smothering under this African queen Goddess, his useless pulses were fading away and she smiled at his hands which pushed, weakly and fitful, at her beautiful sculptured, oiled hips and then fell away, completely limp, all movement ceased, but Arusi did not move. She remained seated on his face for at least another three minutes making sure her deadly smother was complete, and it was. She lifted herself up from the face under her and calmly walked towards the exit of the set.

Mia could not imagine anything like she had just witnessed, Arusi was absolute perfection of the female form, incredibly beautiful on every level, lovely but deadly, she thought then, "Shit!" she cried, "I almost forgot!" she spouted out loud quickly shifting her camera view to his now, very soiled crotch area. "There it is," she whispered, "just what I wanted to see, totally involuntary, wish I could have it. Now I have to figure out how to get it to order. Mm," she pondered.

CHAPTER 60

Li Jie was becoming more and more frustrated; the details of the project Mia working on, were eating him up inside and he was convinced she was on the verge of something special. He went over the events in his head of the visit she made with him, desperately trying to piece together anything that would give him a lead. It was impossible for him to hack into the electronically stored research records and she had been very vague about her investigations regarding the Grottoes so, what could he do?

He even thought about using his manly charms and seducing Carol in some way, but he had already concluded she was a passenger on the other Bus and men were not her thing. His only deduction was Mia's involuntary reaction in the Grottoes to the mural depicting 'new life' and he knew this had something to do with what she was now indulged in, but, what had she discovered? Deciding there was not much to go on there, at the Lab, the only tentative lead he had was the recent events with the intruder and assault on Carol. He wondered if there was a connection there somehow and decided to do some of his own spy work on his upcoming mainland leave, the following Monday.

He alighted from the staff boat in Mersing at around 10:00 hrs and began making his way towards the Police commissioners' office, his only lead to West. He didn't have an appointment but found the commissioner outside of the police station with a soccer ball having a kick around with two young boys, despite his corrupt dealings financially, he was a family man and well-liked and respected by the locals. He found this approach made Police work much easier and reduced the number of locals deciding to break the law.

"Good day to you, Police commissioner, sir," said Li, "I wondered if you could spare five minutes for me?"

The Police commissioner bid good day to the two boys and answered, "Do I know you?"

"Not directly, sir," he replied, "my name is Li Jie and I work on Tengah Island in Mr Allard's laboratory and I have come here for my leisure break."

"What can I do for you?" asked the commissioner.

Before he could reply, just then, a car pulled up, a Hotel car with the logo 'Maylay Lodge Resort' emblazoned on the side and the rear blacked out window slowly lowering to reveal its occupant, Alex West.

"Sorry to interrupt, commissioner Chan," he said. "Just letting you know I'll be checking out later today and on my way back to my business in KL, I'm at a dead end here now, no point me being here."

"Glad to hear that, Mr West," replied the commissioner with elevated, audible emphasis, "get on with your business and forget what happened over on the Island and stay out of trouble!" he added, cautioning him with his finger and smiling.

With that the window went up and the car drove off towards the Hotel complex.

"Now," said the commissioner, "how can I help you?"

"Oh nothing," Li replied calmly. "I just wanted to say hi, I knew you had a good relationship with our Lab on the Island, I'll be on my way, don't want to hold you up from your important Police work."

"Good day then," the commissioner replied.

Li had what he wanted, how lucky was he that, he didn't have to ask any questions at all, he had only caught a glimpse of West when he was taken from the Island after the incident but, had seen his name on the security log in reception at the Lab, everything had just been confirmed, just the person he was looking for.

The commissioner out of sight, he hailed a taxi and headed for the Maylay Lodge resort and Spa.

CHAPTER 61

Li entered the main Lobby of the resort Hotel, it was in a 'hideaway' style with dark wood beamed high ceilings, it reminded him of a remote hunting Lodge. It was very high end with low wooden stools and tables, all of the staff wearing their matching uniforms. The accommodation was separate villa type structures and located around the resort making it very private for people who wanted it that way, exactly the reason West had chosen it.

He didn't have to look very far as his intended target was seated at a low table away from the reception desk with a drink and reading a local newspaper.

"Excuse me, sorry to disturb you," Li said apologetically, "my name is Li Jie and I'm a researcher at the Skintakt Lab over on Tengah Island."

West lowered his paper and became very interested in the person introducing himself.

"Have we met?" he enquired, cautiously.

"No sir, not directly but, I saw you when the Police commissioner came to collect you after the incident, I believe we may have some common interest regarding incidents on the Island."

"I'm Alex West," he introduced himself, "please have a seat, this may be interesting."

Li listened to West's story, how he believed something had happened to his friend on the Island and that he believed the woman called 'Mia' knew something about it.

He explained that he couldn't link Mia in any way to his friend's disappearance other than what had come out already; that the location where the T shirt was found was her favourite bathing spot.

In response, Li briefly explained his association with Mia, he was also unable to link anything directly, but, did, however, believe the secretive project she was now working on coincided with the recent events in some way which he didn't have answers to either.

It became very apparent to both that the common denominator linking the two men's suspicions and point of interest was Mia.

"I'm convinced something happened there," West repeated.

"And I'm convinced this secretive project going on with Mia began at the same time," added Li.

"We do indeed, have common ground it seems," said West, "there is no way I can be caught there, on the Island again, but, now I don't need to because, you are there right?" he said smiling.

"Absolutely," agreed Li, "we exchange contact numbers and I will see what I can find out and report back to you, will you stay here or go back to KL?"

"For now, I have to go back and it is very expensive here, having said that, I can afford it but, I need to attend to some matters back in KL; if I need to come back then I will."

The two men parted and Li spent the rest of the day relaxing but pleased with his day's progress.

He figured everything was linked in some way and forming an alliance with West would help his own selfish agenda discovering exactly what was being so meticulously hidden in the Lab.

CHAPTER 62

The next couple of weeks passed without incident, Mia and Carol continued to work with compounds and got closer to a sample cream for testing, at least on the Laboratory grown Human skin. They knew it wasn't harmful but had to follow strict procedures and plough through the red tape associated with something new to market. They would then need to find some way of proving the cream's remarkably unique healing ability, something they knew would be difficult to test and control.

It was Friday afternoon and Mia was just grabbing a coffee from the common area when she received a phone call from Pietro which was unusual as they weren't due to zoom call until the following Monday.

"Hi, Pietro," she answered smiling, "to what do I owe this pleasure?" she enquired. "Want to take me to dinner?" she added, laughing.

"I wish," came the voice from the other end. "No, I'm at the Clinic here in Zurich and I cannot believe what I am being told by my lead infertility Doctor, I'm so excited; the sample sperm you sent over has fertilised every single egg it was implanted into, even ones which had infinitely small clinical chance of success, it's nothing short of a miracle, where was the sample from?"

Mia went silent, she was expecting this result, which is why she sent them for confirmation of her belief.

"Are you there, Mia?" Pietro enquired.

"Yes, I'm here," she replied. "Listen I don't want to say anything else right now, when can you be here?"

"I know and trust you well enough," he replied, "that important eh? I'll be there on Monday, let's have a full brief and update."

"Ok," she replied, "I'll see you Monday here at the Lab, have a good weekend and take care."

Mia had gotten, uncharacteristically, distracted but, became nervously aware of someone uncomfortably close behind her and turned around. It was Li, who had obviously tried to tune into the conversation she was having.

She scowled at him. "Can I help you with anything Li Jie?" she asked him sternly.

"Err no," he replied, "just getting myself a coffee, have yourself a nice weekend," he added, smiling sarcastically.

The relationship Mia had with Li had deteriorated, she didn't like how he was always trying to mind her business and he kept showing up at inopportune and inappropriate moments, she didn't trust him at all but performance wise, in his Lab duties, she had no complaints.

So much had happened since that night in KL and she had kept the whole plethora of events to herself, but, she actually felt the need to let it all out with someone else and she was glad and happy that Pietro was coming to see her, the bond and trust they had was incontrovertible.

Li knew that Pietro would only come to the Island either for a scheduled visit, which this was not, or for something urgent and pressing. He believed he was on to something and needed to share with his newfound accomplice, Alex West.

Pietro instinctively knew that Mia was into something she now needed to share with him, so, he blocked his diary for the whole week and boarded the 10:35 Singapore Airlines flight from Zurich to KL via Singapore, a total time of almost 17 hours, where he would then take his private jet over to the Island on the Monday morning.

CHAPTER 63

Mia spent the weekend preparing for the visit of Pietro and convinced herself that she would tell him absolutely everything, it would be a huge load from her mind and knew he would support her in any situation, the father she never had.

He arrived on Tengah in time for Breakfast in the canteen with Mia and she had invited Carol as a gesture of thanks for the hard work she had been committed to of late and the boss voiced his appreciation and gratitude.

The breakfast was relaxed with small talk, after which, Mia took Pietro to the private meeting room where no interventions to anonymity could be breached. The meeting they were about to have was for no other, for obvious reasons.

"Wow, oh wow!" exclaimed Pietro who had just sat speechless for the past hour as Mia went through everything from the night of the attempted rape and subsequent murder, through the killing of Jordan Price, right up to the altercation with Li the previous Friday.

"I'm speechless for once," he said.

"I, I'm so frightened," confessed Mia, "should I have told you all of this, what are you going to do with me?" she added nervously. "I have killed two men now!"

"I'm only speechless trying to take in and process everything you have just told me, you know my background, our relationship, I've dealt with much, much worse believe me, what you did was all self-defence in my book but, with some incredible, hard to reconcile, connotations," he added.

"Yes," replied Mia, "the guy in the gym was self-defence and totally un-premeditated, but the guy on the beach was murder!" she uttered. "I don't know what came over me, I wanted to test my theory and the opportunity just reared itself and I took it."

"Listen to me," said Pietro calmly, "this guy was a total piece of shit, the world is a better place and young girls safer without him, no doubt, let's put it down to the advancement of science and the human race," he added, smiling.

"But I'm scared, his friend came looking for him, they found his T shirt and then he came back trying to find out more for himself," Mia said.

"They have nothing, believe me, the T Shirt was useless to them, it could have come from anywhere as far as they know, nothing linking it to him, no, there is no connection between you and the missing criminal and don't forget that's all he was, a dirty scumbag criminal!"

"Ok," she sighed, "you always make me feel better."

"Part of why I came, I knew something wasn't quite right with you, let's get some coffee, although a stiff drink would be more appropriate after that story," he said. "Let's have a little recess and then see what we do from where we are right now," he added. "Don't worry, I'm with you all the way."

Mia physically blew out a large sigh of relief, she felt a massive weight had been lifted from her shoulders, talk about the saying 'a problem shared is a problem halved' she thought.

"Thank you," she breathed. "Let's do that, but, just whilst we are here at this point I'd like to show you something that would have gone totally unnoticed from your last 'snuff' production which, by the way was such a beautiful execution," she said, winking. "This will add credence to the incredible story I have just told you," she said.

"Ok," he said, "what do you need?"

"I know you can have personal restricted access to a recording of the event are you able to access it securely from here right now?" she asked.

"Yes," he answered, "I can go via an electronically secure 'Web tunnel', whatever that means, to my records, give me a minute."

Pietro worked his Apple-Mac and pulled up the video recording she had referred to, with a split screen showing the varied camera positions.

"Just go to the very end," she instructed as they watched together.

"There," she said, "pause right there, this camera view, and zoom in to his crotch area. What do you see?"

Pietro saw exactly what Mia was expecting him to see.

"Incredible," he exclaimed, "that's it isn't it, this 'Seeds of Death' you have discovered?"

"Yes," she said solemnly, "I believe it occurs when the male human body's involuntary system kicks in, knowing death is imminent from a certain situation; I wouldn't expect the same reaction if a man was, say, shot in the head, it would be too sudden for the phenomenon to occur."

"So, choking or suffocation as far as you know thus far?" agreed Pietro.

"Yes, I believe so," answered Mia.

"Incredible and fascinating," her listener repeated. "Let's have a break," he added, signing out of his connection securely.

Across the Lab, Li was bedside himself, pacing around and being very abrupt with his assistant Victoria but, there was nothing he could do today, that was for sure, or was there?

CHAPTER 64

After a short coffee break, Mia and Pietro locked themselves back in the meeting room, there was a mountain of issues to discuss that would extend beyond today for sure.

By late afternoon the two of them had concluded that they had two positions with the discovery of the 'Seeds of Death' (SoD) and both, if managed carefully, could be new, incredibly profitable, revenue streams for the organisation. Pietro took to the whiteboard and marked:

SoD

1 Infertility – Incredible potential for older women with impotent partners

2 Topical Cream – Massive potential for alternative to surgery and skin rejuvenation?

"On the first point," presented Pietro, "from initial testing by my specialist at the clinic, he was astounded at the results of both examinations, and practically implanting into donated eggs, actually stating, 'I don't know where this came from but women need to keep a distance from this fluid unless they are looking to get pregnant, it is so potent it has an effectiveness which I have never seen before!'"

"On the second point," he added, "the potential as a topically applied healing and regeneration of damaged skin cream providing potential alternative to surgery is phenomenal," he enthused.

"You say you have physically tried this application?" he asked.

"Yes," replied Mia, "accidentally on myself and intentionally on Carol my assistant, but, she doesn't know what it is or its origins, so, only the two of us know the whole story, wait a minute," she said excitedly.

"What?" he asked.

"You've been in some scrapes in your lifetime, right?" said Mia. "I bet you have some scars from your escapades," she added knowingly.

"I do actually but, what, you want to experiment on me now?" he asked, laughing.

"I'm serious," she answered, "we've done enough here today, come with me and no objections!" she ordered him.

The Lab was empty now, it was late, and everyone had signed out including Carol. He followed Mia to her workstation, and they entered via the PIN controlled door access system.

Mia retrieved a tiny sample jar from the secure, refrigerated cabinet and Pietro knew what she was going to do, so, he lifted his shirt slightly to reveal an aged scar on his lower belly.

"Here's an old war wound!" he pronounced, "Only a small one from an attempted stabbing during a fight in my early days," he added, proudly.

"Perfect," she said.

What they didn't realise was the hidden figure of Li watching in the shadows from behind a pillar through the glass window of her work area.

Mia took a sterile spatula and applied a small amount of the white cream from inside of the jar to the scar on Pietro's skin, one of their initial trial samples.

She sealed the jar and returned it to the refrigerator then, with the tip of her finger, massaged the cream into the scar area until it was absorbed.

"Right," she said, "you will be tired from the travel, take to your bed and report back in the morning."

"Yes Matron," he replied laughing. "Right away!"

They secured the Lab and went off to their respective living quarters, they passed by the canteen and picked up some food to take back with them and agreed for a 9am start the next day.

CHAPTER 65

Li was trying to fathom out what he had just witnessed and couldn't see beyond Mia innocuously trying out a topical cream on her boss, but for what, exact, purpose he had no idea.

The meeting room, he suddenly thought, maybe there is something they left, some notes, a clue, anything.

He checked around, it seemed everyone had signed out for the day so he went inside and turned on the light, there was some empty coffee cups and plates with remnants of the chef's homemade doughnuts and nothing else, but then, he noticed the whiteboard.

In the end of day excitement, Mia had neglected to erase the text on the whiteboard, and he read:

SoD

1 Infertility – Incredible potential for older women with impotent partners

2 Topical Cream – Massive potential for alternative to surgery and skin rejuvenation

Staring at the whiteboard he became aware of somebody humming a tune, coming towards the meeting room so, he quickly took a photo of the board using his phone just as a person entered.

"Oh, I'm sorry, I thought the room was empty." It was the cleaning maid doing her late shift preparing rooms ready for the next day.

"It's ok," Li assured her, I just left my pen in here and it was a gift from my Mom so, didn't want to lose it, have it now, so, good night, dear," he added, leaving.

"Good night, sir," she replied.

He returned to his room unnoticed and sat on the bed retrieving the photo he had taken from the meeting room's whiteboard.

There was nothing strikingly off with what he was reading. Afterall, he worked for an organisation with both infertility and topical skin care interests, but what on earth was 'SoD'? What did this mean? It obviously had some relevance but, to what?

He googled search results and could only find reference to 'sod' relating to grass but, this was an acronym he was sure of it, SoD, something they were referring to but, he had no clue as to what it meant.

He had managed to stir up further suspicions inside himself that they were appraising something that was very special, but equally, he was frustrated as to exactly what, he needed more.

CHAPTER 66

Pietro had retained one of the previously rated five-star suites for whenever he visited, it was normally following long flights and tiresome travel so he was grateful for the comfort it gave him as he sat down to eat the food he had taken from the Chef. The only downside was that the 'Matron', he thought smiling, had asked if he could keep the area where she had applied the cream dry for a couple of hours. He'd taken a shower in the morning so he just decided to relax with a glass of wine from the small cellar he kept there, a limited edition 2013 vintage 'Ronnie Melck' tribute Syrah from one of his favourite Stellenbosch wineries in the Western Cape of South Africa, Muratie winery.

He smiled as he remembered choosing, at random, the edition number handwritten on the reverse label, '69/1200' bottles and joking about it with the 'tasting' manageress. Its notes of blackberry, black fruits and plum with a hint of 'pepper' as he swirled it around his palate for maximum taste was, just what the doctor ordered.

With that, he climbed into his bed and fell asleep almost straight away, he was tired and mentally exhausted from the travel and the day's revelations which had unfolded with Mia.

Pietro awoke to his iPhone alarm, rubbed his eyes to full consciousness and checked the messages. Good, nothing urgent to attend to from overnight. Shower, some breakfast and then back to the meeting room, he thought excitedly and then he remembered. The cream, the scar, he rushed into the bathroom, stood in front of the mirror and lifted his top to look at it. He gasped in disbelief, look at what? There was no scar, it had disappeared with no trace at all, like it had never been there, this cannot be, he thought, just cannot be, how is that possible?

This is incredible, he thought, he had faith in what Mia had told him, but, this was industry changing advancement, his mind raced with the possibilities and applications on top of what he had already considered regarding its fertility efficacy as ground-breaking potential. Then, finally as with all successful business leaders, the recurring 'Ka-Ching' sound of the cash register reverberated in his head.

There was no need for over-excitement as Mia and Pietro reconvened in the meeting room, he already knew that Mia would be aware of the resulting outcome from their little test and she just smiled with the 'I told you so!' look.

"What now then?" she asked.

"Applications are mind-blowing," he replied, "of course there will need to be testing, and security for something like this is paramount."

"Yes, I agree," said Mia, it will require absolute confidentiality and a testing plan the likes and scale of which we have never executed before; and aren't we forgetting something overwhelmingly fundamental here?"

"What's that?" Pietro replied.

"How on earth do we obtain a continuous supply of death sperm, seeds of death, death seed, whatever you want to call it, to continue its development, we cannot just go around murdering men, although some deserve it!" she added with a wringing of neck hand gesture.

"You are right of course," said Pietro seriously and stroking his chin, "we cannot continue until we have a solution to this," he added, over smiling broadly.

"What, you can think of something, some way of getting a supply of the fluid?" she asked.

"I do actually, and it is familiar to the both of us, let us discuss this today and not leave things lying around like we did yesterday, this was careless!" he said, motioning towards the whiteboard.

"Shit!" Mia responded. "Yes, careless, a good job there's not enough for anyone to work with if they were that way disposed," she added gratefully.

"Well let's start as we mean to go on from now and formulate next steps," said Pietro rubbing his hands together with an almost excited look on his face.

CHAPTER 67

Over the next two days, Mia and Pietro brain-stormed the project, but found they couldn't go beyond their inability to secure a regular supply of the 'SoD' which could only be gained at the dying breath of the male species in reasonably controlled circumstances. At this point, he reminded Mia of his 'snuff' events, easily adapted to provide a constant supply. The source and relevance of the 'SoD' itself could never be revealed, that had to remain a secret between them like the unknown ingredient in 'Coca Cola', Pietro had stated. Mia hadn't considered this possibility till now.

"So, that's what you were thinking," she said, nodding her head but, agreeing it could be the solution they needed. So now with the assumption a possible future existed, a continuable source, they concluded that, there would be two cases. One with a supply for the infertility clinic and one for the potential skin cream, the latter requiring the larger quantity and the former requiring 'more quality' from the donor.

The 'SoD' itself was incredibly potent and fertile and the quantities of the active ingredient in each load was large so, they both agreed that, Pietro's 'snuff' events could potentially be used to harvest the total requirement. Also, the quantity of sperm required for the infertility clinic would be much less and it didn't matter if there was a break in supply. This would not be the major source of income stream from the discovery but, would enhance the clinic's credibility and success ratings. Pietro had pointed out, however, that the physical capturing of the 'SoD' would require modifications in that, most of the male victims in his productions were totally naked and the seed would be 'shot' everywhere whereas; in his latest video the victim could have been made to wear some kind of modified, sterile condom under his shorts and no one would be any the wiser other than instructions to his crew as to how to retrieve and deal with it.

They needed a robust method of harvesting the 'SoD' especially for use in the skin cream applications for which the pair had formulated a large list of potential applications, but again was useless without the 'magic' component.

This was going to take time and careful planning and there was no overnight fix, killing men for their dying sperm ejaculation was not going to be straightforward, although, Mia had to concede, Pietro did have a workable idea as the amount of men needed was relatively low due to the high potency levels.

Reading a report Mia had prepared from research done by Carol and based on the fact that the average single release of male sperm contained more than 100 million individual sperms, they agreed that, they didn't need even tens of men per month to provide enough of the active ingredient contained in this 'super sperm' it was so virile.

"As you know, my beautiful prodigy, us men are weak, narrow minded and predictable, the power of the pussy will always prevail, you only have to look at history, even ancient history, Samson and Delilah, Prince Paris of Troy and Helen of Sparta and we all know what happened there!" he said, laughing.

"I know all of that; I'm trying to understand what you mean," Mia replied. "What do you have in mind?"

"Ok," He began, "there are plenty of men with deep desires and I'm excluding right here any reference to paedophilia as all those bastards should be castrated and hung, no, fantasies be it, a certain type of woman, large, petite, tall, small, slim, large breasts, small breasts, legs, ass…"

"Yes, I get it," Mia sighed, "get to the point."

"Tell me," he said, "do you remember an old TV serial held on a remote and privately owned Island where contestants competed for large amounts of money with all but one ending up dead, their bodies disposed of in a purpose built crematorium?"

"Yes, I do," she replied, "it was quite a sensation back then, but what are you saying?" she quizzed.

"Think about it," he went on, "this is exactly what we need, men coming to an Island in total secrecy to fulfil their life-long fantasies, paying for the privilege, lured into the deadly clutches of our hand-picked women, processed right there on the Island; we could even arrange paying audiences as well, just like my productions now, and I wouldn't need to carry out these externally anymore, everything can be done in one place."

"You're crazy!" she announced. "It's a crazy idea, how could it be set up?"

Pietro was unmistakably serious now. "I'm thinking of a group of purposefully and meticulously trained girls, like the 1983 James Bond film, *Octopussy* who led a band of athletic, luscious women trained to dispose of men," he continued.

"Octo who? Never heard of it," she said, "wasn't even born then."

"Yes, accepted, but I'm a huge James Bond fan. We recruit maybe three girls with varying characteristics and demeanours luring their prey into the trap, effectively harvesting our crop; I still have contacts and I know girls who would act in this way," he went on. "There are trained women assassins who already use the power of their sex to seduce men into their web and finish them off, you must have read about men being found tied up who apparently strangled themselves in a sexual masturbation act, I can assure you, some of these were not accidental. Some men actually paid them in advance to die in this way."

CHAPTER 68

"Yes, I am familiar, but we cannot do that here on Tengah," she continued.

"Tengah, no, I agree," went on Pietro. "You know I also purchased Bidong Island after it was closed down as a Vietnamese refugee processing camp, it is still uninhabited, but already has services and some building structures; it is only 27km from here, we can renovate and purpose build a VIP resort and bring our rich 'victims' to explore and realise their darkest fantasies," he went on. "It will be like an Island Paradise, a five-star resort and the girls don't even need to be there permanently, we can do pre-arranged dates over a week period bringing each individual 'victim' on a one way ticket for his fantasy dream, pretty much what I do now, but using one location."

"It could work," replied Mia, "and we cannot move any further until we secure a robust 'harvesting' method, but it will take time and very careful planning and security will have to be paramount and how will we dispose of the bodies?" she questioned

"I thought of that too," he replied. "The facility will be run on LPG gas, so we will incorporate a similar furnace to the one on Tengah, we cremate them, nothing left, not a trace."

"Security?" she reminded him.

"Yes, I will put Wisetzki in charge of security and I have a perfect employee to run the facility, a spinster, one of my most trusted employees and she can carry out her normal day to day duties as Global HR manager at the same time, she will love the location also."

"The less people we involve, the better," Mia stated.

"Yes, Wisetzki for security and you to oversee the vetting, training and implementation of our plan!"

"Do what!" she screamed. "No way, I can't do that, I'm a researcher!"

"And why not?" said Pietro with a challenge in his voice.

Mia tried to think of all the reasons why she could not but, when she thought of all the reasons why she could, they outweighed the negatives and the project was immense with rewards to match.

"Ok," she said, "you get things moving construction wise and I will prepare details of who and how we recruit, train and deploy, I will also instruct Carol to continue with development and a testing programme in the meantime, this way we should be able to move straight into production by the time these things are in place which, I would guess may take up to two years?"

"Agreed," replied Pietro, "but this is worth the investment, I'm sure, weekly team meetings and I will coordinate works and security with Wisetzki who, will need to know the illegalities of what we plan to carry out otherwise he wouldn't be conscious of the levels of security we need."

Mia had dinner with him that evening and he planned to leave the next day, so it was an early to bed night.

However, she was captivated by what he had said about the James Bond film, *Octopussy* so, she watched it and immediately saw herself as 'Octopussy' especially the 'dealing with' of men contemptibly. She looked forward to her new role within the organisation which, as everything else she committed to, would be 100% effort and nothing less.

The next day, Mia bid farewell to Pietro and then met with Carol, telling her to press ahead with current instructions, that she would be around, but working on something for Pietro regarding his other Island, Bidong.

CHAPTER 69

The construction works had gotten underway on Bidong but, being an Island location, progress was slower than the team would have liked but everything else which could be put into place, in the meantime, was progressing.

Mia followed up with contacts given to her within Pietro's network, identifying potential agents. She was surprised by the abundance and quality of women available for further investigation, especially the already security vetted girls for his 'snuff' events including, she was pleased to see, on the initial shortlist, Arusi, and also a highly, Pietro, recommended Japanese MMA fighter and model, Rui from Tokyo.

Rui had received notification that her 'special' services may be required for a new project. She was taking a break where she was a regular 'actress' for a small video company based in Tokyo. The company known as a 'Club', specialised in 'powerful', sadistic women and there was no shortage of willing, masochistic men to play victims. Everything here was also with legitimate, registered actors, disclaimers, certificates etc. everything was above board.

There were six girls like Rui, and they carried out beatdowns, ball busting, female domination, mixed fighting videos which were sold on DVDs shipped all over the world.

The Club headlined itself as the only company showing live, unscripted and non-simulated, action with men being knocked out and put to sleep for real and recorded on camera.

She was only 19 years old, a college student around 155cm tall, deceivingly toned with muscular, athletic physique, very attractive, long jet-black hair and disarming smile. She had just applied a Japanese style figure four leg choke on one of the hired actors and he was snoring between her legs in less than 10 seconds.

These girls knew exactly what they were doing, all trained in MMA fighting techniques and turning grown men to jelly in a matter of seconds if they wanted to and having fun at the same time. During a video shoot there were no scripted scenarios and, depending on the theme, the 'victims', who were not trained actors, would be choked out by the girls several times, being revived in between by slaps to the face and given a brief time to gain their senses, then, put to sleep again. Of course, this was dangerous, but the men were fanatically masochistic and craved forced unconsciousness, 'going out' between the legs or in the arms of a beautiful young girl. Moreover, there was also an abundance of men and women willing to pay for these video productions, many wishing they were, in fact, the victims. Even under these 'semi' controlled sessions there were willing victims who realised they had underestimated the strength and power of the girls and, with a quick bow, had dismissed themselves from any further punishment. Some, however, were very resilient and masochistic taking severe punishment in the form of head kicks, punching, ball kicking, severe abdominal punishment, full weight trampling, forced face sitting and choking.

She had worked with Pietro before, knew the score and it suited her, she was very sadistic, every time, closing her eyes in sheer ecstasy as men went limp between her legs just loving to witness them suffer at her control and choosing, wishing every time she could finish the victim off for good. She, like Arusi, relished the ultimate power and dominance only realised by the ultimate act and she craved for more. She would also be well paid and was looking forward to hearing about the new venture. Her work here providing the closest to real, legal, physical dominance over men she could have.

CHAPTER 70

Rui was adeptly deceptive in her 'non-friendly' abilities, whilst playing the charming, feminine girl, when she wanted to be. She had learned this from an early age when her mother passed away when only six years old and her father took over as the single parent. He tried his best but money was always in short supply and she quite often had to make do with hand me down clothes and second-hand tech, not getting an actual brand-new phone for herself until she was 18. This made her susceptible to bullying at school, being the 'poor girl', and she was often singled out for verbal and sometimes physical abuse. Her father had instilled pride and she recognised his sterling efforts and tenacity in overcoming the odds to give her the best possible start in life. He had recognised the tell-tale bullying signs in his daughter and introduced her to the traditional Martial Art of Japan, Karate, through her uncle who taught at the local Dojo. It was tough for a young girl, but she adapted herself, learned the art, abiding by its key teaching, self-discipline. She embraced her newly found passion, developing it into a skill and progressing through the ascending levels of 'Kyu', meaning degrees of knowledge.

Rui was a sensible girl and she recognised the potency of the art she had mastered and how it had bestowed on her discipline and respect which precluded her from exercising it for selfish acts or gain.

Inevitably though, there was always going to be a first time and she remembered every second and how she desperately tried to avoid the conflict.

She was 15 and constantly taking verbal abuse from a fellow student girl who was basically obese for her age but used her size to gain respect from a 'gang' of four in Rui's academic class. One morning she entered the classroom to the familiar verbal taunts and pointing, and as usual ignored them, continuing to listen to music on her headphones, heading for her desk.

However, today was different, the teacher was late for the class and the day before she had effectively humiliated the head bully in a randomly chosen one on one basketball dribble in the PT session. Of course, Rui was very agile and easily ran rings around the girl and today she was out for revenge and to demonstrate to her friends the consequences for someone daring to cross her.

As Rui headed for her seat one of the 'gang' members snatched her mobile phone from her hand and tossed it to the leader.

"Look what we have here," she bellowed, "the poor girl has a steam-powered phone!" she added, overzealously laughing.

The other gang members joined in laughing and taunting as they gathered around her.

"Ok, please give me back my phone," she requested.

"Oh, please give me back my phone," the lead bully taunted, putting on a 'baby' voice, "take it from me, bitch!" She waved it above her head. "We aren't in the safety of the gym now, are we?"

Rui instinctively knew today was the day, the day when the bully had to make a statement for the allegiance of her followers and also knew there was only one opponent to target, the others were weak and relied on the big girl and she couldn't back down now.

Rui took up a defensive fighting position and the girl lunged at her. She responded with a front kick to her chest effectively pushing her backwards against the whiteboard on the wall.

"Enough!" Rui shouted. "Give me back my phone, I don't want to hurt you."

"Hurt me bitch?" she screamed and tossed the phone to one of her cronies, then pulled a knife from her back pocket holding it in front of her. Rui weighed up the situation, this wasn't life threating as the knife wasn't large enough to kill with a single stab, but she figured she would go for her face or arms, attempting a wound rather than trying anything more sinister.

She began waving the knife horizontally side to side but again Rui had positioned her defensive stance just out of reach, but then, the girl charged forward with the knife.

Rui was far too quick; with her left hand she parried the knife harmlessly upwards and out of her grip whilst simultaneously following up with her right hand crashing her open palm upwards into the girl's defenceless nose. There was an unpleasant, chillingly cracking sound as Rui's palm connected with cartilage and it exploded with blood on impact. The suddenly stupefied girl stumbled backwards clasping her broken nose with both hands, blood escaping between her clenched fingers.

"You've broken her nose," one cried out, but Rui was still in a fighting pose and there was no one present about to challenge her any further.

At that, point the teacher came in for what was an unusual start to her day, but handled the situation professionally; especially as a 'friendly' neutral student had picked up the knife to keep it out of harm's way and confirmed exactly what had just taken place.

Although Rui's father was called, she didn't receive any disciplinary action, the girl bully was expelled and reported to the Police for taking a dangerous weapon into the classroom with intent.

Rui was never bullied again, and she had no intentions of being so, ever!

CHAPTER 71

Events on the Island were mundane and uneventful during the following months, everyone carrying out their duties routinely much to the frustration of Li, who had 'sneaked' around as much as possible but found nothing he could cling to.

Christmas came and went, Mia had a short visit with Lieke for a catch up and they did some shopping together in Vivo City, spending the whole day together.

Lieke was happy with her home-life, spending more time with her hobbies whilst Marco continued with the shipping company. She mentioned that Daan had become the 'model' prisoner, fully repentant and reformed according to the prison parole board, he had even been given leave to do supervised, voluntary work helping the elderly at a high-end care home. "But I don't buy it at all," confided Lieke, "I know him too well, he can be very, very deceptive like a Chameleon changing everything he does to suit the situation, but I would liken him more to the metaphor, 'A Leopard never changes its spots'."

"What are you trying to say, Lieke?" asked Mia.

"He is about something," she replied, "whatever you do and wherever you are, Mia, when he gets out, and he will, early I suspect, with his model behaviour and pressure by his father on the authorities, watch him and be mindful of him, that's all I'm saying, he has a focus and I don't believe it involves being good."

"Don't go worrying about me," Mia assured her, "I can look after myself, let's have another drink before I head for the Landing strip and my ride back to Tengah."

"Good idea," replied Lieke. "I'm so pleased you could find the time to come and see me, this will make my Christmas," she added tearfully.

CHAPTER 72

'First fix' for the new VIP facility on Bidong, including accommodation rooms, had been completed with January signalling the start of 'Second fix' and the project team were expecting handover in late March, time for Mia to begin her selection process and time to brief and appoint the manager for the new facility.

Pietro had identified a long-standing and loyal employee from his Iowa operation, responsible for training and recruitment on a global scale for the legitimate businesses and lead organiser for his illegal ventures, he wanted someone he could trust implicitly and who would manage the programmes and keep any 'outsiders' just that, on the outside.

Her name was Abigail, a spinster in her late forties of Jewish descent, very highly educated and pristine in her suited, immaculate appearance, hair always up, designer spectacles, manicured nails and a very strict boldness, with no suffering of fools' defiance. She had never married, focusing on her career, and had been 'rescued' by Pietro after falling foul of a relationship scam in her younger years, remaining totally loyal to him ever since.

She had been in what seemed a mutually trusting relationship with a man who identified his profession as an investment banker. He spoilt her with expensive jewellery and apparel and, although she was never a materialistic girl, she enjoyed the attention and pampering.

However, this was his front and not the first girl he had played. He became nervous and saddened and she fell for the ruse believing his story that he had been temporarily compromised and needed a large loan urgently. She rose to his aid and willingly gave him almost all her savings, only to then discover it, and he, were a complete fraud. He disappeared from her life without trace and left her almost broke, emotionally and financially, however, she had a friend and that friend was Pietro.

In addition, from Mia's side she had identified and shortlisted two potential female agents, already vetted by Pietro's security system, and had arranged to meet with Abigail in Singapore to discuss practicalities, roles and responsibilities going forward for the new project.

CHAPTER 73

Mia met Abigail for the first time, and they took breakfast together in the Hotel's restaurant. It transpired that both women believed in first appearances, both suitably impressed with the other, a good start to future relations.

Abigail was dressed in business suit with tailored jacket, below the knee pencil skirt, crisp white blouse, neckerchief and moderate heels looking formidable but with a contrasting, approachable demeanour, armed with MacBook pro and writing folder. Mia was out of her casual leggings and sneakers look, and was smartly dressed in black, fitted trousers, white blouse and flat, patent black shoes.

Mia had booked a meeting room and they agreed to meet there in 20 minutes following breakfast.

Abigail had been briefed in full that, additional to her normal duties, she would manage and be the front for the new VIP resort facility which, in itself, would be a facade for the real, nefarious activities to be carried out there.

"I'm a little vexed as to the method we can adopt for recruitment of our 'would be' victims, and how the whole process will evolve and roll out to get us to our end goal," Mia opened confusedly, "does that make sense?"

"Worry not dear," replied Abigail with an assuring nod, "that is why I'm here, trust me, I will put together a comprehensive and meticulous programme concerning security and every detail we need to consider to make this work, I have no doubts whatsoever, I'm looking forward to my new role."

Mia was impressed, this Lady oozed confidence and professionalism and she knew that, if this was going to work, then she was the right person for the job.

Abigail, working with her trusted researcher, had been responsible for the recruiting and background checks of Pietro's 'snuff' event executrixes and already knew both Arusi and Rui.

She pulled up the bios and resumes of the two girls on her MacBook. "Let me introduce you to Arusi and Rui now," said Abigail, "two charming and beautiful girls," she added, winking.

The credentials and reports read immaculately, and both agreed the two girls would be retained for the work planned on Bidong Island resort without question.

"This is a great start," observed Mia, "we already have two agents for our team, but I'm thinking three would be the right number, someone different, a different perspective, I don't know how, though."

"I agree," replied Abigail, "and I have the benefit and privilege of working with our lead researcher Amanda who retains details of all fantasy theme requests."

"Go on," Mia encouraged her, "this is exactly the kind of topics you and I need to iron out."

"Ok, I will relay her observations to you now which I have written here and will quote her directly," continued Abigail. "With regard to 'attraction', in my experience, for many of these weak-minded males and fantasists who think with their dicks, Arusi and Rui satisfy the legs, ass and model bodies brigade, but, we need breasts, huge ones, a BBW, skinny men love to be physically devoured by a large lady and it fits right in, I have endless requests for overpowering female, physical presence and dominance."

"I like that," commented Mia. "I think she has a valid point, if there is a feed of constant requests of this nature and genre we must capitalise, what do you think, Abigail?"

"I agree," she replied, "and I believe I have the woman for the job," she added, smiling. "Leave this with me for now."

CHAPTER 74

Mia returned to her day to day routine on Tengah, and Abigail prepared for her move there, to begin with, and as soon as Bidong was ready: her new home. But first, a stop-over in New York before Iowa, she had someone to look up who had performed previously and been very much requested since.

Li had caught wind of new developments going on with Bidong Island but all he had was that it was a new hospitality related business investment for Pietro Allard and his expanding empire.

Abigail arrived into JFK late afternoon and checked into her Hotel, she only had a 'one night' window, so had arranged to meet with her contact in the Hotel bar at 19:30 hrs.

She showered and dressed for dinner and was waiting in the cocktail bar by 19:15 with a dry Martini over ice served in a heavy cut crystal glass and watching the world go by.

Then, a remarkable change in the atmosphere like a huge gust of wind, as heads, both men and women, turned towards the entrance of the bar. Abigail knew full well what the sudden attraction was, and she swivelled on her bar stool to join in the vista, raising her glass to the plus sized, ebony beauty walking toward her.

It was Dominica, a Caribbean/American plus size model and soft porn actress. She specialised in fantasy wrestling sessions with rich, vetted male submissive victims fantasising being overpowered by a BBW.

She was jaw-droppingly attractive, Swiss Milk chocolate coloured, flawless skin with straight shoulder length, bobbed hairstyle and perfect hour-glass figure, 1.65m in height, measurements of 115-94-104cm, weighing 110kg and with a voluptuous 38G bust.

She was wearing a halter neck, white, ruffled dress, finishing just above the knee highlighting her formidable, thick legs and beautifully sculptured calves, with one arm sleeveless showing her tasteful Leopard print tattoos; her heavy breasts were seemingly desperate to escape from the tightly fitting enclosure and her stunning black heels with diamante ankle straps and across her instep showed her perfectly manicured toe nails.

I don't think there's a man in this room who wouldn't be at her feet on command, Abigail thought, just what we are looking for to complete our formidable team.

Most men at the bar were daydreaming, hoping that Dominica was headed in their directions, some embarrassingly and visibly preening themselves, but no, she headed for Abigail and they met with a genuine embrace.

"You look magnificent, dear," said Abigail, genuinely.

"Thank you," she replied, "I do the best with what God gave to me and some I added," she said, laughing, "so do you and it's lovely to see you."

The two women had dinner where Abigail went into the basics of what was being planned, to see if Dominica wished to be in on the project which she accepted enthusiastically. "Just love giving the men what they have coming to them," she said.

The last production featuring Dominica had been where she was given a free rein in the total beatdown of a skinny, white German male whose fantasy was to be beaten up by a large Black female and he was not disappointed even though he wasn't able to tell anyone afterwards about his experience. Abigail remembered how she had really gotten into the role, tossing him around like a rag doll, picking him up, slamming him onto the floor, following up with full weight butt drops onto his beaten body. She continued for more than half an hour and of course he had begged her to stop, but this had fuelled her obsession even more, she choked his neck between her massive thighs, blood gurgling from his mouth and before passing out releasing him to continue her full weight butt drops onto his face and chest until he wasn't moving, literally having to be signalled he was dead already. It seemed sheer brutality and merciless, sadistic conviction attracted more interest from the hand selected clients tuned in.

CHAPTER 75

Dominica had been in and out of relationships with casual activities in between, back in her early twenties, and up until then, believed men were just physically more powerful than women. Her final encounter became a more and more abusive affair and she would be punched and kicked more times than she would have cared to remember. Then, one day, as her 'partner' after a drinking session became aggressive with her, she snapped, launched at him with her full weight, slamming him against the wall banging his head. He slipped unconscious to the floor and from that day onwards she decided no man would do anything like that to her ever again, in fact, she decided to be the one handing out the punishment to these cowards and making them pay.

"There's more to add and we need to refine your technique somewhat but that is covered in the training programme we are planning," said Abigail. "I still receive enquiries about you, but I know you are just what we are looking for and will get back to you with more details in the next few weeks."

"Perfect, I need a new challenge," replied Dominica. "I miss the 'real thing', I'm tired of role play, pretending, so, getting 'real' willing victims is turning me on, cheers!" She laughed and finished her drink.

The two parted and Abigail took an early night ready for her flight into Iowa the next day, for her, it was a 'fly to' State and she was looking forward to a scenery other than Corn.

Mia received an update from her following the meeting with their newest recruit and she was pleased with the progress, believing they could finally pull things together. She knew Abigail was absolutely dedicated and Pietro's unfaltering faith in her was well justified.

"So, all you know is that some work is being done on Bidong Island, some VIP guest and resort facilities and a new skin product is being developed to be produced in Singapore; is that correct Li?" asked West toward the end of his zoom call with Lie Jie.

"Yes, that about sums it up but, I do believe this new product development is linked to Mia's work and/or discovery, everything's happened since she returned from Gansu Provence last year," Li replied.

"I will keep vigilant and update you if I have any more, I know we will uncover something, I guarantee it!" he concluded and ended the call.

CHAPTER 76

Pietro was busy and, besides overseeing the physical works with the team, had met with his chief 'snuff' researcher, Amanda, and told her she would continue to report to Abigail either, as now, remotely or make a move to the Island to work physically together. He added that recruitment would be very similar as usual, but any 'filmed' events for external viewing clients would be held in one single location. She didn't really have any family to speak of and as a 'retiring' dominatrix was happy to take up the offer of relocating to Bidong. This suited Pietro as she could carry out other duties which would be required in maintaining and running the new resort facility, the fewer the staff multi-tasking, the better.

Following discussions with Mia regarding the physical capturing of the 'SoD' on ejaculation, he had taken her advice and instructed one of his trusted Laboratory technicians at his infertility clinic in Zurich to develop what he described as a 'new' version of the extensively used common condom. He explained that it wouldn't be used for contraceptive purpose during sexual intercourse activity but strictly for the collection of 'touchless' induced ejaculation. He wanted the 'device' to be fitted to the male genitals and be secure to withstand physical movement, be flexible to take up an erection and prevent ejaculated contents from escaping. It needed to be robust and, when removed, have the ability to clinically 'seal in' the ejaculated semen for transfer into the normal receptacles used for storing and transporting of sperm samples as currently employed.

He was not disappointed in the resulting item although it didn't resemble the 'simple' condom he'd expected at all as he went through the presentation with the technician on a zoom call.

"There was no way, the common condom could stand up to the rigorous and physical demands in the brief you gave me," said the technician, "in my opinion using a condom for intercourse is like trying to pick your nose with a boxing glove on and thank goodness this isn't to be used for penetrative sex between two people!"

"Not heard that idiom before but I can relate to it somewhat, continue, what have we got? It resembles incontinence pants," Pietro said bringing him back to the point.

"Yes, exactly, I took the design from a readily available design of incontinence pants made from natural latex rubber but I pressure-welded this flexibly compliant 'tubular' insert into the pants where the penis will be inserted, reinforced at the base where the 'shaft' of the penis will be gripped, forming a seal, the teardrop shaped end will catch the resulting sperm and is large enough for 'king-size' ejaculations; they will be one-use only as I suggest that the appendage extension tube be cut to remove it together with the contents and then hermetically sealed. I'm assuming the wearer will be compliant on removal?" he checked.

"Oh yes, very compliant indeed," said Pietro reassuringly.

"Oh, and in addition, I'm ashamed to admit it, sir but I have tested it as I knew that would be your next question, but, under the conditions you wish it to operate, I am satisfied that it will do the job you are asking of it."

"Fantastic, real dedication to the cause," laughed Pietro, "no, seriously, great job, have some made, say 20 pairs to begin with, and have them shipped to Tengah."

"Ok, sir, will do," and the call was ended.

Pietro knew sperm samples were anonymous when used to fertilise eggs, but they were obliged to keep records of donors at source. So, there would be legitimate donors recorded but the actual samples would be replaced by the custom harvested, 'precious' seed, this way the facility in Singapore could legitimately receive these samples without any suspicion. He would ensure that the 'victims' would be fitted with these incontinence type briefs prior to their fantasy scenario on the grounds of being part of Health and Safety protocol protecting the participants, he was pleased with the progress.

CHAPTER 77

Carol received positive reports on the resulting cream they had developed which contained the 'super' ingredient. She had advanced to human subjects and conducted 'patch testing' over several days of applications with the Lab staff with no adverse effects whatsoever. She had completed toxicology tests and as there were no 'colour' additives, she had basically covered all of the sampling requirements knowing that the total ingredients were intrinsically safe. The governing body, FDA, did not have the legal authority to approve cosmetic products and/or ingredients prior to market release nor was a set list of tests applied. It was the manufacturer's responsibility, however, to ensure safety of the product when used in the recommended way. With regards to colour additives, these had to be approved by the FDA but there were none qualifying in the product requiring this approval. So, they were good to go. What they didn't know was what could the cream do besides replenishing skin damaged by scar tissue. If it could be used as an anti-ageing cream as well, the sales would be phenomenal; so they needed more testing to find out.

"'Crows feet'," blurted Carol.

"What about them?" Mia replied. "I know it's the term used to describe the fine lines and wrinkles found at the outer corners of the eyes but?"

"Yes, and as you know there are two variations, static and dynamic, dynamic mainly caused by facial expressions which are cute and then suddenly singing a song about Crows feet.

"Have you been drinking, Carol?" asked Mia, laughing.

"No," she said, "just a line from a track of one of my favourite eighties bands, but imagine if the cream works on wrinkles, static ones, the ones that are there all of the time, women would pay in gold to stem or remove these!" she said excitedly.

"Yes, we need to see what else our 'magic' cream is capable of, arrange a testing program through our normal agency, get them to provide a sampling of 'older' demographics for this and we will concentrate on facial and neck wrinkles, then work out a robust testing regime programme as we always do."

So far, the incredible results they had contracted from the complete rejuvenation of skin pertaining to scar tissue in the case of Mia, Carol and with Pietro, consisted of a formulation with high concentration of the 'Magic' ingredient. This was not the way forward, they needed to reduce the content and it would help immensely with the amount of SoD they would require for production. The last thing they needed, on an economical scale, was a 'once' application, so the aim had been to minimise the amount of the 'active' ingredient to a micro, miniscule level. They were looking for a daily application, say over a two-week period, for the cream to do its job. This way they would be able to sell many more pots of the cream which, was always top of any brief for a new product, $$$$!

They now had samples to test with the reduced amount of added 'SoD' and it was a critical stage of development. "On it," replied Carol, smiling. "I could do with mainland trip for a few days."

"You're in charge, and deserve the break, keep me in the loop," concluded Mia.

Carol made the necessary arrangements with the agency and travelled to Singapore to supervise the initial testing.

CHAPTER 78

Abigail's stay on Tengah was shorter than anticipated, the works on Bidong had finished ahead of schedule and apart from a few aesthetic touches the 'resort' was ready for trialling and accommodating the initial start-up staff. Advanced comms had been installed together with the latest surveillance and security systems overseen by Wisetzki; there was nowhere where anyone could be unnoticed in the populated areas of the facility.

Amanda was also on Tengah now and the two of them, with Wisetzki and Sparkplug as hired muscle, were setting off by boat headed for Bidong with their luggage and personal belongings. It was a big move for the two girls but boasted a solid working and personal relationship. Both women were looking forward to the solitude and peace the Island had to offer, it suited them, but foremost was hard work and dedication. They arrived at the newly reconstructed jetty, the same that would welcome its future guests to the resort. The design was a welcoming rustic timber jetty leading to a single storey reception area and main building with staff accommodation and leisure facilities, bar/bistro, spa, gym and small pool with jacuzzi. The five guest rooms were luxuriously appointed as individual Lodge type buildings, again single storey, and of timber construction. As dual-purpose use, Pietro had planned to hold any high-level business-related meeting negotiations there, when required, and the facility would charm any of these visitors, showing his elaborate hospitality. There was an outbuilding with LPG fired boiler and service equipment and, uncharacteristically for such a small conurbation, a furnace capable of taking larger, disposable items.

Amanda was also excited to see her suggestion of an espionage type scenario put into play, like 'murder mystery' events, but with fictitious spies on the run from beautiful female assassins being pursued and tracked down for their secrets. She was very methodical in her work and on several occasions had received enquiries regarding this but, only working with a smaller indoor space, it hadn't been practical before. Now, Pietro had trusted in her judgment and had constructed a 2km long, 'Forest trail' leading to a purpose built, filled with tech, Log Cabin. Now, she could offer the opportunity to simulate an escape by a male spy trying to flee his captors and being stalked by the would-be assassins. This also facilitated drawing the victims away from the main areas where seclusion and isolation would create less opportunity for the limited uninformed employees to witness any questionable incidents. Things were coming together. All they needed now were the guests and the lovely but deadly femme fatales, or female agents as they were to be called.

CHAPTER 79

Things were moving ahead rapidly now, Carol was busy in Singapore organising product testing, they used a retained agency who provided and vetted, paid volunteers for advanced product sampling based on the requirements given to them by her as project lead. They were all bound by NDA agreements and well paid for their services so, disclosures were very rare due to them wishing to be retained by the agency, for some it was their primary income source.

The testing regime covered a seven-day application period. The selected 'volunteers' visited every day and received an application of the test cream, returning each day where Carol would record the progress and results. She had selected four candidates for the testing against skin wrinkles: ladies in their late sixties and one younger lady with a small scar on her shoulder which she had been self-conscious of for many years.

It was going well, and as always, Carol was very efficient reporting back to Mia that she believed she would be able to gauge the amount of 'SoD' required in each product to give the desired effects for the user. This was great news and with no adverse reactions, testing was ahead of the planned schedule, they would need 'SoD' soon.

Mia had arranged for Arusi, Rui and Dominica to come to Tengah with the intention of accompanying them to Bidong for a two-night, three-day, briefing, orientation and training and was forced into employing Li and Victoria to take over her routine duties. She was happy though, because nothing involved the 'SoD' project and they would continue to work in their own allocated workstations with her Lab locked and secured whilst she was away.

CHAPTER 80

The next day, the four girls boarded the motor launch from Tengah to head over to Bidong Island.

"I assume everything went well yesterday?" Mia asked the motor launch driver.

"Yes, madam, all delivered safe and sound and Sparkplug will come back with me on the return today," he added.

Boat or Seaplane was the only way of reaching Bidong so, at a steady 10 knots, it would take less than two hours and the sea was like a mill pond, it was going to be a relaxing couple of hours.

They arrived on Bidong in the early afternoon, greeted by the frantically waving and beaming face of Sparkplug who had been watching out for their arrival.

"This is Sparkplug," Mia announced, "he is a hero and one of our most trusted employees."

"Aww, Miss Mia, I just do my job," he replied, his face reddened with embarrassment.

The three girls instantly weighed up the innocence and big heart associated with Sparkplug and made a huge fuss of him, much to his absolute delight, as he carried their overnight bags up the Jetty and into the reception area where Abigail and Amanda were busy arranging the office area.

Abigail was immaculate as always, pristine and in business attire, Mia had never seen her otherwise and took note of the effect 'Power Dressing' had over people. Amanda, on the other hand, was in jogging pants, T shirt and sneakers, her hair in a silk, brightly coloured cap.

Introductions were made and briefly with Wisetzki, who was permanently, at least for the time being, in residence, passing through the Lobby fleetingly, but with a more pronounced lingering 'catching of the eye' between himself and Dominica which did, however, not go unnoticed by Abigail's constant, attention to detail.

Mia had gone through the agenda with Abigail and was happy to allow her to take over the briefing.

She had told the group that the evening would be totally relaxed, casual dress, no strict protocols, a 'get to know' each other gathering highlighting the importance of togetherness and teamwork. The relevant work would begin the next morning.

"You will meet in the kitchen," announced Abigail. "The fridges and freezers are well stocked for now and there is fresh meat and seafood just brought at the same time as you which Sparkplug has put there. The three of you can decide together what we eat tonight, and preparing food together is a real avenue for, getting to know each other."

This was a temporary 'catering' arrangement as Mia had briefed the Chef on Tengah that he would recruit an additional two 'kitchen hands' and form a team of three which would be seconded to Bidong as and when there was a need.

"That would be four of us!" quipped Mia holding her hand up in a school child type gesture and grinning. "I'm in as well."

"And I will be your barperson for the evening," announced Amanda, giving a thumbs up.

Abigail was very pleased with the responses she had just witnessed with her first assessment of the group, the assembled team of girls was already developing into something special and she knew this was going to be vital, and even life depending, going forward.

The visitors were shown to their rooms which were part of the main reception area building, not large, but self-contained and very comfortable.

Sparkplug returned with the boat back to Tengah, still smiling from the hugs he had received from the girls as he left. He was a very happy young man, couldn't stop himself from continually sniffing his jacket taking in the lingering perfumes from the girls.

Wisetzki continued with his work checking and rechecking the security equipment especially with the addition of the outdoor 'trail' ordered by Pietro. This had been a real test, but cameras were installed, concealed and covering every metre right up to and inside the purpose built 'hideout' Log cabin at the end. HD quality recordings could be made at any time either for surveillance purposes or viewing options.

He would not be involved in the 'gathering' that evening, it suited him as he was tired and ready for his bed and Mia had assured him there would be food for him to take back to his room later that evening.

She also took a moment to reflect on where they had gotten to and she was pleased and proud to be where they were now after all the planning and hard work by everyone involved.

CHAPTER 81

The girls met in the kitchen, all but Dominica casual with joggers, sneakers and loose Ts, all with hair tied up ready for cooking. She wore a brightly coloured pair of skin-tight leggings, looking like they had been sprayed from a can, hugging tightly her plus size figure and sumptuous ass and a top struggling to retain her huge breasts with no bra. "No prisoners ever," she commented laughing with the girls.

But, there was no hierarchy here, they just organised each other and allocated different tasks, they had agreed to cook Ramen style dishes with fresh Prawns, and fillet of beef with noodles and side salad, together with some freshly baked bread brought from Tengah earlier.

Abigail was right, cooking together really was a 'team' event; there were laughs, impersonations of singers using wooden spoons and 'talking' prawns.

Within an hour, the food was prepared and ready to serve. Abigail had joined them in the dining area and Amanda had taken a drink order so, they sat down together and shared the freshly cooked and prepared meal.

It was a cordial atmosphere, very relaxed and convivial with 'shop talk' banned for the evening. They all went through a personal introduction and a brief CV of their lives to date and toasted each other; this was going to be an amazing team, thought Abigail, and these girls will look after each other.

"Sorry to interrupt," came a voice and face peering around the door smiling.

It was Wisetzki; he had finished for the evening.

"Someone mentioned there would be some homecooked food going spare?" he asked in his best *Oliver Twist* voice.

"Yes, of course," replied Mia and she began to get up from the table but was beaten to it by Dominica.

"I'll show you," she said, "come with me to the kitchen," she added, more instruction-like.

"Thank you," replied Wisetzki. "I'm starving, could eat a horse between two bread vans!"

There was a blank silence and exchanging of confused glances around the table.

"Sorry," he apologised, "it's a saying I picked up working in England, just means I'm very hungry."

He made sure he followed Dominica which, she knew, was to take in the view of what could only be described as her magnificent ass twerking from side to side inside the tight leggings; she smelt like a perfumed garden.

They reached the kitchen area. "I'm Dominica," she introduced herself holding out her hand.

"W, Wisetzki!" he stammered taking her hand.

"Wisetzki?" she quizzed. "Parents didn't like you or something?" she added, smiling.

"S, Sorry," he replied, "that's my surname and everybody uses that."

"Well, I will be different," she responded. "What can I call you? What's your first name?"

"Oh," he replied, "Thomas, but Tom is fine."

"Pleased to meet you then, Tom," she cooed.

They released the over lingering handshake, Dominica showed him the food, wished him good evening, and returned to the dining room.

She had read him immediately, he was nervous with her, she knew he was ex-military and could take more than one guy out at the same time with his bare hands, tough as nails but, with her, like putty.

She had always known her feminine, sexual power over men and this was typical, a real tough guy, accustomed to being, the dominant one but not with a woman like her.

She returned to the table and no one else batted an eyelid but Abigail did not miss anything, she was as sharp as a knife and would keep an eye on Dominica and Wisetzki; she knew this could be a potential weakness in the set up.

The meal ended with high fives between the team of girls

and Abigail was happy with the first gathering and warned them to be sharp and ready early the next morning.

Abigail and Amanda now did their part and cleaned up the dining room, loaded dishwashers and wished each other a good night.

CHAPTER 82

Wisetzki only felt this way, adrenalin hype, elevated pulse, under two conditions, one as he was about to begin a potentially deadly op, and two, encountering a certain type of woman. There was no deadly op looming, but he always knew that women with a certain demeanour and aura affected his senses this way. And, being brutally honest with himself, Dominica made him feel very weak to the point where he would gladly fall to his knees before her.

He cleared his mind the best he could, took the food and went to his room but after retiring to his bed, sleep just wouldn't come over him. It had been a long time since he had suffered any kind of 'woman' induced insomnia, he just sat upright and recalled the last time.

Succeeding his time in special ops activities, he was still young with fire persisting in his belly. He couldn't accept peace keeping or ceremonial duties, he had to be in the thick of real trouble so, he put himself up for hire as a mercenary.

He recalled the evening, receiving the call from one of his select, retained employers a Greek shipping magnate. The sea journey between Cape Town, South Africa and Europe was drastically reduced by using the Suez Canal and entry to the Mediterranean Sea but had the disadvantage of transiting off the coast of Somalia and the risk of Pirate incursions. However, this highly illegal and sometimes lethal activity had dwindled considerably of late due to the allowance of armed guards allowed to travel on board and transit the Suez.

His employer had a vessel ready to sail from Port of Cape Town to Genoa in Italy with a legitimate cargo. However, in addition, there was also an accompaniment of illegal passenger cargo on board in the form of four girls recruited to train in Italy to become high end call girls. It was part of a discreet but, legally fronted, Italian 'Modelling Agency' operation where girls were selected under their own, completely free, volition in South

Africa, who saw their future entertaining rich clients and making a better life for themselves operating on a commission basis.

Although a legitimate, commercial cargo vessel, it was equipped with very comfortably appointed, discreetly hidden, cabins away from the main crew quarters and self-contained. The same method of transportation had worked many times before but Pirate activity off the Somalian basin had increased recently, so Wisetzki was hired to travel with the ship.

He had landed in Cape Town and made way to the ship due to sail that evening and act as a legitimate guard as far as the crew were concerned. It was not his brief to interfere or interact with anyone on board other than the Captain and he had his own cabin.

He was aware that there were four passengers on board also making the journey together with six crew including the Captain, so he was fully briefed on the headcount he was hired to protect.

He was told that the additional four passengers on board would not be seen and would remain in the discreet accommodation for the whole journey. This didn't bother him; he was being highly paid for his services and didn't need to ask questions if he was aware of the total number of people in his care.

The Somali Pirates operated and infiltrated larger cargo vessels from small skiffs using hand-made wooden ladders to scale the sides, but these were not capable of making the journey from the mainland under their own steam. A larger boat would travel to intercept any targeted vessel, towing at least two of the skiffs. When in range, the faster skiffs would be launched an accompaniment of three, often fully armed, Pirates on board each.

The Captain had announced for the crew to be extra vigilant as they were entering the Somali basin waters and heightened risk of Pirate activity, but he hadn't reckoned on it being quite so soon.

"There's a skiff gaining on our stern around one Nautical Mile out," shouted the rear observer lowering his binoculars. "Looks like Pirates!"

The Captain alerted Wisetzki to the danger and ordered the crew to man the fire hoses whilst increasing the vessel to full speed.

Wisetzki, armed with an M16 rifle equipped with single shot M203 Grenade Launcher, made his way to the lower, open deck, area of the vessel.

The observer reported that the skiff had peeled off and was following its intended path towards the Port side increasing speed; and believed three pirates were on board armed with Russian Kalashnikov AK-47 rifles.

"They're heading for the Port side," announced the Captain, relaying the information from the make-shift observer, "make ready the water hoses!" The crew were not trained for this, they didn't work for a large shipping company where mandatory training would have been given. They were doing their best under the traumatic circumstances but in heightened state of panic and confusion mistakes were inevitable.

In no time at all the faster skiff was matching the cargo ship's speed and the ladders were being made ready in an attempt to board the slower vessel.

The skiff moved in alongside and the water hoses were trained on it, the Pirates began firing shots trying to stop the operators of the high velocity water jets aimed at them, bullets ricocheting around the ship's steelwork.

Wisetzki had seen enough and moved into action, "Water hoses?" he questioned to himself. "Fuck this!"

He screamed out a warning, took aim, and fired the grenade from his gun. "Have some of that instead!" he said to himself.

Boom! There was a flash of bright orange flame and plume of thick black smoke, the broken in half skiff just stopped moving, engulfed in flames, and three badly charred pirates were face down in the water falling behind the forward moving vessel.

Cheers went up, fists were shaken and there were pats on the back for the beaming Wisetzki, that is until someone pointed out a second skiff just drifting in the wake of the ship, abandoned.

Where had that come from? he thought, but more importantly, where had it been?

He made his way quickly to the Starboard side and, to his horror, saw a ladder hanging from the side rail.

The Pirates had made the first skiff almost a decoy, counting on the confusion and attention, a second had split and gone to the opposite side, its feral passengers now, potentially, amok on board the cargo vessel.

Wisetzki raced for the Bridge knowing it would be the first target and he was right.

He walked straight onto the Bridge without hesitation and the Captain was already being held with a knife to his throat by a gangly Somali, his rifle over one shoulder hung by a strap.

"Stop! I ki…" was all he got out as Wisetzki raised his rifle, simultaneously launching a high velocity piece of lead directly into the Pirate's forehead.

His mouth was still open as he was trying to finish what he wanted to stay but he just crumpled to the floor dead, releasing the captain unharmed from his grip, the knife falling harmlessly to the floor.

"My God!" cried the Captain. "You could have shot me with all you had to aim at," he yelled, shaking.

"Never in doubt," replied Wisetzki, calmly, "there's always a window, a sweet spot, when someone is taking the trouble to concentrate on making a demand and I took it whilst I could."

"You really are worth the exorbitant fee, aren't you?" stammered the Captain.

"Not over yet," he said, "I believe there's at least one more somewhere on board, take this revolver and get everyone else on the Bridge and seal it, I'm going to find them." He left the Bridge.

CHAPTER 83

He knew the other assailants would have headed below decks, especially on hearing the unmistakable crack of his weapon as he despatched the first Pirate to his fishing ground in the sky.

He would be searching for hostages and, with all crew accounted for and with the Captain on the Bridge, there were four left, the hidden contraband only he and the Captain were privy to.

He made his way carefully past the crew quarters until it seemed the corridor ended but, now it did not, and he heard the 'rat a tat tat' of an automatic weapon, resounding thuds, breaking of furniture and girls screaming.

The secret compartment door was open and had been unlocked as the girls had heard gunshots and tried to investigate. The Pirate must have them now, or worse, he thought to himself.

"Put down your weapons, I am Vessel Security," he shouted in perfect English. He entered cautiously, slowly poking the door fully open with the muzzle of his rifle, expecting carnage or worse but could hardly believe his eyes.

Three of the girls were now huddled together, crying but the fourth, a strikingly statuesque black girl dressed in sleepwear, stood over the dead Pirate, a kitchen knife dripping with blood grasped in her hand, and watching the last embers of blood pulsating out of a gaping gash in the side of the Pirate's neck. She had managed to remain hidden when he first entered and, when his back was turned, she pounced, thrusting the kitchen knife into his artery, causing him to convulse and fire his weapon into the ceiling.

Wisetzki took control of the situation, taking the knife from the girl whose name was Adofo, and assuring them that it was over, and they were safe. He knew that if any more Pirates were on board, they would have shown themselves as they would have no intent to be carried out of the Somali waters, it would be pointless. The girls were aware of the secrecy under which they were travelling and agreed it should remain that way.

The idea was to remove the body into the common corridor and seal it off once more and whilst the other three began tidying up, Adofo offered to help Wisetzki remove the dead Pirate out of their quarters.

This was the first time he had been affected by a powerful black female, he was instantly drawn to her femininity which she knew and wasted no time letting him know.

She leaned into his ear. "I'm so fucking hot after that, my pussy is tingling and craving some serious attention," she whispered.

Although taken aback, he just knew what was going to happen and it did. For the rest of the Journey, Wisetzki would sneak Adofo from her hideaway and into his cabin for the hottest and most consuming dominant sex he had every encountered. She was insatiable and both physically and mentally demanding.

Then he remembered how they reached Genoa and he never saw her again, the Black Nubian goddess he lost sleep over for many nights.

It was happening again with Dominica.

CHAPTER 84

It was a beautiful day on Bidong Island, Rui and Arusi had been for a run and Dominica had worked out in the gym, running not being her forte, all before breakfast, which they had sorted individually and were already in the meeting room. Wisetzki was also up and about to ensure total security for the meeting and seminar even though risk was low, Abigail had insisted 'alert' level, and this was what he did.

Amanda manned the reception area keeping an attentive watch on the CCTV and the girls were joined by Abigail.

"I enjoyed our evening last night and believe we will make a great team together for this brand new and exciting venture we are about to embark upon, so, welcome to today and the work begins now!" said Abigail.

"I am going to hand over to Mia now but, before I do, this is the defining moment right here right now," she continued, "complete, confidential exposure, we have an incredible story to share with you, full disclosure is the only way you will understand completely, so, we are under maximum security and critically, 'non-disclosure' is paramount; it doesn't get any more serious than this, it goes beyond any individual events you have been involved in previously, if you are not comfortable with this then, leave now, do you all understand?" she checked.

The girls were very serious now and in professional mode, they all accepted.

"Ok," said Abigail, "with the visual aid of a slide presentation, Mia will brief you fully attending to any questions at the end, we must all understand our roles and responsibilities, over to you, Mia."

"Thanks, Abigail and welcome again, ladies," said Mia, "what you are about to hear is nothing short of incredible so, full concentration please," she pleaded.

For the next two hours, Mia began right at the beginning of the trail of 'SoD' from her 'kill' back in the gym in KL right to where they were today with Carol in Singapore doing advanced testing and the whole point of this team's existence, the harvesting of the 'Seeds of Death'.

"And there you have it!" she concluded.

Total silence, you could hear a pin drop in the room, astonished expressions, no words.

Abigail was the first to speak, "We will take a break now, I suggest you all do your own thing, absorbing what you have just been told, take a coffee, juice or whatever and we meet back here in 30 minutes where I am sure there will be questions and clarifications," she instructed.

Mia was, as ever, impressed with her flawless management skills and she needed a break also, the memories flooding back of the journey she had made over the preceding months.

The 'break' Abigail had suggested was just what they all needed, and they reported back ready for a serious Q&A session.

CHAPTER 85

"Ok, the floor is totally open, no questions and/or observations are silly, we have to nail this right here this week," Abigail warned.

With the science accepted, which was not really their area to worry about, she was surprised at the simplicity they all assumed as Rui opened the questions.

"You have told us that, this 'end of life' ejaculation, totally involuntary, occurs when the victim is either choked or suffocated as far as you know right?" asked Rui.

"Yes, that is correct," replied Mia. "I first experienced it defending myself against a would-be rapist where I felt I had no choice and I choked him to death."

"Nice one, got exactly what the bastard deserved," said Rui. "I can choke someone out in a few seconds, and they are effectively asleep, but we have to go beyond the 'passing out' stage of course whether suffocating or choking to get this effect?"

"That's right," said Mia, "both of you have killed and know how it goes but you will never have noticed what happens when death comes, I have re-watched Arusi's latest smother kill, which was so incredibly beautiful by the way, and his pants were soiled with the ejaculation."

"Thank you," responded Arusi, "so, we stick to choking and/or suffocating our victims to death?"

"Yes, for now or until we discern more, I definitely know these methods work," answered Mia.

"So, all we have to do, in a nutshell of course, is to dispatch the men that come here to play out their fantasies either by choking or suffocating them to death and catching this 'SoD'?" Dominica asked.

"In short, yes," replied Mia, "Abigail, Amanda and I will be responsible for selecting the 'victims', getting them here and briefing you on their individual fantasies."

"How can we be sure that this final ejaculation will not spill anywhere?" asked Arusi. "It will be difficult for us to ensure this as we will be attached to and concentrating on the other end, their breathing and consciousness apparatus?" she asked, sadistically laughing.

"We have this covered," replied Mia, "one of Pietro's technicians has designed a method of catching and preserving the fluid we need by ensuring the victims are wearing an undergarment apparatus to capture and preserve it, you do not need to be concerned with this, you just do what you are best at."

She went on to tell them that this undergarment would be specified as part of the brief on the day of their fantasy, part of health and safety, so they would willingly wear it totally unaware of what its true purpose was.

"Sounds straightforward to me," said Dominica, "it's pretty much what we have done before, we lure the victims into their fantasy and finish them against their will, obtaining this 'SoD' in the process which, you say, happens automatically anyway, we don't have to 'wank' it out of them?" she added, grimacing.

"Exactly right," said Mia, "you girls just get to do what you enjoy, stay here on the Island for the session and get highly paid for your services and dedication."

"We even plan on some 'doubling' up as Amanda often receives a fantasy with two girls," concluded Abigail.

"So, we could even team up!" Arusi said excitedly.

"Perfect," laughed Rui, "a two on one kill!" she added, rubbing her thighs.

"Will any of this be screened live as it is now?" asked Arusi.

"Good question and in short, yes," replied Abigail, "we want to maintain the huge cash influx obtained from our 'snuff' events, with paying customers. We could have Wisetzki choke the men to death with cheese wire, but this is not what our audiences wish to see," she went on. "We chose this method of harvesting the 'SoD' as a cash win-win all round and for your benefit. We will select certain 'kills' for live broadcast, these you will have to play out the role as requested; however, and despite the role play asked for by the client, if it is not to be screened then you can finish them off as fast as you like, it's not as if they are going to be able to complain to customer services is it?" concluded Abigail, smiling.

The group laughed, Dominica adding, "They won't get to fill out the satisfaction survey at the end for sure!"

"Or tick the smiley face of their choice icon, I don't think there's a choice of skull and crossbones," added Rui, again drawing laughter from the team.

Hard to believe, thought Mia, these three girls were lethal, armed with both beauty and seduction skills, the human version of the 'Venus fly trap'; more, she smiled, the ultimate 'honey trap', perfect. She was excited and a little aroused, if she was honest, about her new role as the modern-day version of 'Octopussy'.

"We will wrap up here," announced Mia, "same routine for dinner, and tomorrow I want us to meet in the gym where we can share our tried and tested techniques for choking and smothering the life out of these cretins."

The next day, Mia spent the whole time with the girls in the gym where they practiced and demonstrated on each other the different choking and smothering methods they could employ, together with some self-defence tips, especially from Mia and Rui with their knowledge of MMA fighting.

They returned to Tengah, arriving in the afternoon, leaving Wisetzki, Abigail and Amanda to maintain the Bidong facility.

Mia drove Arusi, Dominica and Rui to the airstrip where Carol had just arrived in the Lear and they would depart for Singapore and take their respective flights to their home destinations remaining on standby for their first assignments.

Mia drove Carol back to the Lab, stopping for a few moments in a secluded spot to engage in a very long, passionate, no tongues barred, kiss and a promise to 'catch up' later that evening in her apartment, it had been a while, they both agreed.

CHAPTER 86

Li and Victoria were dining in the Bistro, they had both been working extra hours, taking up some of the slack in the Lab, due to the re-assignment and resulting absence of Mia and Carol.

"Tell me, Victoria," said Li, "do you know what Carol has been conducting away from the Island? And where, in the City I believe, these past days? Seems a little covert to me."

"I don't think so, Li, it's no secret that the company is in the final testing stages of a brand new, and I hear very innovative, topical skin care cream; Carol has always martialled this development stage and routine before a new product is introduced onto the market," she replied. He was frustrated, Victoria didn't know any more than him, he just harboured suspicions he couldn't and wouldn't share with her.

"I have witnessed new products coming to market through our R&D, I get that, but this one seems to be attracting more layers of security for some reason," he went on.

"Again, Li, I think you are reading more into it, this is a crucial stage for any new product, you don't want it leaking to, say, a competitor so I believe it's business as usual, stop concerning yourself with it and pour me another glass of wine, mine is empty!" she answered.

"Of course," he apologised, "proper Gentleman, aren't I?" he quipped.

After a very civilised and convivial dinner with Victoria, she said her good evenings and retired to her room.

Li always thanked the Chef in person after every meal and he went to the kitchen to find him, unusually, a little distraught and cursing inanimate objects.

"Everything ok, Chef? I just came to thank you for the food this evening, something bothering you?" he enquired.

"Oh yes, sorry," he replied, "just a little stressed and despondent with the recruitment I'm trying to sort out, I don't seem to be able to find anyone suitable, it would probably help if I had contacts in Mersing, but I don't."

"Recruitment for what?" Li asked. The Chef told him that, on certain occasions there would be a need to supply a team of up to three catering staff for hospitality events on Bidong Island when 'paying' guests would be hosted by Pietro and, thus far, the candidates he had found were not up to the roles.

Li struggled to hide his jubilation as a scheme unfolded quickly inside his head, this was it, a chance to get someone on the inside on Bidong to find out what was going on there.

"I believe I may be able to help with that," he offered. "I spend my leisure days in Mersing and through a mutual friend have gotten to know the Police commissioner there who, in turn, knows everyone, I'm sure he could help and coming from him, their credentials would be unquestionable."

"Now, that would be really helpful if you can, thanks," said the Chef.

"No problem, leave it with me and I'll get back to you," said Li, disappearing quickly.

CHAPTER 87

He couldn't dial the number fast enough, making two fumbled attempts before getting the ring tone and verbal response. "It's Li, I told you we just needed to wait for the right opportunity, and it has happened right now," he said to the caller.

"Ok, slow down, glad to hear," replied West from the other end, "I was wondering when we would have some luck, tell me."

He repeated that, as they had discussed, something was about to happen on Bidong Island but, he couldn't find out anything other than it would be a VIP resort facility.

With the absence of quality information, they needed someone there, on the ground, to report back with any link relating to unusual activity and if it had anything to do with the death of Jordan Price. He explained that the Chef was looking to recruit two service/kitchen staff for Tengah with occasional duties on Bidong Island itself.

"I'm sure you can suggest and help with that via the commissioner, then one of them could be 'ears and eyes' for us when called upon to work on Bidong and also report back any unusual activity whilst based on Tengah," he concluded.

"Well done," said West, "this chef is looking for two staff and the Police commissioner is always looking to place local people in gainful employment, he will see this as a favour from me to make up for what happened when I was caught on the Island and the embarrassment it caused him, but, he doesn't need to know anything beyond that."

"So, you will make contact with the commissioner and make the necessary arrangements and I will arrange for interviews with the Chef on Tengah once you have the candidates?" checked Li.

"Yes, I will be in touch soon," he concluded.

West wasted no time at all arranging to return to Mersing to meet with the Police Commissioner who was completely sold on the 'do good' gesture he had proposed to him.

Nepotism goes hand in hand with corrupt officials throughout the world and extended family provided candidates for almost anything. The commissioner offered the opportunity to a daughter, Nina, and son, Bujang, of two of his cousins twice removed. They were both experienced with kitchen and catering work so, on that front, were suitably qualified for the roles.

Nina was in her early twenties still living at home with her parents, husband and two small children, she worked all hours she could gain in a local Hotel and café style restaurant, familiar with both kitchen and hospitality duties. Bujang was understudy to a chef, also in a local restaurant, and was 24 years old, single and a little wayward. He had been in trouble with his Uncle, the Police commissioner, for very minor offences so, he put him forward for the role to widen his horizons and afford him better opportunities.

For Nina it was an easy choice, sometimes business would be sluggish at the Hotel and she would be laid off for periods, having to find any type of work she could, so an opportunity like this gave her more stability and guaranteed income to support her family. Bujang, on the other hand, really embraced the chance given to him by his Uncle and was determined to do well.

He had been introduced to West as the instigator of the opportunity, so thanked him personally.

The interviews were set up, the Chef visited and was satisfied with the candidates and arrangements were made for the two to be based on Tengah and, when called upon, to make up the seconded team working on Bidong.

As agreed with West, Li arranged to speak with Bujang once he was settled on Tengah.

Li told him that there had been some suspicion of espionage within the operation and as he was to work at both facilities would be a great help in reporting back any suspicious activities he may encounter.

Bujang didn't want to disappoint anyone, after all, he was new and looking to impress so, when dollars were added into the equation, he was happy, especially as he wasn't being asked to be proactively snooping around. The young chef felt he had made an immediate ally and he could still concentrate on the duties allocated to him by his new boss, the Head Chef. He was determined to make something of himself, maybe gain some opportunity to work elsewhere in the world if he proved himself.

CHAPTER 88

After a night of catching up, Mia and Carol met the next morning for the test program debrief, report and recommendations.

Mia was very, very pleased as her trusted assistant consistently delivered on her expectations. She reported that everything went to plan and the formula they had composed for testing had performed better than they could have hoped for. The strength of the active 'SoD' element behaved with complete prediction and over the seven-day period, results had been consistently progressive. They would await feedback for the next seven days but there were no adverse reactions to daily use; it was as though their discovery somehow genetically reacted in the right levels for every application. The test on the scar tissue was conclusive and had completely regenerated, identically matching with the surrounding skin after the sixth day. The wrinkle analysis was also very successful with noticeable results after the seven-day period. Carol recommended a further reduction of the active 'SoD' ingredient so that more cream applications would be needed and hence more sales. She did not believe this would have any detrimental effect on its overall effectiveness.

"It is, unbelievably, so non-complex," she began, "we have what is basically our bestselling moisturising cream compound with the addition of our 'magic' ingredient, it remains an incredible find and development. Barring any setbacks from the testing in the next week or so, the product will be ready, and we need to address strict menu formulations with controlled production."

It was agreed that she would be deployed to the factory to supervise the initial set up and first production batches. The only requirement left now was the supply of 'SoD' to make it all happen and Abigail, Amanda and Mia were working to make that happen.

CHAPTER 89

Carol was very much enjoying her 'change of scenery' excursions, whilst passionate and satisfied working in the Lab on new compounds and formulas, she was grateful for the chance to travel a little, albeit another, relatively short, trip over to Singapore and the factory.

She arrived at Changi Airport and was collected by a driver who took her directly to the production facility, she had requested a tour of the plant with the facility's manager, especially the newly installed, dedicated line for the new skin care product.

The Singapore facility was the Jewel in Pietro's portfolio of manufacturing plants, fully ISO certified in both 9001 and very importantly 14001 environmental versions. Zhang Wei was the model employee and had worked in many of the organisation's plants, cutting his teeth before being appointed manager of the flagship facility. He was a chemist with qualifications in chemical plant operations, a slight man in his late fifties, grey hair with seasoned complexion and large, black rimmed glasses. He was married with two grown up sons who also worked within the organisation and was a gentleman unless intentionally crossed and the workforce respected and enjoyed his command.

"Mr Wei, pleased to meet you in person at last, I know we have spoken on the telephone and on video calls but this is better," Carol said as she greeted him warmly in the reception area of the plant.

"Likewise, Miss Carol, and please call me Zhang," he replied.

"Ok," she answered, "and in that case I'm just Carol," she added smiling.

The handshake was firm and sincere and mutual respect was instantly given and received.

"I know you are keen, but first some tea and I have arranged for the driver to take your luggage to the Hotel and get you checked in, I will take you there later," he said.

Carol was treated to some Jasmine tea and water biscuits and then put through the compulsory factory safety and orientation video presentation.

She was issued with PPE and Zhang took her into the plant itself.

She was expecting clean but the place was immaculate and the phrase 'So clean you could eat your dinner from the floor' immediately sprung to mind.

There were polished stainless vessels and containers everywhere with automated lines transporting jars from the intense heat and then an E-Beam sterilisation process to filling, capping and labelling ready for packing. They had just installed AI (Artificial Intelligence) technology for content and volume quality assurance QA and this was also to be used in the newly installed line for the new product.

Zhang escorted Carol to the new dedicated plant area. It was the largest production line they had and, until recently, used to produce a very long-standing volume product now shifted to another facility. Complete overhaul and refurbishment had been carried out with many new 'state of the art' pieces of equipment including, as he had mentioned, AI. Large as it was, he had been briefed regarding the sensitive nature of the new product and hand-picked staff had been chosen. There was increased CCTV security installed together with biometrically controlled area entry systems.

Carol was impressed and Zhang was the pinnacle of dedication, she knew everything was in good hands.

As she had remotely supervised, an ultra-secure room had been constructed with entry only possible for Zhang. This would be where the 'secret' ingredient would be kept and she would brief him on storage, addition quantities etc. In effect, for every batch production he would personally add the ingredient, and no one would know the quantity, source or nature of it.

Zhang was fully empowered; he knew the gravity and potential this new product addition could bring to his company and he also knew what competitors would do to get their hands on it if, indeed, it matched up to their expectations.

The tour over for the day, Zhang took Carol back to the Hotel and left her to her own devices promising dinner together the following evening.

She was grateful for the time, got settled in her room, showered, caught up with Mia and ordered room service before settling down. She had to be ready for an early start back to the plant the following morning and the next two days of finalising and instruction, concluding with a very small batch size, production 'test' run and proofing.

CHAPTER 90

Everything was a 'go' and Pietro had told the team that the facility on Bidong was ready, all they needed now was its first client to prove and test the months of hard work and dedication.

Amanda had received a follow up from a single, 35-year-old male from Atlanta and big fan of live WWE who had requested the possibility of being in a 'live' match, but with a Lady Wrestler, "diva", he mentioned. He wasn't any kind of wrestler himself and said it would be more a 'fantasy' style, match with little or no fightback or resistance on his part. He basically wanted to be wrestled into submission against his will, but, in a ring style situation and in addition a 'live' commentary broadcast over speakers as it was happening.

Amanda had carried out all the background checks and he had the potential to be the first 'victim' to come to Bidong Island as a paying guest.

His name was Graham, now to be known as subject zero, a recluse who had been living alone with his elderly mother who had passed recently and left him her estate. He wasn't rich but it meant he could sustain himself without working and watch as many DVDs of his WWE heroes as he liked; he was a perfect fit. He was around 1.5m tall, slight build, healthy, own teeth and a receding hairline, not much to look at but, he wasn't interested in making friends or relationships.

She would arrange for Dominica to travel to the Island a couple of days ahead so that she could supervise the construction and authenticity of the ring and set up in the gym.

Wisetzki was on hand with security and seemed more happy than usual when he discovered that it was her featuring in the production. He was to make sure that phone or internet signals would be strictly password restricted. Satellite location would not be possible, messages in or out by the victim from any device, although, would have already been screened and tech confiscated, before arrival.

Pietro and Amanda had secured a lucrative paying audience as usual which had attracted a lot of attention and in the end had to cut down on the original interested parties. It seemed WWE RAW was going to take on a whole new meaning and people wanted to see the spectacle where the 'stalking' and 'merciless' displays of dominance would in fact, be authentic.

Abigail had arranged an evening check in for the victim, a briefing and meal before the 'action' the following day and everything was in place with Mia agreeing to take the part of commentator.

He flew, regular service, into Singapore which would be his last traceable journey and he boarded Pietro's Lear Jet for onward travel.

He was aware of the security protocols when asked to surrender his phone and any other communication devices which he had already agreed in the T's & C's beforehand.

He had no reason to suspect subterfuge, this was his life-long fantasy and these people were helping him to achieve it. The Lear was flown for around four hours to hide the location of where his end destination might be, eventually landing on Tengah at the small Airstrip away from the Lab facility. There it was met by a small Seaplane and he was transferred, in darkness now, to Bidong where Abigail was ready to greet him.

She welcomed him, Amanda had checked that the funds he had promised were in the bank account and proceeded to escort him to his Lodge accommodation arranging a meeting at 20:00 hrs local time for the briefing. After settling in he met with Abigail and Mia and they took him to the gym to show him the set up. He was thrilled, "It's just so life-like," he commented, "ropes, corner stools, lights and a table for the commentator, it's perfect."

He didn't have any clue as to the 24 UHD cameras focused to cover every angle of the arena and that, his 'match' would be screened live to a discerning, paying audience.

They agreed that, he would spend the next day relaxing and was to report back to the gym changing rooms at 21:00 hrs for his 'ring' outfit the following evening and wouldn't meet his opponent until the MC announcements. He was so excited he could hardly sleep but with nothing to do the next day he just spent the time daydreaming of his defeat by a competent female wrestler.

CHAPTER 91

Everything was set, the paying audience were confirmed as logged on and streaming live from the ringside whilst subject zero was being prepared in the changing rooms by the senior stagehand. He was given bright red shorts, socks and boots, with an electric blue Lycra top with a gold 'Lightning' bolt emblazoned across the front and a red face and head mask shaped to leave his hair protruding from the crown. Underneath his shorts he had been instructed to wear the now refined and very comfortable soft, latex rubber pants designed by Pietro's technician on the pretext that, should any blows be accidently misdirected into the groin area, these would help protect him and his wellbeing was of prime concern. He suspected nothing, felt like he was being looked after to the highest degree of safety and satisfaction and his heart was beating out of his chest in anticipation.

I hope she is full bodied and formidable, he thought to himself as he walked into the now, brightly floodlit ring area, climbed through the bottom rope and into the ring itself.

Mia was hidden from any camera view but sat ringside at a small table with headphones and a microphone.

As he entered the ring, the stagehand played the canned audience cheering loudly and he responded in full role play, stretching on the ropes and parading around the ring in adulation of his 'cheering fans', he was in his element.

Then, Mia in true MC style and voice expression, "Here, fight fans, welcome to the main event of the evening, we have in the Blue corner 'The Flash' out of Atlanta, Georgia, our strong and favourite challenger and we expect it to be brutal!" she exclaimed.

He strutted around the ring soaking up the canned atmosphere and then stood in his corner as the lights were dimmed. Music began to play, and a single spotlight suddenly picked up a figure walking towards the ring and as it got closer, he became totally dumbstruck almost freezing in awe. Of course, it was Dominica but, to him, his dream wrestling opponent, a 'Women's RAW WWE Goddess'.

She was dressed all in white, thigh length boots, PVC one-piece Basque and matching G String and soft elbow length fingerless, evening gloves. The contrast of her chocolate skin, shiny straight 'bob' style hair and immaculate make-up completed this statuesque woman opponent.

He was transfixed; she was a powerhouse. He couldn't have asked for more; she was exactly the 'wrestler' of his dreams.

"And now the Champion!" Mia announced. "In the Red corner, and wrestling out of New York, our man destroyer, 'Dominator She'!"

The crowd cheered and Dominica strutted confidently around the ring, then headed towards him, stopping and turning around she slowly bent forward and touched her toes in front of him.

His gasp was clearly audible at the sight in front of him, her powerful chocolate thighs appearing above her white boots, the material of the tiny G String disappearing between the cheeks of her delicious, sumptuous ass, he could only stare.

Dominica went to her corner and Mia announced, "This is for the title with only one left standing at the end, there are no holds barred but, no scratching or biting, the match ends when one wrestler cannot recover and is done, is that clear?"

They both nodded, "Then let's rumble!" she announced.

CHAPTER 92

The bell sounded loudly, and the crowd cheered.

Dominica knew she could squash him like a bug in seconds but she had a plan to start slow and easy, giving him some confidence before going into the more violent moves. After all, this was a money making, live streamed event so, she had to play the game.

They met in the middle with the traditional clasp of fingers as she towered above him.

"That's 'gotta' hurt!" announced Mia as the fingers of The Flash were bent backwards, forcing him down onto his knees in front of her. She used her knee to push him over and onto his back and stood, hands on hips, waiting for him to get up.

He wasn't dazed at all, there was no strike power from her knee; it was just a 'showboat' move.

They circled around the ring for a while and he lunged at her a couple of times in a 'rugby' style move which she just side stepped and helped him on his way to the floor once more.

Dominica then began using some of her skills, showing him how to bounce off the ropes and run from one side of the ring to the other, warming up in the process.

He'd always wanted to do this and began using the opposite sides of the ring, as they passed in the middle a couple of times he was enjoying it until, suddenly, he hadn't noticed Dominica stop in the centre of the ring and, as he went to pass her, she straightened out her arm and caught him in the throat with a 'clothes line' move.

This was his first introduction to real wrestling pain, for a few seconds he was suspended in mid-air, his head at a standstill with Dominica's flattened hand in his throat and his legs still trying to transport him to the other side of the ring, something had to give. Of course, she stood firm as he crashed down onto his back, dazed at being caught with a 'real live' move and clutching his throat. She rolled him over onto his front and mounted him, putting him into a 'Camel clutch' pulling his head back by the chin.

"Now it's heating up!" screamed Mia excitedly. "That's a brutal clutch and he's in pain."

She wasn't kidding, he was grimacing from the painful hold and wondering quite what had hit him, it felt like a freight train.

He tapped violently on the floor and eventually she let him go, falling face first onto the mat. He continued to play the part and managed to get up onto his knees. She grabbed him by the arm, pulled him to his feet and flung him against the rope once more and as he recoiled back towards her caught him with her knee in his stomach, doubling him up on his knees again, gasping for breath from being winded.

"She has him down!" screamed Mia, the Flash heard, although he was still dazed, he was like a rag doll and feeling real pain but he decided this was what he had asked for.

"The Champion is behind him now and coiling those white, gloved arms around his neck, this looks like, yes, a Rear Naked Choke, his head is up and her forearm is in under his chin and locked with the other at the back of his neck, he's in trouble now!" she continued.

She sat down, pulling him back onto her and wrapping her thick thighs around his waist, crossing her ankles then, squeeze time as she applied the choke.

"He can't get out of this," screamed Mia, "he is desperately trying to prise away her arms, this is a sleeper, he's going to go out," she continued.

Desperate he was and she was right, he had no chance of breaking the hold, he tapped, he pawed at the deadly arms forcing him to sleep.

"He's going out!" Mia said. "She's putting him to sleep right here and now, his eyes are rolling, that's it, he's snoring," she added excitedly knowing the feeling it gave her when an opponent went limp.

She immediately released the choke hold, not wanting the match to end here, he flopped unconscious to the floor where she lay him on his side.

Darkness had come over him. He had never been choked out before but it was a short period and he awoke quickly, wondering what had just happened as he came to his senses and remembered where he was and what was going on.

Dominica just stood preening herself, adjusting her gloves and boots and repositioning her thong waiting for him to come around for what she had planned next for the hapless victim.

She went easy as they restarted, putting him into some arm and leglock moves on the ground until he tapped, she wanted him to feel a little more confident again and it worked, he had felt as though things had gotten a little extreme but now he felt better again. That was until from a standing position she pulled his head down just as her knee was coming up, crashing into his face.

"Ooo!" shrieked Mia. "That's a heavy knee to the face and he's on his back again, we have first blood, looks like from his nose, seeping down his mask," she went on.

He clutched his nose, once again dazed from the brutal knee blow. She walked over to him, picking him up by the hair to his knees and delivered another knee blow, this time to the side of his head, he went crashing to the floor.

"This is one sided now," screamed Mia, "he is defenceless, she can do whatever she likes, I have a feeling this is going to be very brutal."

And brutal it became, Dominica was in 'kill' mode now and totally 'lost' in the part.

"Please, I've had enough!" he screamed from his foetal position on the floor. "Ring the bell, I want it to stop!" he gurgled, blood now seeping from his mouth, he pleaded.

"There is no bell!" she shouted to him. "There is no 'enough'." As she dragged him by the hair again across the ring leaving a trail of blood behind him. He was flat out looking at the sky and totally dazed from the onslaught.

Then, 'splat' as she dropped across his body with her full weight knocking any remaining air he had right out of his lungs, spitting blood into the air.

Mia was taken back on one hand at the brutal beating happening in front of her, but, at the same time aroused by what Dominica was doing to him.

He managed to roll over onto his stomach and lay trying to get some strength back repeating he wanted out, he wanted it to stop, this was not what he signed up for.

Of course, that didn't matter, and he didn't have the strength to run away as she circled above him.

She sat down facing him, lifted his head up by the hair and snapped her massive, powerful thighs around his neck in a forward, front head scissor.

"She's back to choking him," Mia announced, "God that's tight, look she's squeezing the blood right out of him."

He was totally out of it but still conscious as he gurgled between her lethal legs, hands pushing weakly at her crushing thighs, blood dribbling onto them.

She controlled the choke, she knew she could finish it right here in this position but didn't want to yet, she had a different finish in mind.

She released him again before he passed out and he lay on the mat totally defeated.

"We're waiting for the finish," announced Mia, "I sense it's coming, he's her bitch now totally at her mercy." He was and there wasn't going to be any.

Dominica turned his head to the side and lifted it from the mat. She knelt, wrapping one leg under the back of his head forming a guillotine, the back of his neck resting on her calf and his throat trapped under her inner thigh, in her crotch, and then she sat down on his throat. To complete the move, she straightened out her other leg in front making sure her full weight was bearing down on him.

"Oh my God!" shrieked Mia. "What a choke, he's not going to get out of this, I can almost hear the pressure." She was right, he was done totally, no resistance, he clawed weakly at her thigh but Dominica just sat looking nonchalantly straight ahead, hands on hips, feeling the power.

He gurgled and choked as the deadly hold took its course, she looked up, eyes closed, as his hands fell away limp and his legs stopped kicking but she remained, unmoving and calm, for a further two minutes and he was dead under her heavy thigh.

She uncoiled her leg from his throat, climbed out of the ring and headed back towards the changing rooms, her work done.

He lay face up on the mat, eyes open and choked to death, Mia looked on thinking it was so surreal, the contrast of a man in a bright 'flash' emblazoned wrestling fantasy costume splattered with blood and really, really, dead.

She was first to him and, with a pair of scissors, cut away his shorts to reveal the latex rubber undergarment.

It was perfect, the inner tube teardrop end was completely full of the 'glowing' fluid she had experienced before, a total success and first harvested sample of the 'SoD' as she cut the tube away to seal and retain its contents.

She left the scene and the body was taken care of that same evening, together with everything he had brought with him to the Island.

The first 'kill' was over and proven, Pietro had watched online together with Abigail and Amanda; Mia was satisfied, their strategy was going to work.

CHAPTER 93

"That was some show!" complimented Wisetzki as Dominica passed him by the locker room on the way to the changing rooms. "You look magnificent and glowing," he added, gulping and unable to hide his admiration of her feminine prowess.

She was in an elevated state of arousal from what she had just carried out, she was very high and with no further thought, removed her thong, sat down on the bench with her back to the wall, spread her legs open and looking straight at Wisetzki calmly said, "Get over here on your knees and lick my pussy!"

He didn't say anything or even hesitate, within a couple of seconds he was on his knees in front of her, hands on her thighs, his tongue buried deep inside her womanhood, licking at her puffed labia like a starved dog.

She reached forward, positioning her hand on the back of his head pulling his face deeper into her gaping sex.

She was already sopping wet from the kill, he found her large, swollen clit and took it into his mouth, sucking on it then licking, sucking then licking. Throwing her head back in ecstasy she orgasmed on his lapping tongue forcing her hips forward towards his willing mouth, coming right there in the locker room. Then, after a short recovery, coldly, "You shouldn't be in here," she said, "I will take this up with you later."

"Anything you say," came the reply, he was hooked, she knew it, but was satisfied for the time being and he had to be slowly teased, just what she needed after the huge adrenalin rush.

CHAPTER 94

After all the months of planning and dedication, the work seemed to be paying off. Abigail chaired the follow up debriefing after the event and shortfalls were identified with remedial actions listed for future events.

Chef had recruited the two kitchen hands and Abigail, Amanda and Wisetzki were permanent residents of Bidong, but with Wisetzki commuting between there and Tengah on a regular basis which suited him.

Abigail had announced that Amanda was working on active leads, Bidong was ready for business, Mia and Carol were satisfied that their trials with the new skin care product could be controllably extended with no failures or setbacks whatsoever to date, and Carol was in Singapore supervising the plant ready for the start up production.

They had decided to brand the new skin cream 'Seeds of Life', which Mia felt was very apt as it represented the story behind the murals she had witnessed in the Grottoes of life, resurrecting from death, albeit, a commercial version.

The marketing department were working on a launch strategy with advertising, endorsements and testimonials down to packaging and presentation. As a beauty and cosmetics company, 'Skintakt', would always exhibit at one of the largest industry exhibitions worldwide, 'Cosmoprof'. This year, perfectly, it was scheduled to take place at the end of the year in Singapore, seven months hence, so this was the targeted launch venue.

The 'SoD' harvesting was working with military precision, Abigail supervised every event with all victims being flown onto the Island for a maximum two nights' stay; some were broadcast as live streaming 'snuff' events and others were not. The agents were used according to the requests, and Amanda made sure there was a rotation of the girls ensuring equal financial reward.

Rui carried out a 'harvest' where the victim requested an arranged fight outside of a Japanese 'college' with the girl who thought she was tough. The scenario was an argument in the college classroom with an agreement to settle the dispute once and for all. Later in a remote spot, there would be a fight with no witnesses and no holds barred, the fight ending when one of them could not continue. Abigail had arranged for Wisetzki to be hidden near to the pre-arranged area, a clearing near to the Log Cabin at the end of the trail in case Rui found herself in trouble. However, he could only watch in amazement at her fighting skills, Abigail's fears were totally unfounded as the fight lasted less than two minutes, Rui choking him to death in a Japanese figure four leg choke after putting him down with kicks to the head and body, he was no match at all. The time it took her didn't matter as there was no paying audience and no complaints to the customer service department. Easy work, she had thought, now I have the rest of the day and tomorrow to swim and sunbathe, what a job!

CHAPTER 95

Aside from the proving of the harvest system, Amanda had been credited with the earlier suggestion of a 'spy/espionage' scenario, by Pietro agreeing to the construction of the Forest trail leading to the purpose-built safe house, the Log Cabin. As lead researcher, she had reported that this was a popular request from the more discerning wealthy enquirers, imagining themselves as a James Bond type character. Up until now the scenario had been untested so when she received the perfect request, Amanda pushed it through the vetting procedures and directed the scenario arrangements personally. Pietro later described it as the most intriguing production to date with much praise received from the paying audience. Although their sole and ultimate objective would always remain the acquisition of 'SoD', this mini-production, or short spy film, captured the imagination and interest of his viewers, creating even more demand and hence, more dollars!

The crafted scenario featured Arusi playing the part of a black Femme fatale where she was sent to retrieve a formula from the victim who was 'holed up' in a 'safe house'.

The 'victim' was a white male in his mid-sixties and an absolute film buff of the 'femme fatale' genre. He knew every female actress to ever portray the seductive, charming but, extremely deadly character in the movies. His age, however, took him back to his first crush and that was the renowned actress Pam Grier and her role as *Foxy Brown* in a 1974 film. He believed this woman could get anything she wanted from the power of her sexuality and it led him to writing a script with an ambition to play it out. He had been widowed for many years, lived alone with no heirs but with more than enough money from his meticulously managed property portfolio to make his dream a reality.

Plaguing him for a long time, and with the stark realisation that, in this day and age 'nothing' was beyond the power of money, he had answered an ad and subsequently been put into contact with Amanda who, convincingly, assured him of the possibility of converting his personal fantasy into a reality. He would play the part of 'Richmond Bowler', an eminent government scientist who had developed a formula for a horrific chemical weapon the likes of which, had never been seen or imagined. He was being pursued by a vicious foreign power and the only physical existence of the formula was in his possession stored on a very complex and super encrypted flash drive, the code to which only resided in his head. The story began as he was travelling on a light aircraft en-route to a secluded airfield but with the knowledge that he had been compromised with an unwanted, welcoming committee already in waiting. The only person he could trust was a female agent who, he believed, was working for the same side and she had given him the exact time to bail out of the aircraft and rendezvous with her in a 'safe house' where he would find respite and safety.

Of course, she was ultimately a 'double agent' and would sadistically torture the information from him using her feminine charms by way of the classic slipping of a drug into his drink to subdue him.

He had sent his script to Amanda and she had discussed it with Arusi whom she thought would best fit the bill. Arusi loved it, she had always been a 'wannabe' actress, dressing up playing out a scripted character role, and this was right up her street.

CHAPTER 96

Everything was set, the victim was prepped even down to the role play beginning with him discarding and concealing a real parachute whilst checking around to make sure he hadn't been spotted. It was dark and the reality of the setting spurred him on deeper into the role as if it was really happening. He could smell the semi-sweet aroma of the naturally wooded clearing as it settled in for the night after a warm, humid day. He carried a small rucksack with his laptop and the flash drive. "Richmond, you have to focus on your objective," he said out loud and pretended to check a 'mock' location device apparently following a signal that would lead him to where his 'accomplice' was waiting.

Of course, his path to the cabin was assured, even dimly lit, they didn't want anything to happen to him well, not yet anyway, as Amanda and Mia watched his journey from the cameras in the office.

On reaching the cabin he again checked around before knocking with a 'rat a tat' rhythm on the wooden door.

The door creaked open slightly on its false, patina-look, rustic hinges.

He was taken aback, smitten involuntarily by the most exotic fragrance ever to dance with his senses, he literally sucked in more air through his nose, yearning further intoxication. This was the scent of a woman like he had never experienced before, and at such close proximity.

"Richmond! Richmond," a voice whispered loudly.

He came to his senses.

"Err yes, Miss Brown, Richmond," he stated.

"Quickly, inside," the voice of an angel, he thought, reverberating back at him.

He entered the cabin, heard the door locked shut behind him and turned around.

The room was warm, totally occupied with the same heavenly aroma he had experienced earlier and lit by a log fire and one small orange glowing table lamp.

His eyes adjusted to the setting and he savoured, for a fleeting second, the most jaw-dropping moment of his life. Arusi was dressed in a stunning light caramel coloured, ruffled, sleeveless evening dress finishing just below the knee with matching, conservatively heeled pumps. On her arms she wore a pair of elbow length matching gloves and in her left hand, held at chest height a crystal glass with a warming honey coloured shot of whiskey. Her hair was in a tight bun on top of her head and with her make-up subtly toned to match her outfit she truly looked the period part he had imagined.

"I'm glad that you made it safely," she cooed, "you are safe here, no one knows we are here, do you have all of your belongings?" she quizzed gesturing towards his rucksack.

"Yes," he replied, "everything is good," he added, nervously.

"Take off your coat and bag and relax for a while, I will pour you a drink," she suggested.

"Yes, I will, I could do with a drink."

Arusi went over to the drinks trolley, nonchalantly slipping a GHB (gamma hydroxybutyric acid) 'dating' drug into his drink and handing it to him.

"Cheers, this is to our partnership together," she toasted, raising her glass.

"Cheers!" he replied and, still in acting mode, playing out the next part where she drugged him, downed the whole glass.

He was wondering when to start faking his being drugged when he heard, "Are you ok, Richmond, you look a little dazed and confused."

He tried to look at her but seemed to have trouble focusing, he squinted his eyes, trying to clear the optical haze he was experiencing, to no avail and he became disoriented.

"What's happening to me?" he uttered worryingly. "I feel very…" his last words before slumping like a freshly punched insentient in a boxing match, from his seat on the edge of the sofa, onto the floor, he was out cold.

CHAPTER 97

As he came to. "What's happening? Where am I? I suddenly felt dizzy and don't remember why and, why are my hands and feet tied?" he stammered, gesturing, struggling to gain his senses and wrestling with the rope binding his wrists behind his back. He was sitting upright on the floor with his back leaning against the sofa.

"Mr Richmond Bowler, government scientist, you are back with us, now you need to tell me what I want to know," said Arusi, calmly but firmly.

She was seated on a chair she had pulled up in front of him, but, was this the same girl? She had removed her dress and released her hair from the bun, and it was draped over the front of her shoulders. She was wearing a one-piece, white Teddy and sat crossed legged, the shoe on her raised foot dangling provocatively out of its heel.

"Now tell me, I have the laptop and the flash drive there on the sofa behind you, all I need now is the password," she said to him.

He was disillusioned and shocked, surely this wasn't supposed to happen? He had been drugged for real and tied up while he was unconscious.

"No, this is a game, a fantasy script, it's not meant to be real, it's, it's gone too far!" he stammered.

"Not real?" she replied leaning forward. "A game? Oh, this is very real, and I need the password!"

"But I don't have one," he replied.

"That's what I thought you would say, of course I didn't expect to get it straight away and I like it like that," she purred, running her index finger down the bridge of his nose.

"What do you mean? I don't have anything to say, please untie me, I want this to stop now," he pleaded.

"Let me show you how this works," she replied.

Arusi moved to sit down behind him on the sofa draping her legs over his shoulders then, leaning forward to circle his neck with her lithe, silky brown arms, applying a perfect rear naked choke.

There was no warning or slow tightening so he could adjust to the situation, she just pulled back on the arm under his neck and gripped the forearm of the other and choked him out within a few seconds, releasing her grip when he was snoring involuntarily.

He began to regain consciousness with the slapping of his face by Arusi now sat on his knees and looking into his terrified eyes.

"As you can see, I am not playing with you, this is not a game, I believe we can get your disk unlocked anyway but, I love my work, now! The password!" she shouted slapping his face one more time.

"This is a mistake," he repeated groggily, as he returned to a more lucid state from the sleeper, dizzy and confused but, what could he do?

In his mind, he came to the conclusion that, if he played along some more and gave her a password, any password, it would end and be like a realistic fantasy realisation after all, he had paid a huge sum for this privilege.

"Ok, I give up," he stammered, "the Password is 'MondRich upper case M, upper case R and 100%."

"Better," she answered. "Let me try."

Arusi slowly stood up in front of him, his face level with the V of her crotch where her shapely, muscled thighs met. She moved over him and lay stretched out behind him on the sofa and pretended to enter the code on the keyboard of the laptop behind him.

"Seems I'm not getting through to you," she purred seductively, arching her leg so that her foot brushed his mouth tantalisingly.

For a moment he thought that, if he wasn't so terrified, he could enjoy what was happening but he wasn't, and he didn't.

Arusi stood back up and then sat down once more on top of him over his knees, facing him.

"I don't like violence," she said, running her finger down his face and looking him straight in the eyes. "But it seems the only way."

"What!" he cried. "Please don't, I don't know what you want from me," he begged.

CHAPTER 98

Arusi leaned back and slapped him hard across the face, his head snapping to the side with the force.

He yelled in pain but she lined up his face to a straight position and delivered another, then another, with blood now appearing at the corner of his mouth.

"Please stop!" he begged but she was just warming up as the flat of her hand turned into a fist and she began putting her full weight into each blow.

She lined up his swollen face for each blow, taking her time and ignoring his grunts and pleadings until he was unresponsive, and his chin rested on his chest, he was out cold. The cameras were still rolling and the audience always demanded severity, she lifted his head by his hair and delivered another blow to his unconscious form, again and again. She was clearly enjoying herself but, didn't want him dead yet, so she got up and drank some water before throwing the remains into his bloodied face. He shook and woke once more, trying to squint through his eyes closing from the swelling around them.

"Now!" she screamed holding his head up by his hair once more. "One more chance. Give me the fucking password!"

He was dazed and beyond any form of conversational ability, he just groaned in agony.

"So be it!" Arusi concluded. "I do not need you anymore, my organisation will break your secret code anyway."

She lay at the back of him once more, lifted his head and curled the back of her knee around his throat, locking it with the other one under her in a Japanese style, rear, figure four leg choke, recently taught to her by Rui.

She hardly needed to squeeze, the weight of her body and the constriction applied through the technique she skilfully applied was enough. He bucked around for a few seconds, blood gurgling from his mouth and was still.

Arusi maintained the Anaconda-like pressure on his neck and throat making sure he was dead.

She uncoiled her silky legs from around his throat and stood over him putting one heeled foot on the back of his slumped head.

"I just love my work," she announced as the lights faded to dark and the production was over, especially for Richmond Bowen.

Again, Mia supervised the collection of the special liquid from his undergarment and all had gone to plan.

Wisetzki had worked tirelessly supervising security and was satisfied there had been no breaches in all events thus far, he was, however, particularly looking forward to the next event which would feature, yes, Dominica.

CHAPTER 99

"So, let me get this clear," clarified Li, receiving an update from Bujang who had just returned from Bidong, "you noticed something which, didn't make sense, am I right?"

"Yes, sir," he replied, "I was instructed to take out the garbage, which is near to the incinerator, first thing this morning as we tidied up, cleaned and prepared to leave. We don't operate the furnace ourselves because it is very hi-tech, but I spotted a flashing light so went to look at the control panel. I saw an amber light indicating that it was still warm, so it must have been used the night before when I had all of the rubbish to be incinerated with me," he reported.

"So, you think the furnace was used to dispose of something other than the garbage the night before?" Li asked.

"Yes, sir, that is the only thing I can think of," Bujang replied.

"Thank you," he said, "these things are exactly what I want you to report, well done. Continue to be vigilant when you next go to Bidong, here is your reward, just continue your duties now

"Yes, sir; thank you, sir," he replied.

Back on Bidong, Abigail and Amanda sat down with a coffee to carry out their customary post CCTV check. This was standard procedure instigated by Wisetzki following any visitors to the Island and their subsequent departure and there was 72 hours' worth to get through.

However, this was very important as he was only one man and they relied on the tens of CCTV cameras operating in key areas to maintain the net of total security.

It was late afternoon and Wisetzki was preparing to take the seaplane back to Tengah, excited that when he returned, so would Dominica.

"Hi Wisetzki, this is Abigail," he heard from his comms unit. "Before you leave, please come and take a look at this footage from today."

The security chief headed over to the reception area and office where Abigail and Amanda were viewing the CCTV data and watched the screen.

"Umm, what is he doing by the furnace?" asked Wisetzki. "Interesting, that's Bujang, he has no business there, right?"

"Not in that exact area," replied Abigail, "he would take garbage to the area adjacent and leave it there for disposal but, no business at the actual furnace, Amanda operates it after every event and when everyone has left, apart from the special disposals which you take care of."

"Ok, thanks, and well spotted, keep the footage for now and do nothing else, I will talk with him next time I see him but don't see it as a serious threat, maybe just curiosity," he replied.

Wisetzki left with the stage crew, Amanda and Abigail went about their post event duties and then to prepare for the next event, unusually, only two weeks hence.

Li reported back to West who was in KL and he was very excited with what he was told.

"I knew it!" he stated as they talked on the phone. "There is something going on with these furnaces, that's why I went probing in their lab facility and here we have another incident, there is a connection, I'm sure of it!" he exclaimed.

"But what do we do?" asked Li.

"You must find out when Bujang is next going to the Island and I will come to Mersing where we will meet in advance," he said.

"That will be difficult because he only gets 24 hours' notice, although, I suspect that the Chef will know sooner than that," he added.

"You must get closer to the Chef and find out when they will next go, the more time we have to plan something, the better, see what you can find," instructed West.

"Ok, will do," replied Li and ended their call.

CHAPTER 100

Mia, together with Carol, had a zoom call with Pietro where they reported all 'good news', everything was going to plan, and the 'SoD' collected was way ahead of any production forecast projections.

Carol had found a way to extract the 'active' ingredient under microscopic conditions in such infinitesimally small quantities that each 'SoD' collection yielded vast amounts of what was required and meant that, the 'Octopussy plan' as named by Pietro, was more than sufficient for their needs.

"Fancy a tumble on the mats and then some?" quirked Mia, winking to Carol.

"Sure, just what I need," she replied, "it was hard work over at the factory and nothing to do in the evenings," she added, smiling.

"Ok, let's do it!" she concluded, and the two girls went off to prepare for the gym and the start of their 'girlie' evening.

Wouldn't mind getting between those two, thought Li as he watched them leave for the day, but he was going to eat in the Bistro and see what he could find out from the chef. He invited Victoria to join him and arranged to meet her there later in the evening, their relationship purely platonic.

He ate with Victoria and accepted her excuses to leave when she had finished her food, she wanted to read up on material relating to the project she was working on before the next day. Li was disappointed he hadn't been able to find out one shred of information regarding the project Mia and Carol were working on but hoped to pursue his suspicions in other ways, starting with Chef that evening.

"I've noticed it must be difficult for you to plan catering and staffing arrangements for your away team attending Bidong on occasions?" Li quizzed the Chef as they sat alone together, everyone else having left the Bistro.

"Ah you've noticed," he replied. "It's ok, I have a regular shipment of supplies going to Bidong for our permanent staff there and typically 10–14 days for any special requirements, like extra guests and things like that."

"I was involved with recruiting Bujang, so I like to think he is happy in his work, that's all," said Li.

"Of course, and so do I but, I am instructed to only tell him and Nina the day before, something to do with security!" replied Chef, sighing and rolling his eyes.

"You remember his Uncle is the Police commissioner in Mersing?" Li asked him.

"Yes, I do," replied Chef. "I like him, nice family man and Bujang has been very reliable so far."

"Can I ask a favour for his Uncle?" asked Li. "He is trying to arrange a special, 'Surprise' family gathering and wants to make sure Bujang will be able to attend, not wanting to arrange things when he was not available."

"I suppose it can't hurt this time," said the Chef, "after all it is only 10 days from tomorrow when we have to go over to Bidong and I know how close these families are, life is all about family right?"

"You've got it!" he replied. "So, 10 days tomorrow you all depart for Bidong?" he checked.

"Yes," said Chef, "please don't tell anyone I told you, Wisetzki might shoot me," he added laughing and mimicking a smoking gun with his fingers.

"Of course, not," said Li, "it's just a family thing, totally harmless," he finished.

They said good night, the Chef back to checking his kitchen for the next day and Li off to report straight back to West with welcoming information which, he was surprised, came very easily amid the apparent, extra layers of security Wisetzki had put into place.

CHAPTER 101

"So, Daan, we would like to welcome you today to this extraordinary parole board meeting," announced the Prison superintendent, "I do, however, have to make it clear that this meeting in no way constitutes or should be construed as consideration for enhanced earlier release, is that understood?"

"Absolutely, sir," he replied, humbly, "I am grateful for your communication and feel privileged and honoured to be afforded this meeting."

Daan was confident and very relaxed with a genuine demeanour and maturity as he sat facing the three-person board. He was very well groomed and probably the most physically trimmed and fit he had ever been in his life. He had been rewarded for his 'exemplary' behaviour and progress to the tune of, a non-scheduled meeting with the Prison Parole board and intended making every possible use of the opportunity.

"I've worked very hard and come to terms with my past heinous act, something which I will regret for the rest of my life, with a realisation of the effect this had and must still be having on my victim," he added, shaking his head.

"This is one of the reasons we meet today, partly based on your ongoing, official periodic, mental and physical evaluations and the attitude just demonstrated in your responses just now; a complete acceptance and repentance for your past actions is always a good sign of your attitude to our comprehensive rehabilitation program here," the superintendent continued.

"Sir, I've accepted my position and penance with a very vivid, realisation of the reasons for it and although I cannot turn the clock backwards I'm hoping I can seriously contribute only good to my society in the future," Daan replied.

"All areas considered, Daan," he continued, "as you are aware, your father is a very valued and respected businessman and upstanding member of the community making charitable contributions and offering start-up jobs for under-privileged citizens. In addition, he has made some financial donation to your victim and although this cannot be determined as 'compensation', it was accepted in the way it was offered. As you know, he also pledges and guarantees your employment, housing and behavioural monitoring should early release be sanctioned."

"Yes, sir; thank you, sir, I'll keep on working and continue to do the best I can whilst I'm here," he answered.

"I believe you will and have, I'm right in saying you continue to chair one of our inmate therapy 'free speech' sessions where fellow inmates can express their thoughts and talk about rehabilitation as you have embraced?" he asked.

"Yes, sir, I view my time and purpose here as a new beginning for me and like to share my positivity and motivation with others in similar situations," he replied.

"Ok, all is good, continue with your sterling work and we'll see what the future holds, thank you, Daan," the superintendent concluded.

"No, thank you, sir," he replied holding out his hand, which was taken with a firm handshake.

Daan returned to his now solitary cell, completely satisfied and pleased, lay on his back on the canopied bunk and looked up, smiling at his motivational card wedged into a crack which, read quite simply: 'Mia the fucking Bitch!'

CHAPTER 102

It appeared as though being wrestled into complete submission by a powerful woman was a very popular fantasy requested by submissive men and an easy one to stage for Abigail and her team.

From Dominica's recent performance there was, also, enough vetted viewers who couldn't subscribe last time, on a waiting list for another such event, eager to participate in a new one, hence, the shortened time period between events.

It was literally a carbon copy, so Abigail had everything in place as per the previous event and fully expected it to go ahead without a glitch. Another happy person was Wisetzki, who always received a list of every person attending the island for any event at any one time, when he saw that Dominica was the selected agent.

Alternative plans also in progress were those of Li and West, who had arranged to meet in Mersing the preceding weekend together with Bujang, both taking their main land leave together.

Li just made small talk with him during the crossing, wanting all relevant discussions to be heard by all, face to face. He did explain that this was not to do with his Uncle and reiterated that the financial arrangement was with himself and West and his Uncle would not be present today.

They met in the Lobby of West's Hotel and sat down together with drinks in a quiet, secluded booth area.

After introductions, pleasantries and praise for his work so far, West led the meeting.

"Tell us," he said, "exactly the steps, instructions and duties you are asked to do when you go to Bidong for the special catering events, be very precise and don't miss out, any details, ok?"

"Yes sir," Bujang replied and he continued, "I am told on the day before that the next day I will go to Bidong sometimes with Chef, but always Nina depends on the amount of visitors cooking requirements which I can handle if the numbers are few, it varies. So, we arrive in the morning and prepare everything for the following day's necessary meals, Nina puts out fruit and makes sure that the guest accommodation is properly prepared for a guest arrival."

"How many guest rooms are prepared?" asked Li.

"Only ever one actual guest room, but there is normally one other lady, not the same one every time, plus sometimes there are others in addition to Miss Abigail, Miss Amanda and Mr Wisetzki," he informed them.

"How many 'others'?" asked West.

"Sometimes it's just one, but other times there are two, once even three, oh and Miss Mia is mostly also there but we never really see them at all, we are kept to our duties and Nina has never seen an actual guest, we are just told what to do by Chef and we do it."

"Who exactly is this 'other' lady, or ladies?" asked West

"I'm not sure, but Miss Amanda told me once to get one of them some juice after she had been jogging and said she was like doing some company training there," he replied.

"And how long do you stay there, typically?" asked Li

"We're typically there for three nights leaving on the fourth day, but again it varies," he answered.

"And you travel back with everyone who was a visitor?" he added.

"No, sir," replied Bujang, "only people from Tengah use the boat, everyone else uses the aeroplane which lands on the water, I've only ever seen it leave, never arrive."

"That's interesting," stated West "so, who arrives and who leaves on the airplane, you have no idea?"

"That's right, sir, we do our job, what we are told to do, and then leave," said Bujang.

"What about the security?"

"That would be Mr Wisetzki," he replied, "he always tells us what we must and must not do and the areas where we can and cannot go and we are not allowed out of our rooms when our kitchen work has been done until the next day."

"So, the last time, when you said that the furnace was still warm, when you took out the trash, that was just something odd you noticed, correct?" asked Li.

"Yes, sir, I am authorised to take out the trash but only to deposit it in a certain area and not touch the furnace, it's very complicated you see and I wouldn't want to mess things up, I like this job," he replied.

"Yes, that's fine," said West. "You are doing a good job and we just want you to carry on and do what you have been doing, reporting back to us anything which you feel might be odd, ok?"

"Yes, sir, I will do and thank you, sir, I can go and see my family now in town?" Bujang responded.

"Yes, of course," replied West, "but, you tell no one of our arrangements, ok?" he checked. "Including your Uncle."

"Yes, sir of course, I understand," he replied and with that, left the pair of them in the Hotel Lobby.

"So, if I have this right, 'The others' are already on the Island when Bujang arrives in the morning and 'The guest' or VIP of which, there is only one, arrives late that evening and normally stays there at least one night before leaving," said West.

"I believe that is correct," said Li, "we have no clue as to the details of these 'guests' just that, there seems to be a lot of work and other visitors for just one person at a time. I wonder if it could be drug related and if these are high ranking members of some kind of Cartel?"

"I agree," said West, "they are important, whoever they are, and I intend to find out," he finished with a determined look.

"We have a few days to plan," said Li.

"Yes," he replied, "but I intend to be on the Island the day before Bujang arrives, I have an acquaintance, a marine biologist, who legitimately operates a dive boat and although he's not allowed to moor on the Island itself, he will be able to get me there and be around when I need to leave. I will take my own small tender and can silently row over to the island from his boat."

"You'll have to be very careful and use the darkness as your shield," said Li, "but it sounds feasible. You can take some supplies and equipment with you and camp there until everyone comes and goes and from what Bujang has mentioned, he thinks that only the main areas are CCTV monitored, so there's many places to stay hidden overlooking everything."

"That's the plan, I don't intend getting caught, I'm going to observe what I can, from a distance this time, note the comings and goings, reconnaissance etc. Now, let's have some lunch," he quipped, "I'm starving, meeting over."

West made arrangements with his dive friend, but was told that if he was caught on the Island, he would deny all knowledge and if he did not return at the time and place they would arrange he would not wait or search for him.

West was more than happy with this; such was his obsession to find out more of what had happened to his friend Price and he was certain something more than hospitality was taking place on the island of Bidong.

CHAPTER 103

West boarded the adequately proportioned and capable dive boat, having below deck accommodation more like a cruiser really, with his 'friend' in the early morning. They arrived off Bidong by midday and the boat was anchored, his accomplice Ray wanting to get a dive in for that day. Ray was an Australian national, qualified as a marine biologist. But this was to satisfy his own passion for the sea-life rather than an official scientific study, which had long been performed off the island resulting in over 4,700 species of fish to try and photograph and catalogue for himself. He was in his early thirties, single, tall, athletic build, sun-tinged skin, a mop of jet-black wavy hair and a smile fit for dentistry advertising.

He made money from his underwater photography from within the tourist industry but, being an only child, was mainly funded by his adequately wealthy parents, providing him with the beach life he had always wanted.

He had gained the necessary licenses and permits for diving off the reef of the Island and wasn't going to get into any trouble that would result in these being taken from him. However, it was West who had introduced him to government fishery officials in gaining these permits, which money alone couldn't buy, so he felt he had a debt to satisfy. That said, he was aware of West's sordid activities back when he chartered boats for 'leisure' cruises. This was how they had met in the first place, he didn't approve, would never support, and for that reason was less of a friend for him than the other way around.

The sea was still, like a millpond, with virtually no swell, the weather was good with clear skies and a no moon night in waiting.

West remained below deck, keeping out of sight and taking the opportunity to get some sleep ready for his 'mission' to the Island. He was still fit and more than capable of paddling his small boat over to the Island, setting up a small, discreet camp and observing.

Their boat was moored offshore to a small sandy cove inlet, just around a small headland away from the jetty leading to the main buildings, and he was awoken by the sound of a propeller aircraft at low level.

He jumped up and grabbed his binoculars, still staying hidden on the steps to the deck, he watched as a seaplane appeared very low above the water and disappeared behind the headland, landing on the calm sea. The first external visitors had arrived by air and were duly noted by West. Ray was on deck having completed his dive and they agreed to have a meal and prepare for West's departure in the small tender towed behind the boat as sunset was scheduled at 19:00 hrs.

CHAPTER 104

Wisetzki welcomed and checked in the arriving party consisting of two stagehands, an IT specialist, Mia, and of course, almost melting on the spot, Dominica who was dressed in skin-tight leggings hugging her magnificent ass, down her powerful thighs to the shapely calves and sneakers. A tight-fitting T under a light fleece jacket, with her heavy breasts straining the material, completed her outfit and she rewarded Wisetzki with her very disarming smile and 'knowing' look.

"Ok," he announced, "everyone is familiar with our set up, there is food laid out for you, but, I know you've travelled so I would assume early nights all round, Amanda and Abigail will brief you at reception, can I be of any further help right now?"

Everyone acknowledged him in acceptance except for Dominica who said, "I'm a little restless, the travel gets me that way, is it ok if I get some air later, maybe a walk along the path to the Log Cabin and back, it won't interfere with your security?"

"Err no that's fine," stuttered Wisetzki, "as long as I am made aware, much of that pathway is lit and I will gladly be on hand to escort you," he said, recovering his tone of authority.

"Thanks," she replied, "I appreciate it, I feel so worked up, need to expel some frustration, around 7pm?" she added, giving him a definite command.

"Ok," Wisetzki concluded, "everyone is sorted, let's get you all checked in and made comfortable, if you wouldn't mind leading the way please, Mia?"

"Of course, this way," she replied but hadn't missed the exchange between Dominica and Wisetzki at all.

CHAPTER 105

West was ready as the sun disappeared below the horizon and darkness fell, clad in a tight-fitting dry suit. The tender was duly loaded with a small one man ridge tent, warm clothing for the night time, food supplies, small gas cooking burner, some fresh water enough for the three-night vigil he had prepared for and a short wave radio to connect him with Ray back on the dive boat.

He slipped into the rubber, air inflated tender and made the short journey to shore under darkness heading for the small white lit beacon placed there earlier in the day by Ray, his only, extra, agreed contribution to the incursion.

He had ferried the waterproof, battery operated small lamp under water to the shore where had placed it in the centre of the beach. It would be invisible during the day due to the sunlight but, would become clearly visible at darkness as the only light on the shore at sea level.

He pulled the boat up and onto the small sandy beach, unloaded the large military style backpack containing everything, and then concealed the dinghy out of sight behind a convenient rock with some palm leaves.

He then set off upwards, skirting his way in a curved path and using a specialist torch with narrow divergence to light the way. He utilised the same procedure he had learned, stalking prey whilst hunting, treating the lit buildings as his quarry to evade discovery. The terrain was rough but manageable and he was shod with military style boots easily navigating the rough ground between clumps of forest. As he progressed further up the incline, he began making his way back towards the cluster of buildings which were now way below his position. He was confident his navigation technique had succeeded in avoiding exposure and found a perfect spot for camp. It was a small clearing right above the lights of the buildings below him with a good view yet far enough away, it was working out just as planned. He made camp, feeling pleased with himself, believing his efforts would reward him with at least, some kind, of final closure for that of his missing friend and maybe some retribution if his hunch was founded.

CHAPTER 106

Securing all risks from the arrivals first, Wisetzki proceeded to make his way to the Log Cabin at the end of the man-made trail and went inside. It was so much more than just a 'shack', it was a comfortable, traditional log cabin of pine construction with electricity, small kitchenette and bathroom and a wood burner for authenticity. It was furnished again with pine constructed armchairs and an abundance of animal furs making it resemble an Alaskan style hunters lodge. He may have been wrong, but the look he had gotten from Dominica made him decide to light the wood burner and make the place receptable and cosy, for what, he would have to wait and see.

He made his way back to the reception area and it was around 7pm when he saw her, letting Abigail know she was going to take a walk along the trail for a couple of hours to chill out from the travel.

"Here's Wisetzki now," announced Abigail, "Tom, Dominica is just heading out for some 'me' time, just letting you know someone is out and about until curfew at the scheduled 21:00."

"Sure," he replied. "I am around if anyone needs me."

"I'm going to head to the cabin," she said, "if it's not locked I might just chill there for a while, I love the smell of the Pine, perhaps you could check on me a little later?" she added with a look that was more of an instruction than a request.

"Err, yes, of course," he replied, "whatever you say, and yes the cabin is open, I tended to it earlier and lit a fire for you," he added almost buckling at the knees, his heart was racing, this woman! he thought.

Dominica set off down the trail and Wisetzki went to Abigail's control desk to make sure he could pick her up on the CCTV, not forgetting to disable the cameras in the Cabin itself.

"Just so that you know, Abigail, I'm running some diagnostics on the lodge's internal cameras so they are offline for now, but I will make my way, personally, down there to

250

make sure Dominica is all right and taken care of," he said to her.

"Ok," she replied, I bet you will, she thought, "we'll confirm everyone is secure at 21:00 hrs, see you later."

Wisetzki set off but, further above, West couldn't make anyone out as he scanned below through his binoculars. He could see a 'snake-like' trail of lights in the trees leading to the rooftop of a small lodge type building with wood smoke gently leaking from a chimney but that was all.

Wisetzki reached the steps and door to the log cabin, he could barely breathe, these rare feelings had returned to him, he wouldn't have been in this state about to infiltrate an armed gang stronghold, but, this woman had something over him, she knew it and so did he.

"It's me, Tom," he announced, pushing the door open slightly.

He could see the orange glow of a flame from the open wood burner, a definite candle lit glow from within and although not cold outside a contrasting homely warmth.

"Come," Dominica replied.

He went inside, instinctively latching the door with the heavy wooden stay and adjusting to the light within the lounge area of the cabin but could not readily concede if he was hallucinating or, not.

Dominica was sat on her haunches, on a beautiful white mountain goat hide, hands on hips and completely naked except for a colourful band of traditional African waist beads, a sign of femininity and sensuality. Her hair was braided, tight on top with a long ponytail at the back, but, strung over her shoulder. Her brown lightly oiled skin glowed with the light from the scented candles she had prepared, and her heavy breasts hung, unsupported, her large nipples protruding outwards.

He was transfixed as he stared at this beautiful goddess, could not find any words, but it was Dominica who broke the silence.

"Time for worship," she whispered. "You will take off all of your clothes and then crawl over to me on your hands and knees, is that clear?"

"Yes," he stuttered back.

"Yes, Mistress!" she corrected him, "say it!"

He was done, she could have ordered him to hang himself and he would, he was totally under her feminine spell. "Yes, Mistress," he repeated.

He stripped naked revealing his very athletic body, battle scars and, almost perfect, washboard belly.

His circumcised cock, although not huge in length but with a very commendable girth, hung for now but was already twitching with that tingling feeling in the heavy balls hanging below.

"Crawl to me now!" Dominica commanded as he got down on his hands and knees.

He crawled across the partially rugged floor over to where she was seated on the goatskin.

She knelt upwards to face him and ordered him to kneel up also.

Then, looking straight into his bewildered eyes, she reached out with her perfectly manicured fingers and began rolling his already erect nipples between her fingers.

He sighed with pleasure as she began pinching, mildly at first, but then with more pressure.

"I am here to be worshipped, I am your supreme being and that is the way of things, is that understood?" she asked.

"Yes Mistress," he choked.

"First my breasts and you will follow my commands, do not deviate from them," she added.

CHAPTER 107

Dominica knelt upright, hands on hips, as Wisetzki cupped her heavy breasts in his large hands caressing the soft, oiled fleshy mounds working his way to her huge erect nipples jutting out like mini rockets.

She closed her eyes as he leaned forward and began rolling his tongue around her dark areolae making his way to her protruding nipples flicking his tongue over one then the other.

She tensed slightly as he took the first nipple right into his wet, warm mouth, gently sucking and working his tongue in circles over it. Her nipples were hard from his increased attentions and she moaned slightly in approval at his dedicated, gentle play, caressing her own womanly hips with her hands.

"Enough!" she suddenly said abruptly and moved into an all fours position on hands and knees thrusting her sumptuous ass upwards and looking forward eyes closed.

"My lower back," she said, "your tongue!"

He positioned himself, moved her beads towards her upper torso and began dragging his wet tongue down her spine to the start of her sumptuous ass and hips. Her skin was slightly wet but he gladly drew the moistness into his mouth, desperate to taste her heavenly black body. His cock was hard, very hard, and it protruded out horizontally from his own body, wet with small beads of precum.

Dominica lowered herself at the front onto her elbows, parted her thighs slightly and bent her hips downwards forcing her huge ass into the air in front of his face.

"Tongue my ass!" she ordered him, "part my cheeks and get your tongue deep inside my ass."

He didn't hesitate for a second, such was the urge to taste as much of this woman as he could, and he buried his tongue deep inside her puckered anus. Dominica groaned as his tongue began fucking her ass, in and out, as he held her cheeks spread so that he could delve as deep as possible. Her aromas were musky and violating, intensely erotically, his senses, it was as though he had tasted something he just couldn't get enough of.

He was very proficient, his military dive training meant he could hold his breath for extended periods which added to the continuity of his ass tonguing technique.

Once more Dominica ordered him to stop and she lay down on her back, knees drawn up resting her head on a soft Rabbit skin cushion.

"Now it's pussy worship time," she cooed, "get to it."

He lay down in some difficulty, due to his massive, throbbing erection, but managed to position himself, his face between her powerful thighs.

Hands behind her head and eyes closed she felt his tongue begin gently and tentatively flicking over her swollen labia. He reached under her legs and gripped her hips for support, gently pulling her towards his willing mouth.

The first taste of her sex burst onto his tongue it was like honey and he was the 'Honey Badger'.

It parted her labia and he moved upwards seeking out her swollen love bud, isolating it, and began administering dedicated treatment. He rolled her clit around with his tongue and then began sucking it into his mouth, still applying the rolling movement with his wet oral appendage.

Then, as he felt more juices on his chin, he withdrew his tongue to watch the white creamy liquid oozing from her lips. He lapped at them like a dehydrated dog, rabid up and down, from the bottom of her sex up to the swollen clitoris begging for more attention.

The juices licked and swallowed, he returned his attentions once more to her clitoris, sucking it into his mouth like a mini penis.

Dominica began to moan, clutching the goatskin rug between her fingers, he had the rhythm and he stuck to his task unrelenting until she tensed violently thrusting her pussy hard against his sucking mouth and tongue and orgasmed in his face.

He held on to her clit, sucked into his mouth, until the spasms subsided and she relaxed herself sighing with sheer orgasmic release.

He lay, his head resting on her mound for a few minutes until she said, "On your back!"

He lay down on his back on the hard wooden floor, his cock jutting upwards and throbbing, but he didn't care, he spread his hands out to the side in complete submission as she stood over him feet either side of his head, facing his feet.

She slowly lowered herself down, parting the cheeks of her wet ass over his nose, her pussy covering his mouth settling down fully on his prone face.

A muffled sigh from him as her juices sealed his mouth and nose. Was this what she did? he wondered. He knew he couldn't push her off if he wanted and he certainly didn't want that as he felt her hand firmly grasp the base of his erect penis.

He couldn't breathe but, he didn't care as she slowly began wanking him, her oily fingers gripping his shaft up and down, up and down, his balls were reaching boiling point as he began pushing at her mountainous hips unable to budge her one inch.

"Cum for me!" she ordered him. "Cum for me now!"

He was running out of breath, feeling weak, but his orgasm wasn't, her expert wanking was far too much for him in this state and it wasn't long before he shot a huge load of white sperm high into the air as he bucked beneath her.

"Good boy," she cooed, "someday I will allow you to fuck my pussy, but, not today." And she lifted herself from his panting face, covered in her white creamy love juices.

He lay exhausted and trying to reflect on what had just happened and the effect this woman had over his very being, one thing was for sure, he was hooked.

She told him to clean up and get dressed then escort her back to the accommodation area that she had to prepare for a performance the day after tomorrow.

He escorted Dominica as instructed and there were no words, just an understanding for now, and then returned to secure the cabin.

CHAPTER 108

West decided to call it a night, he was determined to see as much as possible the following day where he expected the boat from Tengah with Bujang on board and hopefully the arrival of the guest or guests later in the day.

He awoke early having had a comfortable night out camping and prepared himself a breakfast of tinned soup cooked on the small burner and served in his multi-purpose billycan, it was 8am and he prepared his look out point, focusing on the jetty area.

Sure enough, as expected, it wasn't too long before he spotted the small cabin cruiser arriving from Tengah and berthing alongside the small jetty. From his position and high-powered, military grade, binoculars he could identify the visitors as Chef, Bujang, Nina and his recent adversary, Sparkplug, helping with the many boxes of supplies. They were greeted by Wisetzki and he noted everything he was able to see with time and number of arrivals etc.

Chef, Sparkplug and Bujang made several return visits to retrieve all the supplies and, on completion, Sparkplug boarded the boat with the driver, and they left for Tengah. Events were as Bujang had reported back and he now had to wait for the arrival of the seaplane, hopefully providing some answers as to who and what any guests would be visiting the island for.

In the meantime, Mia and Dominica were supervising the setup of the wrestling arena as used before and setting the scene for the event the day after tomorrow.

Wisetzki was very occupied, checking and rechecking cameras and keeping an eye on everyone. He took no chances when it came to security but, he had to admit, Dominica was his weakness and he was grateful she wasn't around, instead she was going over some of the requested script with Mia for her upcoming performance.

The weather was mild and comfortable for the time of year with clear skies, West had checked in with Ray who had just finished his dive for the day and everything was going to plan, it was around 4pm when he was alerted to the unmistakeable humming of the seaplane engine.

He picked up the arriving plane, now skimming over the calm waters and landing very comfortably on the calm water. There was a distinctive pick up in the engine buzzing as it manoeuvred the craft into a securing position at the jetty.

Steadying himself with his binoculars he focused on the area of the jetty where he noticed three people waiting for the plane to be secured and doors opened, two women and a man. The man he recognised as Wisetzki and one of the women, Mia, but the other he hadn't seen before: being Abigail. This he noted, as this third person hadn't arrived in the past two days, so she must reside permanently on the Island, he was slowly putting the picture together.

The door of the plane was open but his full view of the alighting, male, passenger was obscured by the reception party with Abigail welcoming him with a handshake. She must be in charge, he thought to himself. He was able to make out that the guest was a male, quite tall, and wearing a beige linen suit with a matching Panama hat but that was about all he could manage, however, he was able to note that the plane was only carrying one person and with luggage enough maybe, for two to three nights at the most.

As the group left the Jetty area and headed towards the reception area, he lost sight of them but his gathering of information was pleasing, and he was satisfied with the day's work.

The visiting guest had specifically requested a day of relaxation which he paid the extra for, wanting his fantasy session the day after, so he was shown to his guest lodge and would spend the following day relaxing by his personal splash pool and taking the hospitality offered.

This meant slightly more work for Wisetzki whose objective was to prevent any interaction with unsecured staff such as Chef, Nina and Bujang.

CHAPTER 109

The following day, West had an absolute, uneventful watch with nothing to note or record. He had been tempted to move closer to the buildings for better reconnaissance but he decided to stick rigidly to his plan of 'hide and observe' on this visit to the island, his main objective being avoiding detection.

Suiting the paying audience time differential, the event on Bidong was scheduled for 6pm, being seven hours ahead of Europe and the majority of the discerning viewers. This was good for Wisetzki as it was within the hours of darkness; Abigail and Amanda were manning all CCTV and he was 'roaming' from area to area ensuring tight security. He did, however, coincidentally find himself in a good viewing position to watch Dominica in the main event. She looked magnificent, her white costume and boots once more contrasting with her flawless black skin. She was always on top, totally dominant, dragging the victim screaming around the ring. She liked to see blood and his nose was already broken and gushing from the blows inflicted by her elbows. In his total defeated state, she began playing with him like a cat plays with a mouse, allowing him to crawl towards the ropes before dragging him back to the centre of the ring for more punishment, hearing him begging for mercy from each hold she put him into. He was lying face down on the canvas totally exhausted and trying to breathe through his bloodied nose and mouth. Dominica strutted around the ring, hands on hips, forcing her heavy breasts outwards in a display of dominance. Then she sat down in front of his face and lifted his head from the canvas by the hair.

He managed to open his eyes and stare pleadingly into hers. She opened her huge thighs and dropped his head between them, his neck tight into her crotch and crossing her ankles. Gurgling sounds came from her crotch as she tightened her grip on his trapped neck and blood oozed from his mouth. What energy he had left was diverted to his legs as they began thrashing around and his hands went weakly to the huge thighs constricting him but, it was futile, he couldn't have broken this grip with all of his strength never mind in this state. From trying to prise them apart to pushing ineffectually his clawing, desperate hands fell away limp, his legs just twitched, and he convulsed involuntarily as she choked the life out of him, he was done. Wisetzki was transfixed, she was so beautiful yet so deadly, but he still felt the uncontrollable stirring in his own groin area.

CHAPTER 110

The 'clean up' was initiated immediately with military style precision, Mia first retrieving the precious liquid from the choked victim.

West was aware something different was going on from his vantage point from the amount of buildings with lights on compared to the night before but, exactly what, he couldn't determine. He made notes of timings for lights coming on and going off and a point of note was the illuminating of a small building away from the main cluster of buildings and, from his discussion with Bujang, he thought it could be the waste disposal area and incinerator which he found very interesting.

All but, permanently, night lit areas were extinguished by 10pm so West prepared for his final night in hiding, having confirmed he would rendezvous with Ray at sundown the following day.

He woke early the next day as he didn't want to miss the evacuation from the Island of its visitors. The first transport to arrive was the boat from Tengah with its returning passengers, Chef, Bujang and Nina. He watched as, again, Sparkplug was on hand to help with the empty catering cases and with all on board he watched the cruiser leave for Tengah.

Around an hour later he heard the seaplane approach and berth at the jetty.

He then counted five people go on board the seaplane but he was angry and disappointed with his plan, because, he had not been in position to count the number of arrivals when he viewed the plane arriving from Ray's dive boat. He couldn't identify whether the 'guest' who had arrived alone had now joined this group leaving the island, although, there was no one dressed smartly as before. He did, however, conclude that if the guest was important enough to arrive alone, then, he would be leaving alone and who and for what purpose were this unidentified group now leaving Bidong? He had missing pieces from his jigsaw but had the VIP left the island, was he still there or had something happened to him?

These questions went around in his head but, one thing he was certain of, there was something 'untoward' going on at this island location and he was convinced it was linked to the disappearance of his friend. West was already planning his next visit as he packed away his things ready for descending back to his inflatable at nightfall to rendezvous with the dive boat.

All visitors departed and accounted for, Wisetzki met with Abigail to check any anomalies recorded by the CCTV footage to close out the security report for the event.

"The seaplane pilot reported a small cabin cruiser moored just around the headland when he turned for his course heading this morning, I checked it out from the headland and it is a boat going by the name of 'Ozzy-Ray'," does it check out?" he asked Abigail.

"Yes it's registered to a 'Ray Jones', he's a local marine biologist cum photographer and he has permits to dive on the reef but is not allowed to visit the Island itself, he comes fairly regularly and stays maybe two to three nights at a time is it a problem?" she replied.

"Ok thanks" replied Wisetzki. "I'm not happy it's around when we have an event on the Island but I guess we'd be exposing ourselves to scrutiny if we tried to ban him at certain times, so no, for now, leave it but I'll investigate more if it is around at our next, upcoming, event."

CHAPTER 111

Despite being over subscribed for the amount of 'SoD' required for the new skin cream, Pietro was having 100% fertility rates in his 'older' clients at the clinic. He was charging premium rates, so he encouraged Abigail to stage regular events to provide sufficient quantities for infertility applications. The clinics were rated on success data with attention and emphasis on the efficacy of the treatment in older, less fertile, clients. The newly found fertility wonder he had gained was raising the clinic to unrecorded success rates and wealthy couples were flocking, desperate for children of their own. What a revelation Mia's discovery was turning out to be, he mused.

On her return to Tengah, Carol had informed Mia that she had arranged a zoom meeting with the marketing heads regarding the fast approaching exhibition and the launch of their product.

Carol had already briefed her that, product wise, everything was ready to proceed with a limited launch.

She had refined the ingredients, particularly the quantities of 'SoD' required for each small jar pack size, to such a degree that they already had enough of the 'magic' ingredient to cope with any forecasted demand for the product. She had balanced the effectiveness of the cream with the economies of scale of the user and very cleverly come up with two versions. The first labelled 'Seeds of Life Repair' and the second 'Seeds of Life Maintain'. Each of the versions came with user instructions but, basically, customers purchased the 'Repair' version which would, over a two-week period using two jars, completely rejuvenate scar and wrinkle tissue. Then, they would use on an ongoing basis, the 'Maintain' version which, of course, contained no SoD ingredient, just a basic moisturiser. The rationale behind this was that people would be so amazed at the effectiveness and results of the 'Repair' version that they would carry out any maintenance regime suggested, for fear of reversing what they had done. Carol had overseen the initial production with only one person, the long serving plant manager, responsible for the 'adding' of the magic ingredient to any batch production and kept in a very secure, refrigerated unit. She always smiled when she thought of this, likening it to the 'secret' ingredient known to only a handful of people which went into the recipe for Coca-Cola.

Mia and Carol attended the online marketing call and it was the most positive and exciting launch in the history of any division within Pietro's group of companies.

They had arranged to take the largest, centre floor, space in the whole exhibition arena and the marketing media covered both electronic and physical with thousands of e-mails and DMs sent from the huge database of subscribers. The visual campaign featured a single white dove sometimes depicted in the Moses story but, this time, carrying a small seed in its beak, signifying a life after darkness or disaster. The theme and branding carried across all the media providing a consistent message and Mia was very pleased with the outcome.

CHAPTER 112

So, everything was in place and the only thing left to do was to arrange the physical manning of the exhibition stand. Customary in most organisations, representatives were often selected from its employees as a reward and motivation towards the company they worked for and Mia decided to choose some of the Lab staff. 'Cosmoprof' typically attracted more than 40,000 visitors from over 129 countries and ran over a five-day period. This meant that she could devise a 'shift' programme where staff could attend on a two-day basis with a one-night stay, all she had to do was arrange the people and their attendance timings.

However, she had a personal issue with one attendee, and that was Li, but she couldn't be seen to isolate him out of the event when his close colleagues would be included.

Mia and Carol chose the staff and arranged to give the marketing team responsible for any press or non-public visitors the necessary product training and awareness to be able to answer the questions of would-be visitors to the stand in the form of a one-day presentation seminar.

At the seminar, Carol presented the new product together with its features and the most astounding benefit of anything she had ever worked on. She went through the timeline from development to Lab testing, to physical testing and the unfounded results to its launch programme.

Everyone knew that something special was happening with Carol and Mia working strictly together and on one project; no one more so than Li who listened to every single word of the presentation.

As expected, when the presentation reached the Q&A section it was Li Jie who spoke first.

"First of all, congratulations on what appears to be some kind of 'Miracle' cream, the potential is phenomenal, I cannot even begin to guess, but, how does it work, what is in the recipe which, can give these kind of results? Nothing I know or have heard of can do this," he said as everyone in the room waited excitedly for the answer.

"I will take this one, Carol," Mia stepped in quickly. "We have discovered a new ingredient which is naturally produced and in force with nature which, with tireless work from our colleague Carol, we have refined to be incorporated into one of our existing, basic moisturising products."

"But how does it work and what is it?" asked Li again.

"I will answer in two parts," Mia responded, "the first is that the cream works in unison with the body's own regeneration of new skin but has the uniqueness to actually accelerate and rejuvenate damaged, or age-onset deterioration, of skin; In the second part, and I think you should know better than to ask, the 'what is it' part remains a proprietary secret and will never be made public or, to any member of staff other than myself and Carol, does that answer your question, Mr Li?" she concluded with a definite challenge in her voice.

"Err, oh, yes," he replied. "I'm just so excited, of course a company would never reveal a breakthrough like this to fall into the hands of any competitors, I understand, thank you for answering my questions."

Li dealt with, and silenced for the time being, Carol handled the rest of the audience questions mainly around application regimes and what it could and couldn't be used for.

Everything was set, attendance schedules and accommodation/travel arrangements made, everyone was excited to be part of the new product launch, proud to be part of it. All except Li, of course, who wanted more, and he was angry at being put down again by Mia in front of everyone, he was beginning to like her less and less by the day.

That evening Li went through his notes and had an update from West on his successful first visit to Bidong Island, he was planning to return there as soon as possible and asked Li for the heads up, when Chef would next be going there. Li knew that there was still much secrecy and continued increased security in the Lab where Carol spent 100% of her time, and from this deduced that whatever the secret related to this new product was, it continued to be manufactured there. He repeatedly stared at the three letters in his notes and was convinced 'SoD' held the answer; imagine if he could get hold of it and sell it to a competitor? The potential for this cream was mind-blowing and a competitor would stop at nothing with no payment being too great to secure it, but how could he get hold of it? He wasn't able to gain access to the actual Lab, but he knew that manufacturing of the cream was in the Singapore plant, so there had to be a time when the ingredient was transferred from Tengah to the manufacturing facility. He decided that could be his window of opportunity right there.

Exhibition arrangements were well advanced and planned to military precision with developed editorials issued to all the major publications in the cosmetics industry. Already, requests for interviews were flooding in, the product was already being talked about and its launch much anticipated and with high expectations.

This was pleasing for Mia as it would be the pinnacle of her recent months and months of hard work culminating at the world renowned and famous cosmetics industry flagship trade event.

She had one more diary fixture to complete before then, and that was a Bidong Island event, the last one before the exhibition.

CHAPTER 113

The events on Bidong were working like clockwork with Abigail and Amanda doing most of the organising but Mia still felt the need to be there and be the one collecting the 'SoD' from the killed victim. This time the paying client had requested a 'two' girl scenario so Mia decided to bring all three of her agents with the aim of a catch up and debrief with an upcoming, short term break in the events schedule due to the product launch. She had also arranged for a meeting with Wisetzki for a brief of the plan to utilise them as extra security for the exhibition, blending in as visitors for the set up and duration. It was going to be a non-screened event so it was much simpler to arrange and there were less visitors to deal with. The client had a fetish for black girls, in a dungeon type scenario, so Dominica and Arusi would deal with him and the set up would be minimal, he would arrive in the evening and the scenario carried out the following day.

Li had been contemplating his theory of how, whatever the secret ingredient was, it was refined in the Lab on Tengah and somehow transferred to the Singapore manufacturing facility. He had also noticed that Carol was extraordinarily busy following the Chef's return from Bidong Island duties; could it be that, whatever this 'magic' ingredient raw material, it was obtained from the Island itself or brought there by the arriving VIP guests?

Whichever, he deduced that Bidong Island was involved somewhere in this jigsaw and he had made a point of referencing this scenario with West, who was planning his next incursion to the Island. Li had already sweet talked the Chef into a heads up of the next planned trip so West was well informed. The pair concluded that, something was obtained from the Island during these 'VIP' events, that it was transported to Tengah, refined and processed and, subsequently, further transported to Singapore. Logistical journeys created opportunities for interception and a lasting thought from West was that he had no proof the visitor he witnessed arriving on the Island ever left, fuelling his suspicion of what might have happened to his friend.

He was all set to revisit Bidong, transport was arranged with Ray and scheduled to arrive the night following Chef's arrival earlier in the day. Chef had informed him that the visit on this occasion would be three nights and he was more determined than ever to find out more of what was happening there.

At the same time, Abigail had made all other necessary arrangements for the arrival of a visitor. Also arriving the day before were, Mia, Rui, Arusi and Dominica, with someone's groin area again, fluttering regarding the latter.

CHAPTER 114

West arrived just offshore from the cove around mid-day and, whilst Ray dived on the reef, kept out of sight awaiting darkness.

At nightfall he retraced his previous journey successfully and made his way to the camp site area he had used before and got settled for the night. He checked down below and the only lights he could see were coming from the main buildings, so he climbed into his sleeping-bag ready for the next day.

He woke early and made some tea with biscuits from his pack, it was a beautiful sunny day with clear skies and warming up very nicely.

He was alerted by the familiar sound of the Seaplane approaching and took up his position with a clear vista of the jetty area where the plane would settle on its skis.

With his high-powered binoculars he could make out people but without much definition, however, this time there was only one passenger alighting from the craft, again, a smartly dressed man with a small suitcase and briefcase. He was met by Wisetzki and Abigail who took him to the reception buildings and the plane left.

He knew that there would not be much to see now but he stayed alert and vigilant, just like his potential adversary, Tom Wisetzki.

"I've noticed that the dive boat is back and moored just offshore again, Abigail," Wisetzki said to her.

"Oh," she said. "I didn't know but, then again, that's your job," she fired at him smiling.

"Of course, fully accepted," he replied, giving her the thumbs up. "I have much to do securing our guest and locking down for tonight but tomorrow I will take a closer look, I don't like its presence coinciding with us receiving a visitor."

"Yes, I agree, thanks, Tom," she replied. "I will get Amanda to remain extra vigilant on the cameras from now."

"Ok, work to do," he said and left her office.

The following day he checked on the position of the dive boat and it was still the same, he even saw a diver getting back on board, cleaning his gear, and then relaxing in the hot sun, not too alarming, he thought but would maintain vigilance.

In the meantime, West had managed to catch sight of some of the current visitors to the Island and sensed that something was being arranged and it was imminent so, in the late afternoon, he decided to make his way down the slope, hidden by trees, and make his way to the outbuilding he had assumed was the incinerator shed. Although void of any secret service type training he was very nimble and dressed in camouflage jump suit with stout boots for the shaky terrain. He made extra sure he was avoiding any CCTV cameras but knew the closer he got to the building the more likelihood there was of being seen. He managed to find a covered position opposite the doors to the incinerator and waited for nightfall.

He remained there patiently and had just reached the conclusion that nothing was going to happen when he heard the sound of a motorised vehicle of some sort and, sure enough, a quad bike appeared in view with a trailer hitched on the back.

He stayed silent and in position but nearly gasped out loud when he saw that on the trailer was a body bag and it was not empty!

The rider got off the bike and opened the doors to reveal the incinerator, amber illuminating lights came on automatically and he pressed some buttons on the control panel. What appeared to be fans began to whirr into life. He then opened a chute, went to the trailer, lifted the body, put it inside the chute, closed the door, pressed some more buttons and stood back, looking around vigilantly.

West could not believe what he had just witnessed, he was right, that was a body, it must be the visitor, he's been cremated and this is what will have happened to my friend, he concluded to himself.

Wisetzki was patrolling around the incinerator waiting for the cycle to complete and West feared he was going to be compromised, he had to get this information back with him and bring the authorities.

He decided to retreat back deeper into the trees and, as he did, he broke some loose twigs underfoot but he didn't look back, he carried on up the slope heading back to his camp which was difficult in itself in the dark.

Wisetzki heard the sound of the breaking twigs and was at the spot in a flash but he found no one. He searched with his high-powered torch, physically sighting the newly broken branch, it could have been an animal but his instincts told him something more was at play this time. He ventured into the trees and upwards but concluded that, in the dark he would be at a disadvantage to track anyone.

West eventually found his way, with some luck, back to his small camp and was pleased with himself. He would stick to the plan of laying low until nightfall tomorrow and making his way back to the dive boat on the arranged night. He only had the short-wave radio for communication but he wasn't going to tell Ray about what he had discovered, he had to keep it to himself for a little longer.

CHAPTER 115

The following morning, Wisetzki was a little fatigued, having paid more dutiful respects to the demanding Dominica that evening, but met with Mia.

He told her what had happened and that he was going to investigate around the shoreline opposite to where the dive boat was still moored.

She told him to keep her informed and that she had the three girls should he need any help.

Wisetzki made his way around the headland and from above spotted the small sandy beach right in the line of sight to the dive boat, so he made his way there. It didn't take him long to discover a small inflatable hidden behind a large rock and covered in foliage. He had judged correctly, someone was on the Island and, if it were him, he'd wait till nightfall to get away. I'm going to find you before then, he pledged in his mind, and I have a starting point from last night, this is what I do.

He updated Mia and she told Rui and Arusi to get their beach bags and towels and do some sunbathing at the cove where Wisetzki had found the boat. She made Wisetzki aware that, she believed, the perpetrator was the same person as had shown up on Tengah, the one seeking his friend and that he couldn't be allowed to get off the Island at any cost.

"And if he shows up in the meantime?" asked Rui.

"I'm sure you girls can look after yourselves," Mia replied, "be discreet and have fun, he doesn't leave this Island!"

"Now I am really Octopussy!" she said to herself smiling

West was beside himself and couldn't wait to get back to his boat by the shore, he had already packed everything away ready but knew he needed the cover of nightfall. Or did he? He was contemplating just taking a chance and rowing in daylight to Ray's boat when something else made up his mind.

In the distance he could just hear the faint popping of a motorcycle type engine and he knew straight away that it was

the quadbike he had encountered the night before. He knew
it couldn't be ridden to where he was located, but that its rider
would be getting as far into the trees before continuing on foot
and he couldn't be sure he hadn't been spotted the night before.
He couldn't risk it and decided to make his way down to the
sandy cove, retrieve his inflatable and paddle to the dive boat
even though Ray would probably be underwater taking pictures.

He skirted around avoiding a direct path but when he broke
through the brush on to the small sandy beach he was taken
by surprise.

He could see where his boat was still hidden but lying on the
soft, golden sand adjacent, basking in the sun, was a beautiful
black girl in a tiny bikini, her silky skin glistening with oil from
the radiance.

He didn't sense danger but wasn't sure whether to run back
into the brush or make out he was lost from the boat moored
just offshore; and who were these girls there? On a tiny beach
on a private Island, he assumed guests of the owner.

Arusi broke the silence, "Hi I'm Rusi," she purred.

"And I'm Ru," came a voice from behind him and he turned
his head to see there was a tall Japanese girl with jet black hair
also wearing the tiniest of bikinis well, almost.

On any other day he would have blessed the Lord, imagining
it could only have been his birthday.

"What are you doing here?" he asked putting down
his rucksack.

"We could ask the same, but it's ok," Arusi replied and
offered her hand out to him, "aren't you going to help me up?"
She smiled suggestively to him.

West took her hand and Arusi, very ladylike, rose from
her position and stood close to him, looking into his eyes, he
was mesmerised.

She reached out and put both her arms over his shoulders,
clasping her hands at the back of his head.

"We can all be friends," she said. "I think we could even
have some fun," she added smiling but, at the same time, pulled

his head towards her and simultaneously brought her knee up, crashing painfully into his testicles. He groaned and fell to his knees holding his crotch, not even dreaming of defending himself from the incoming, searing roundhouse kick to the side of his head from Rui.

He lay crumpled on the ground, conscious but dazed. Rui reached down and grabbed a handful of his hair, Arusi his arm, and they dragged him towards the sea. He was heavy for them in his prostrate form but, once they reached the water, it was easy as they waded out to deeper water with him trying to lift his head to avoid swallowing sea water.

Everything had happened so quickly, and he was too dazed and shocked to have any fight with the two girls.

At waist deep, Rui turned him onto his back as he floated between them, his eyes blinded by the sun.

Arusi pushed him down deeper, straddling his throat in her crotch between her thighs and clamping tightly whilst Rui straddled and gripped his midriff in the same manner.

He kicked like a fish out of water as Rui stood, hands on hips, looking down at the drowning face between her legs, his white face contrasting her beautiful black thighs.

It didn't take long before his legs slowly stopped kicking and bubbles came out of his mouth as he looked up with terrified eyes, through the water, and then calm as the warm seawater filled his lungs and he drowned in the shallow water between Arusi's legs, West was done.

The girls dragged his body up the beach and behind the rock, Rui contacted Wisetzki to inform him they had eliminated the threat and there would be another body to dispose of.

West was identified by both Mia and Wisetzki and as the dive boat was a regular, licensed visitor they had no reason to suspect he had an accomplice, more like he had just paid for the ride and, anyway, they hadn't seen anything of him if anyone investigated.

Ray was totally unaware of anything untoward happening as he surfaced from his dive and made ready for the arrival of his stow-away.

He waited till dark and when the time came for the rendezvous and West didn't show, he left for the mainland. The deal had strict rules, Ray wasn't to know West's business on the Island and knew that, if he didn't show, then that was that, he would forget anything ever happened between them.

CHAPTER 116

Li was very frustrated, he couldn't get the answers and now, his only accomplice was unreachable; he had tried West for two days and nothing. He couldn't raise any kind of alarm because it would expose him knowing about his partner's incursion to the Island and he couldn't have that. Instead, he decided, somehow to try and obtain information himself regarding the new product about to be launched. He knew more facts now; some part of it was refined in the Lab on Tengah and subsequently transported to Singapore.

He had his schedule for the upcoming exhibition, and it meant that he would have time back in the Lab when both Carol and Mia would not be on the Island. Wisetzki would also be on permanent duty at the exhibition and, therefore, security reliant on his number two, not in the same league.

He needed PIN access codes and began thinking around how he was going to get them, but first he needed to reconcile how valuable the information would be to a competitor and more importantly the financial reward he could gain from 'selling' it.

Li knew from presentations, secrecy and project time disbursed into the launch of this new product, that it was very, very special, something no competitor could boast and potentially worth millions of dollars. Of course, competitors would analyse the formula but, he also had an inkling, that it could take years and even then, the source of its unique active ingredient may never be discovered. He decided it was worth much more that he could ever make working in a Cosmetics Research Lab.

Li had retained contacts from previous 'off the record', but low level, leaks where he had supplied much lesser, sensitive information and one of these came up with a lead. Within the industry it was no secret that 'Skintakt' was about to launch a skin care/treatment revolution, unmatched and unrivalled by anyone so the big guns were feeling for any information. He was put into contact with an 'agent', effectively a hired spy, secretly contracted to one of the largest competitors in the market and he arranged a face to face meeting in Mersing at his next shore leave.

Li met with the representative in a small café by the harbour, he had raised huge interest from the cosmetic giant he worked for and had permission to negotiate with full authority and autonomy. It was no secret through the media that a ground-breaking skin cream was to be launched at the upcoming, international exhibition and would have a huge impact on the market.

Of course, at this point, Li could only offer the potential of usable information and/or a sample so he had to base his offer on what he thought he would be able to obtain.

The agent knew that Li had the potential to deliver so dangled a huge Carrot for his consideration based on supplying formulas, research notes and a sample of the ingredient which no other company had.

Li outlined his plan from completing his rota at the exhibition, returning to Tengah whilst Mia and Carol were both still in attendance, to getting into their Lab and retrieving what he needed. He would then need a commercial flight out of Singapore to London where they had agreed the exchange would take place.

The offer was more than he could have dreamed of and he was determined this was his opportunity to make it for life and would do everything he could to make it happen. He provided dates and times he believed he could carry out the crime and all was agreed.

CHAPTER 117

Mia was assisting with the setting up of Skintakt's huge and impressive centre stage stand in the Singapore Expo exhibition hall, with two days to go to the formal opening and Press day, when she received a call from Lieke.

"Lieke, how are you, so good to hear from you, I'm launching my new skin cream product this week," she said, excitedly.

"Yes, dear, I've been following in the media, I am very proud of you but, this isn't a social call," she replied solemnly. "Daan has been released from Prison!" she announced outright and then, silence.

"Mia, are you there?" she enquired. "Did you hear me?"

"Err yes," replied Mia, "it is sooner than expected but, it was going to happen someday."

"Yes, it's an early release due mainly to his regretful and remorseful attitude together with exemplary behaviour in the prison, on top of that, his father's guarantees and lobbying, he doesn't have his passport back so he can't travel out of Singapore," she informed her.

"Ok," replied Mia, "I appreciate the call and know it must be difficult for you being his mother."

"About that," Lieke responded, "I didn't mention before but, he isn't my child, Marco had an affair with, believe it or not, a local prostitute, everything was hushed up at the time and she was paid off, I brought him up as my own from birth he doesn't know so, you mean every much, if not more, to me than he does." Mia was shocked, this was the first she had heard or even imagined of this, but she had always wondered why his father was so attentive and forgiving towards him. Also, he didn't have any psychological or physiological traits of the kind, to the endearing and respectful Lieke.

"I'm sorry," said Mia, "thank you for confiding in me, I know Daan has said some things but, really, I'm not worried, I will stay alert."

"Yes," replied Lieke, "stay safe, dear and you can tell me all about your new product very soon."

Mia wasn't over concerned with the news, she knew Daan had a grudge but he was also just released, would be under strict supervision and wasn't that clever or stupid, or so she thought.

She reported all potential security threats to Wisetzki, and this was no different, this was his job and he was the best at it.

So, Daan was free, his 'Oscar winning' like Prison performance was exemplary and he was very pleased with himself. With any fit, full blooded male an obvious craving following incarceration and forced celibacy would certainly involve sexual release with a partner in waiting, or even the services of a prostitute, but not Daan. He had one woman on his mind and that was Mia, he still carried the motivational card he had kept in his cell as a reminder of the sole cause of his demise and ruined life, revenge his only focus. He knew she would be in town for the exhibition and the timing could not have been better, he already had a plan, he just needed to know where she was staying.

Currently at set up stage, the exhibition hall was full of contractors, electricians, carpenters, carpet fitters and stand builders; it was organised chaos and security was difficult to exercise.

Daan dressed himself in overalls and a homemade 'Exhibition Contractor' Lanyard, picked up a cardboard box and walked into the halls after finding the location of Skintakt's floor space.

He hid his face behind the box he was carrying on his shoulder and approached the stand, she was there, he couldn't believe it.

His anger and hatred began to bubble up inside of him like a Volcano preparing to erupt, but this wasn't the time or place, he just needed to confirm her presence. He walked past the stand hurriedly just as Mia looked up. It was one of those fleeting moments where one freezes on the spot like having seen a ghost. Was that Daan, could it possibly have been? She came to her senses and he was gone, just someone carrying a box with his back to her, a trim figure, it couldn't have been him, he was much heavier build, she concluded, just her mind following the call from Lieke.

What she didn't know was the effort Daan had put into his transformation and the fixational obsession he had with exacting revenge on her. She worked until late and her Hotel was within pleasant walking distance so she was glad of the fresh air but, what she failed to notice, was the character keeping a safe distance behind her. Continuing ahead, once she entered the Hotel, Daan now knew where Mia was staying.

CHAPTER 118

The grand, cosmetic industry showcase opened and, as expected, the focus of attention was the Skintakt stand where crowds of people both exhibitors and visitors flocked with the Press to hear about the, much publicised, revolutionary skin care cream.

Aside from the marketing team and Mia there was Li, Victoria, Carol and two other Lab staff members manning the stand for the first two days, and then, a change around for the final three with the exception of Carol who was scheduled for the full duration. In addition, Rui, Arusi and Dominica had been given exhibitor passes by Wisetzki and the brief to just mingle with the crowds around the stand area and watch for any unusual behaviour, reporting back to him, who himself stayed inconspicuous with his presence. The most talked about attraction was that Carol and the marketing team had organised for a model to be a live experiment as a demonstration of the cream's unbelievable skin repair properties. This concept was totally revolutionary and billed almost like a bygone circus act, the bearded lady or the jungle raised boy, observe the transformation in real time! The model had a small burn scar on the underside of her upper arm caused again through the common, accidental misuse of a hot hair tonging device when she was in her teens. The Press were gathered like vultures around a fresh kill. The show belonged to Carol and she began by introducing the young model, allowing her to tell the audience the history and details behind her burn scar. Then, certain, random people from the audience together with a representative from one of the largest industry magazine publications, *Global Cosmetic Industry* were invited on to the stage where a leading plastic surgeon confirmed the authenticity of the burn scar. Photographs as a 'before' were taken, and then, Carol applied a specially formulated, stronger version of their released product directly to the scar tissue. She knew this would show results within the time period of the show to the scar area. The cameras flashed and illuminated, video cameras capturing every moment. Carol announced that the model would return every day at the exact same time for a re-application of the treatment and everyone could see and monitor for themselves the progress and concluding result, towards the end of the exhibition. It became the highlight of the entire exhibition and never in its history had a product launch roused so much interest and the media were all over it. Individual bloggers and influencers began posting the first day on Instagram and YouTube, promising an update the next day, there were millions of views.

From a commercial standpoint, enquiries from current non-distributors and outlets resulted in countless meetings for the business team to attend to, it was a proud time for Mia and Carol.

CHAPTER 119

It was the second day with Li scheduled to leave in the late afternoon. He had watched Carol the day before presenting the 'live' experiment to the press and audience at exactly 11:00 and she prepared herself now, in an enclosed area behind the reception desk for staff members only. It was like a mini-storage space where they could keep bags, personal belongings and chargers for their mobile phones etc. He had checked and observed that Carol's phone was charging and so, when he knew she was preparing for the model update, he made a call from a sim only phone he had purchased and then went to where Carol was located out of sight. She was in final preparation for the show answering the ring with the phone pinned to her ear on her shoulder but dropped it. She fumbled for the phone and unlocked it to check the missed caller. "Damn," she said anxiously, "I will be late for my slot and the bloody thing is almost dead."

"Here," said Li, taking the phone from her, "they are waiting, get out there do your stuff and I'll put it back on charge for you."

"Great, thanks," she replied and left the storage area. He had been pressing the screen constantly to ensure it didn't self-lock and he checked.

"Yesss!" he sighed with relief. "It's still open." Knowing she would be busy for at least 30 minutes and not wanting to be found there by anyone else, he left the stand, keeping the phone active.

He remembered what she had said when they were talking about passwords so, finding somewhere out of the way, he began scrolling through the contacts on her phone.

Was it really this simple? he found made up contacts listed as Lab Colleagues with obviously made up, fictitious telephone numbers. He screenshotted them all with his own phone, guessing that the numbers were Carol's disguised PIN numbers. He couldn't be sure but was confident he now had the information to get him into her Lab and workspace documents. She even had phrases listed against certain contacts where these phrases and numbers could be combined, he couldn't wait to get back to Tengah.

He sneaked back to replace the phone on charge before Carol finished her presentation but Rui had spotted him looking around as if checking to see if anyone was watching him. When she saw him dart into the storage area she followed discreetly, just enough to see him crouching on the floor, his back to her, with Carol's pink mobile phone, apparently replacing it back onto the charger. She retreated before he saw her but updated Wisetzki on what she had just witnessed, it seemed some people were not there just to support the company and she didn't really know him at all.

The following day's presentation was more incredible than the last. Carol re-introduced their 'live' model and presented her upper arm for the world to see and gasp in awe. The scar was now barely visible, and she took cleansing lotion to show that it hadn't been covered intentionally with make-up and that it was in fact, the real deal. Again, cameras flashed and the whole stand was illuminated with the bright lights from video and camera recorders. She could hear vloggers and bloggers conducting their own, live presentations. She then applied a further dose of the cream and invited everyone back the next day for what would surely be a complete disappearance of the scarred area on the model's arm.

CHAPTER 120

Meanwhile, Daan was not at the exhibition, he had other things to do today. He was, in fact, lurking in the reception of Mia's Hotel where he had followed her the day before, but he had to get into her room somehow. He knew that Hotel receptionists were trained not to give out client information but had noticed one agent behind the desk wearing a badge identifying her as a 'Trainee'.

He waited for the right moment when her supervisor was showing a client to the elevators and made his move. He rushed to the desk pretending to be out of breath, "Sorry to bother you, dear," he said, "my colleague hasn't turned up at the exhibition today and she's not answering her mobile," he added waving his phone in front of her.

"I have been sent to check she is ok but I don't know which room she is in, I will just call her room from the house phone here in the Lobby if that's ok?"

The young trainee was nervous and knew she shouldn't divulge personal guest information but it was obvious the man was working with her, she thought, and he didn't want to go there, just use the house phone. "Err ok, sir," she said, "what's her name?"

Daan had done his homework and checked the names of the stand officials from the exhibitor handbook. "Mia Romano," he said confidently. Mia had retained the surname from her birth certificate of her Italian father.

"Miss Romano," she repeated. "M Romano, yes, room 7142," she whispered.

"Thank you," said Daan, "you've saved my day," he added making his way to the house phone. He pretended to make the call, after which, he walked past the reception again and whispered to the trainee, "She's fine, thank you, just working from her room."

The trainee acknowledged him and set back to her registering of new arrivals.

Daan found a quiet area to plan his next move, he had to get up to the seventh floor but knew that the elevator would not operate without a valid key card scan on entering the floor number.

He waited patiently for a single person to press the upper floors button on the elevator and the person could only be described as a 'sweet old Lady'. She was prepared, key card in hand and watching the elevator descend on the electronic floor indicator. The elevator arrived and she stepped back to allow its passengers to exit then stepped in swiping her key card onto the pad and selecting floor nine. Daan took his chance, rushed in at the last moment and began fumbling in his pockets, panicking as the doors began to close. "Oh, dear it's here somewhere," he said, "I'm always forgetting I need it for my floor," he added pleadingly.

"I know the feeling, dear, I have mine ready, what floor do you need? And I'll swipe mine, so you don't miss it," she replied smiling.

"Oh it's seven, and thank you, I know I have it somewhere," he added.

"It's ok." She smiled, swiping the card and adding floor seven to the floor stops.

They reached the seventh floor and Daan got out after thanking the Lady for her help. Two out of three, now I need to get into the room, he thought to himself.

He knew that, at this time of day, guests would be checking out with new arrivals due and the housekeeping maids would be busy servicing the rooms.

He went towards Mia's room; the cleaning Lady was inside another room two doors away and he could hear the vacuum cleaner singing away. He was thinking of how he could convince the maid to let him into her room with the 'master' key card, attracting the least amount of attention, but there it was. She had left her master key card dangling on a lanyard on her trolley. He quickly picked it up, swiped Mia's door open, wedged it quickly, returned the key card to the trolley and went inside, closing the door behind him, first putting out the 'Do not disturb' sign.

He had succeeded, the plan had worked, he was inside Mia's room and he sniffed the air loudly. He looked around and noticed the bed, still made, but with one corner drawn back where she had got out of it that morning. He reverted naturally to Daan again, feeling her clothes hanging in the wardrobe, going through her used underwear with all his perverted senses at play. He held up one of her G string panties and said out loud, "You may think you are every man's dream but, today you repay this man's!" And threw them onto the floor. He then got stuck into the well-stocked mini bar, switched on the TV and waited.

CHAPTER 121

It was around 8pm, Daan lay in wait, inside of the room, for Mia to return. He had removed the 'do not disturb' sign so that she was not alerted to the fact, since she had left the room with the intention of it being serviced. He had drunk every spirit from the mini bar and sat in silence in the skyline vista lit room when he heard rather loudly, "Damn where's my key card!" and what sounded like a handbag scraping against the door, someone searching through it. He rushed to the door and peeked through the spy glass in the door, it was Mia. His heart began racing, this was it, it had been relatively simple, she was there, and he would be alone with her. He hid out of sight of the main room in the changing area and waited silently. The door opened, but strangely no lights were turned on even though a second card was located in the electricity slot by the door. Then he heard the door close shut on its automatic hinge. He waited for a few seconds but, still nothing, silence then. "What a day!" Mia announced out loud.

He couldn't wait any longer, he revealed himself in the shadows of the dimly lit room and announced, "Yes, Bitch and it's not over yet!"

"Daan!" she shouted.

"Yes Daan," he replied and at that moment was taken aback by all of the powerful main spotlights suddenly illuminating the room. He rubbed his eyes in disbelief, he could never have perceived the scene now confronting him yes, Mia, but she was flanked by two armed policemen in full uniform, their handguns drawn and pointing at his torso.

"Mr Daan De Jong, put your hands slowly above your head and kneel down!" the leading officer yelled at him. Daan was foiled again, he knew resistance was futile, but he was armed, which would surely increase the severity of the intent. Added that, the fact that he was on probation meant he would certainly end up back in Prison and for a long time.

He was totally silent as he was led out of the room; Mia was calm and not overly distraught as the plan had unfolded like clockwork. She made the call to Wisetzki.

"Yes, I'm fine and he has been arrested," she told him.

"That's good," he replied. "I'm glad you took my advice to fit the handy cam in the ornamental mask above the door in your room; being told he'd been released was a great heads up, you just never know and that's my job!"

"Yes, the live video feed on my phone was crystal clear, I watched him in the room when it alerted me, he's still a nasty pervert," she said. "But I can relax from that one now."

"Yes, I know things like this are traumatic, but he was acting alone so the threat has been eliminated completely, you are safe now," Wisetzki assured her.

"Thank you," replied Mia, "is everything else ok?"

"Just whilst I have you, it may be something and nothing, but I'm meticulous as you know; Rui reported that, she saw Li Jie acting a little suspicious around Carol's phone at the exhibition whilst she was out front. I quizzed her about it and she told me that, he had offered to put her phone back on charge after receiving an anonymous call with a withheld ID and she was in a rush, but when she went back it was till there and on charge," he informed her.

"I don't trust Li, as you know, I will recheck with Carol in the morning if you can stop by before you head back to Tengah late on Thursday?" she asked him.

"Sure, that will work see you tomorrow," he replied.

"OK and thanks again," repeated Mia.

CHAPTER 122

With the 'live' model test on the Skintakt stand creating unprecedented attention and shocking the whole cosmetics world, Li had been contacted several times for an update on his progress and had already managed to renegotiate his fee for the information they sought. He reported that he was in a good position to get what they needed and an exit plan to get it to them in London was arranged.

He was back on Tengah with the knowledge that Wisetzki would not be around till the following day, but, consciously aware his number two would still be monitoring things around the place.

He had studied and checked the screenshots from Carol's contacts list, and it was not difficult to reveal how she listed her entry and security passwords. They consisted of made-up contacts with numbers beginning correctly with region codes etc. but then, random numbers and digits. One contact was actually listed as 'Denni Safecab' – 'Lab Colleague' and this was obviously Carol's PIN number to the storage cabinet 'safe' in her Lab, and others he would be able to try by plugging his laptop into the network and signing in as 'Carol'. He purposely stayed at his station in the Lab until everyone had left for the evening, he had to do it tonight as he was booked on a flight the following evening, first class to London Heathrow. "Working late Li?" Wisetzki's colleague asked as he made his patrol around the Lab.

"Oh yes," he replied, "duty called but, being away has put me way behind, don't worry I'll switch everything off when I'm done here, you can rely on me."

"Sure thing, Li, have yourself a good evening," he replied and left on his round.

He waited until the guard had left, knowing that he would now patrol the outside. There would be no one monitoring the cameras and the footage would not be viewed until the next day when he wouldn't be there anyway. He made his way to Carol's Lab and checked the codes he had deciphered, it was so easy, she may have been an ultra-effective and ultra-intelligent researcher, but her security protocols were non-existent and he guessed the electronic entry key pad door entry code on the first try, he was inside.

Was it really this easy, was she so simple? he thought again as he entered the code for the storage cabinet and it was, first attempt and the door swung open. The Cabinet was arranged very neatly and, from what he could see, date order as he removed one of the sealed, glass vials from its location. Then he saw it 'SoD' with a batch number and date. "'SoD'," he shrieked, "I saw this on the whiteboard, and it had no meaning, this must be the secret ingredient and it's called 'SoD'." He put the vial in his pocket and closed the door to the cabinet, then took out a small flash drive and plugged his laptop into the network. Carol had everything listed in her phone and a professional 'hacker' was not needed to extract anything at all, it was so straightforward as she even had phrases listed to 'hide' passwords. How forgetful must she be for things like this? Li asked himself.

He was consciously aware of the time constraints and knew that the guard would be back to check the Lab was secure for the night.

He managed to log in as 'Carol', but knew it only gave him access to her own backed up personal files on the hard drive and not necessarily 'official' company data and information on the main frame. He searched through endless folders with personal photographs, personal journals, Martial arts videos and tens of music album files listed by artist. Then, he noticed something, he was not a fan of eighties music, but a folder named 'SoD Greatest Hits'? There it was again, 'SoD', it just had to be the key, he thought, but as he prepared to open the folder, he heard the Lab outer door open. He quickly copied the whole folder onto his flash drive, closed everything down, and left the Lab to get back to his own station as the guard reappeared. "I really need to close up now Li," he stated. "Sorry."

"Sure thing, I'm done now, I'll see you tomorrow," he replied and left the Lab.

CHAPTER 123

Late that same evening Mia had a video call with Pietro. He had heard from Wisetzki what had happened with Daan and wanted to make sure she was ok and safe. She assured him everything was ok and at no time, thanks to Wisetzki, was she ever in danger at all and she'd been through much worse.

She updated him on the progress of the exhibition and more importantly the roll out of their brand new, industry changing, product. She could only report good news, everything had excelled beyond anything they had predicted. He recognised Mia's need for some reflection time and listened empathetically as she recalled the fateful night in KL at the gym where she had inadvertently been subjected to the very first application of SoD. How she had passed it off as being the last involuntary yet, perverted, action of a depraved rapist and still, it had led to this. She anticipated awards from the organisers and sponsors of the Cosmoprof exhibition, never had such a launch attracted so much attention. The planning and execution of the live model interaction display and performance was beyond that of any manufacturer in its long running history. Hits and views to both the exhibition, official and personal social media accounts of the many vloggers and influencers had heightened awareness of the Cosmoprof event and stand spaces were already being requested for its next schedule.

The future looked illuminating, this was going to be, potentially, the biggest money-maker in the company's history and Pietro was both pleased and very proud of her endeavour and hard work. This reflection on where they had started and where they were now, was a real reminder that they were on the verge of something colossal and everything had gone to plan thus far, or so they believed.

"It's good to take the time for reflection sometimes," Pietro said, "makes you weary of the trials and tribulations and the application of positive affirmations on a daily basis."

"Yes indeed," Mia agreed.

They went on to discuss some of the other resultant implications and, even though both acknowledged the value of the 'SoD' for infertility use, they agreed, for the foreseeable future, to focus on the cream application to ensure they had enough of the raw, harvested material in meeting demand.

"So commercially we now move to a limited release, not general distribution?" Pietro asked.

"Yes, correct," replied Mia, "the commercial and marketing teams will now press ahead with the program and it is planned that we engage with high profile people in media, movie industry, sports, music etc. to gain endorsement material. This will create heightened exigence; we are preparing our existing lead wholesalers and distributors for this expected demand and of course our factory!"

"Well!" concluded Pietro. "It seems like everything is under our control, nothing can stop us now, everything is forging ahead and it's all down to your tenacity and belief which, of course, will be highly rewarded, 'Miss Octopussy'!" he added laughing.

"Ha," she replied sarcastically. "It all sounds too good to be true, but I sometimes feel that, when things are going so well, something comes up to ruin it, but that's my pessimistic side when I achieve success."

"What could possibly go wrong, our competitors have no clue and will never find out, so don't worry, let us catch up at the weekend when you are back on Tengah, I'll come over when my business here, is done, good night, Mia, and well done, I'm proud of you," he concluded, ending the call.

CHAPTER 124

Early the next day Li, discreetly, hitched a ride back to the mainland, paying the captain of the small supply vessel who had just delivered some food supplies, he had a flight to catch that evening out of Singapore and had absolutely no intention of missing it.

Before the opening of the exhibition, the next day, Mia and Carol sat down privately with Wisetzki who wanted to eliminate any potential security breach with Carol's mobile phone.

She went through the events and steps leading up to Li taking her phone with the offer of putting it back on charge. "Let's look at worst cases, could your phone have remained unlocked as you gave it to Li, giving him access to contacts, folders and the like?" asked Wisetzki.

"I guess it could," replied Carol. "I had opened it to check the caller and I was being called out front it was all so hasty."

"Ok," he replied calmly, "and again, worst case, is there anything which could be of interest to him, anything at all?" Carol was silent and it said everything.

"Carol," said Wisetzki, "you must tell me, it is done now, but I have to assess where we are and the gravity, if it's just that he was able to look at your contacts and stuff then so what?"

She cleared her throat and knew she had to reveal the potential consequences of someone looking through her contacts list.

"Look," she began shakily, "I have difficulty remembering PIN numbers and passwords so I."

And before she could finish, Mia exclaimed angrily, "What, you wrote them down!"

"Woah, slow down," interjected Wisetzki, "getting upset or angry won't change anything, Mia, tell us, Carol," he said.

"No, of course I don't write them down as such, but I use made up telephone numbers disguising PIN numbers in my contacts list and use phrases to remember passwords, it's how I remember them," she added solemnly.

"So, everything is there if the user interprets them correctly?" he asked.

"I guess so, I'm sorry, I didn't think anything like this could happen," she added apologetically.

"Ok," replied Wisetzki, "it's basic security protocol not to ever write anything down, I will look to retina scan and fingerprint access going forward, but we do have a security risk, right now, what of Li, Mia?"

"I don't trust him as far as I could throw him, he's sneaky and selfish and I believe he would compromise anything for the good of himself," she replied.

Wisetzki said that he would contact Tengah and have his man check carefully for any sign of a breach with Carol's station and would use his Interpol connections to see if he could find Li's current whereabouts. An hour later Wisetzki discovered that there had been a log on to Carol's profile the evening before, the 'locked' cabinet had been checked and Li hadn't had the sense to re-align the Vials in the storage cabinet to not leave an obvious gap where something had been taken. Li was nowhere to be found and his phone records were clear, but Wisetzki figured he was using a second mobile for his illicit dealings. There was, however, one e-mail which linked him to a cosmetics competitor, nothing too revealing but nevertheless a piece of the jigsaw he had to complete.

He met back with Mia and told her that the worst scenario and, which he feared was in fact the case, that LI had a sample from the cabinet, some files downloaded from Carol's profile, a link to a competitor and he was basically on the run, but where and how, he didn't know yet.

There was no point in going back to Tengah as he had a hunch that Li would be heading for Singapore for a flight out that day.

CHAPTER 125

Wisetzki had updated Pietro of the situation, Li could be running to a competitor with material and information that could ruin everything they had done, and he couldn't find out where he was.

Pietro agreed to use his own contacts, some in very high office in government, and get back to him.

It was late afternoon as Wisetzki and Mia heard back from him to give the information that Li was booked onto the evening flight out of Singapore with Singapore airlines, First Class, Cabin 1A, to London Heathrow. Wisetzki told Mia that he would head to the airport to see if he could locate him, but it was already beyond the three hour check in time and even if he got to him he wasn't sure what he could do; couldn't gun him down in public, it was after all a reality situation and not a spy movie. The clock, however, continued to tick.

Li knew that, with the ticket he had, it enabled him access to early, priority check in and use of the elite first class lounge. Boarding was direct from the lounge area so he would not be in any public area until he eventually boarded the flight.

Wisetzki had raced to the airport even though he knew there was not much he could do if Li was already airside and if he were in his shoes, that is where he would be.

He went through the motions but the gate was already open to economy passengers, so he knew Li would have already cleared security and be taking advantage of the First-Class lounge.

His efforts were futile, Li had planned his escape very carefully and everything was going for him.

"There was nothing I could do to stop him," Wisetzki reported back to Pietro, "it's difficult when someone is booked first class, you cannot get to them."

"Yes, I understand," he replied solemnly. "We have to assume he's away with whatever he has and, according to Carol, it's only written in her words but it pretty much outlines most of what we've been up to; even the source of our materials, it could be very grave for us." He continued, "Even if whoever is receiving it doesn't want to try and copy, but instead expose us, this is a very serious and grave compromise, I will speak to Mia also and will head for Tengah myself."

"Ok, Pietro, I will meet with you on the Island, goodbye," he replied.

Pietro relayed the gravity and possible consequences of their dire situation to Mia and that he would be there the following day. "We have to work on the worst case," he told her, "I don't need to spell out the potential consequences of this, so I need you to prepare for a crisis meeting to try and come up with damage limitation protocols and ideas."

"Yes" she replied, "there's nothing anyone can do to stop him?"

"No," he replied, "he's already airside with less than three hours to take off and Wisetzki cannot get to him."

"Ok," she replied, downheartedly, ending the call, "I will see you tomorrow.".

CHAPTER 126

Mia went to find Carol who was sat alone staring at an empty take away coffee cup in one of the common cafeteria areas of the main exhibition halls.

She sat down opposite her and apologised for shouting, after all, they wouldn't be where they were without her, but conversely where they were arguably was because of her.

Mia knew there was absolutely no intent from her loyal partner, she was the most honest, dedicated and pleasurable person she had ever worked with in her whole career to date. She hadn't realised the seriousness of the compromise afforded to Li by using her phone contacts to store or remind her of personal security data.

"I even remember when he asked me how to memorise all of the different PINS and passwords we had to remember and I waved my phone, how fucking stupid was I?" Carol said, breaking the awkward silence. "You have every right to scream and shout at me, Mia," she added, "I'm truly sorry." She sobbed.

"Hey," Mia replied taking her hand in her own. "Li was a devious bastard; he's been playing his own agenda all along and he is very good at it!" She tried to console her.

"But what an idiot, what a stupid fucking idiot?" Carol repeated.

"Keeping passwords and PINs like that is not the right thing to do, Carol, but we wouldn't have gotten this far without your efforts and dedication and whatever happens we had a great ride, we've done something amazing," Mia told her.

"How can you ever forgive me?" she asked her.

"Nothing to forgive, no debate, no regrets," she said warmly. "Whatever happens from here and, if it's the worst, we regroup, see what our position turns out to be and we carry on. Pietro is flying into Tengah tomorrow and we plan for the worst case, of which you will be part, I assure you of that," she added convincingly.

"Really?" she asked. "After such a mistake?"

"I remember hearing you sing something about playing all of your cards, holding aces, about losers, winners, it being destiny and as you know I can't sing for toffee, but here goes anyway!" Mia said clearing her throat, and reciting very loudly, the popular eighties Abba hit, 'The Winner takes it all',

Despite the completely out of tune rendition, Carol recognised the song, one of her favourites, and it brought a smile to her face.

"You're right," she said, "you cannot sing, but we are the losers?" questioned Carol, "even if it is just a song someone is singing."

"There's also a 'singing' related saying," Mia told her, "one you will have heard of, being Australian, and that is 'it's not over until the fat lady sings', there are four aces in a pack, even though Li seems to be holding them all. Now let's get ready to clear up, head back to Tengah, and see what tomorrow brings us?" she suggested.

"Ok, Mia, let's get out of here," Carol agreed.

CHAPTER 127

Li sat comfortably in the First-Class lounge, having eaten a first-class meal, and was enjoying a digestive liqueur. He had made a copy of the flash drive which was in his pocket and the other in his small attaché case with the Vial sample, he was all set and confident it was too late for anyone to stop him.

And that appeared to be the case, he wore the biggest smile as he boarded the aircraft. He'd never turned left before at the entrance to the plane and was going to enjoy every minute. He clutched his case tightly and checked his suit pocket for the extra flash drive, everything was in order, he had done it.

"Good evening, Mr Jie, my name is Steven Wang and I will be your personal steward for the whole of this flight to London Heathrow, please follow me to your suite, do you need help with any luggage?" he said.

"Thank you, and no, I can manage my luggage, travelling very light," Li replied.

"Great things come in small packages eh, Mr Jie, or so they say?" he quipped, smiling.

"Yes, they do, they certainly do," he repeated, clutching the case to his chest as he followed the steward.

"Here we are, Mr Jie, your private suite, everything is prepared and as you are travelling light, I have pre-selected pyjama size from your passenger information details, everything should be to your satisfaction," he suggested. Li looked around the suite for the first time, he couldn't believe air travel could be like this or who could possibly afford it. It was like a miniature five-star Hotel suite, from the wall to wall, hand-tufted, luxury carpets to the leather padded compartments, beautifully made-up bed, richly upholstered leather seat able to recline and swivel to suit any requirement, en-suite wardrobe, and a private well-appointed lavatory with sit down vanity counter complimented with a range of toiletries. I can freshen up in the morning before landing and my meeting, he thought.

He certainly wasn't used to this and wished he could make more of the luxury, but he wanted as little interaction with anyone as he could. "Everything is at your fingertips in here, Mr Jie," the steward added, "our selection of fine dining menus, TV and media, workstation, and you can eat or drink whenever you like, just call me."

"Thank you," said Li, "I have already eaten, so my plan is literally to 'freshen up' and go to bed, I don't believe I will need to be disturbed at all."

"Of course," replied the Steward, "just know I am here if you need anything at all. Good Night, Mr Jie I hope you have a deep rewarding sleep."

"Thank you and good night," said Li.

He sat back in his leather seat and reflected on where he had come from right back as a child, how he had mostly accepted what was left over for him and where he was at that moment. Boy done good, I have what I need right here with me and nothing can stop me now! he pondered.

He undressed, showered, put on his complimentary pyjamas and climbed into bed, his case next to him, his jacket close by. Now for a long comfortable sleep and when I wake up, I'll be on my way to never having to worry financially ever again, that's a fact! he mused, closing his eyes.

CHAPTER 128

The Singapore Airlines flight touched down safely into London Heathrow the following day with Li on board and Mia subsequently received a telephone call from Pietro.

"Mia!" exclaimed Pietro. "I'm looking at a news feed, a Singapore Airlines plane has reached London with a dead passenger on board in the First-Class compartment described as an Asian male in his thirties, could it be Li?" he gasped.

Mia replied, as calm as a cucumber, "I can't really confirm or deny that!" she replied convincingly. "But what I can confirm is that Rui just happened to be a First-Class passenger on the same flight!"

There was total silence for a few seconds and then,

"Oh my God! you really did take your 'Octopussy' role, seriously!" he gasped.

THE END